CROWN OF FANGS

CHRONICLES OF PLANE

FAITH JAMES

Cover Design by Arcane Covers

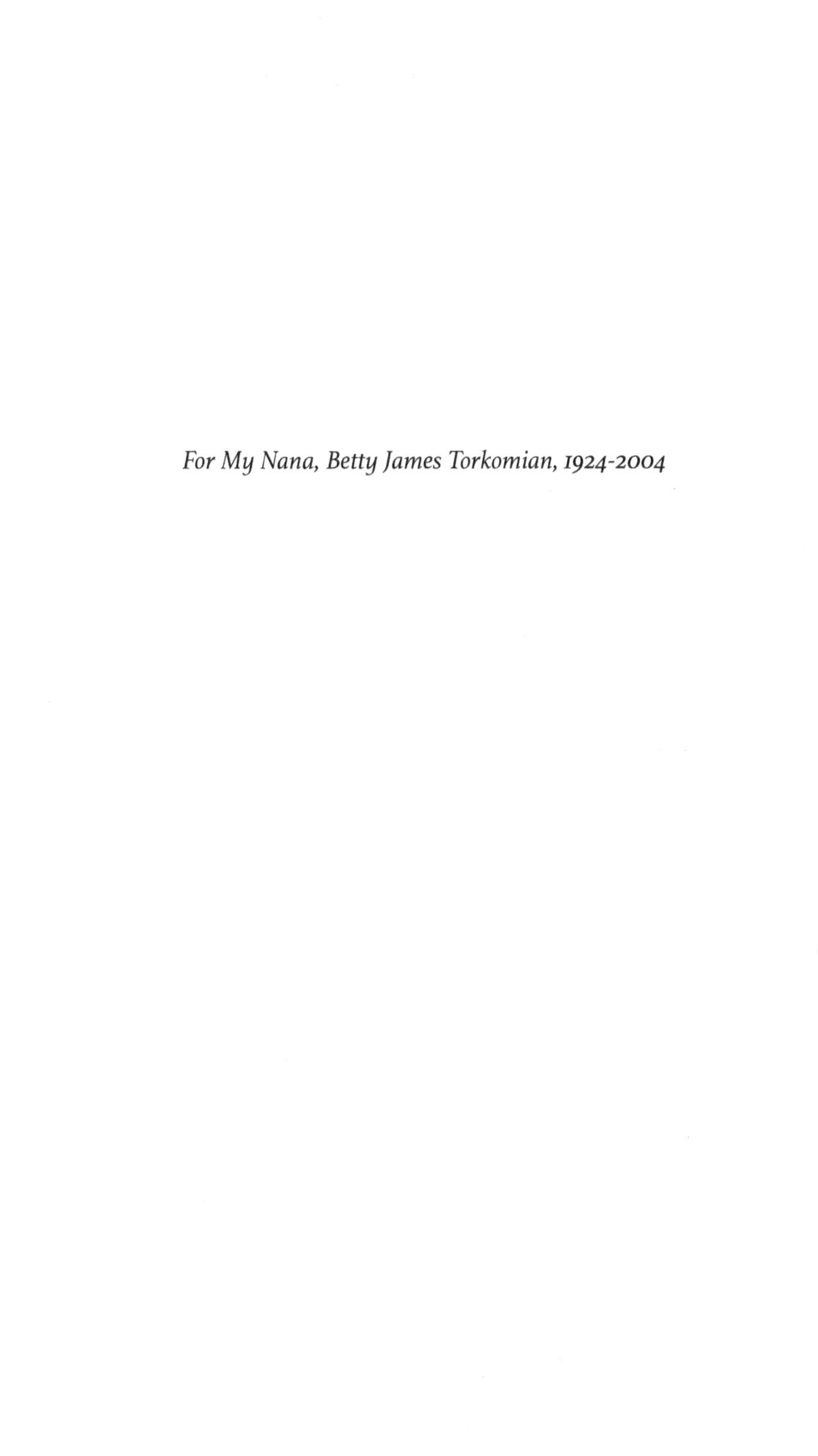

For My Nana, Betty James Torkomian, 1924-2004

1

THYRA

It is Handfasting Day.

Otherwise known as my twenty-first birthday, a day I have dreaded for every one of those years.

Perhaps I exaggerate. When I was born, I did not yet know my birth day would, in future, be used to auction me off to the highest bidder, like a prize sow at market.

"Hold," my nurse commands, interrupting my thoughts. It is not strictly accurate to call Edda my nursemaid any longer, as I have been out of leading strings for eighteen years, but old habits are difficult to abandon. Without question, I grasp a bed post as she tightens the laces of my gunna, as she has countless times before, when there is a feast or festival in my father's hall or a wedding, which I was always happy enough to attend when it wasn't my own. What is different, though, is I notice she takes care to tie the laces beneath my breasts, instead of over them. She is freeing them, instead of binding them.

"Do not worry so, Edda. These suitors will want me whether my breasts look pert or not. They want Father's kingdom, which only I can provide. A good pair of breasts, they can find anywhere."

"You complain too much," Edda responds as she steers me to the stool by my desk. She is a deft hand at both lecturing and pulling and tugging at me so I am made presentable, all at once. "Many a noble lady has found herself wedded and bedded before her sixteenth year. Your father gave you over two decades to yourself, free of the cares of a married woman, not to mention a future queen." To emphasize her point, she pulls my laces with a tug that is even more aggressive than usual.

Edda is a giantess, only a foot or so taller than the average woman, yet stronger than a pair of yoked oxen. But this is not why she is as terrifying as Hel. Since I was small, she has been stitching me into too-tight garments and braiding my hair even more tightly, so my very mind cramps when I think of the intricate patterns she weaves through my tresses. She is also bossy, as only the superintendent of a future queen's formation can be. I have tried many times in my life to disobey her, though somewhere around my sixteenth year, I mostly gave up, realizing my efforts were futile.

"You and I both know Father runs a fool's errand. For once my intended discovers my secrets, he will break the betrothal quicker than a hound rousts a pheasant."

"You underestimate your own personal charms, but more importantly, the might of Vagmar. An alliance with your father is the desire of every other ruler in the Northlands."

She holds my mother's amber-beaded hairpin aloft as if it is a treasure of the gods. I revere this pin as if it were gods-given, but still, I stifle a groan. My mother's amber beads only come out when Edda is preparing to stab my scalp–

repeatedly and viciously–to fashion an ornate knot at the crown of my head.

Her reassurance is not what I wish to hear. My only comfort all these years has been that, once my betrothed discovered my secret, he would break our marriage agreement, risking war with Vagmar just to disentangle himself from me. I should have known better. My wings and my fangs are to be accepted, or at the very least, ignored, in favor of an alliance with the pirate kingdom of the Northlands.

And to be fair, my fangs only protrude when I scent blood. If my betrothed is bleeding in front of me before our wedding takes place, we will likely have more pertinent issues than his distaste for my cursed disfigurements.

I prop my elbows on my desk with a loud crack. Without missing a beat, Edda pushes my arms off its surface, as I knew she would. But I still savor my small moment of rebellion. Usually, I don't even bother fighting against her ministrations.

"You know you must keep your back straight if I am–"

"'To do my braids properly.' Yes, yes. I am well aware, Edda."

I try not to slouch, but not very hard. It is Edda who insisted on a stool to serve as a seat for my desk, so she could style my hair with ease. When loose, it reaches my knees. Many people say it is my crowning glory, but as I am the Princess of Vagmar and heir to the throne, they are rather too generous with their compliments.

I chose not to complain when I was assigned the stool instead of a more comfortable seat, because I did not want to jeopardize the acquisition of my desk. I had campaigned long and hard for it, meaning I'd smiled sweetly and spoke softly for many days, against my wont, eventually wearing my father and Edda down until the slightly shabby and nicked mahogany piece of perfection was mine.

You wouldn't think it would be so difficult for a princess to come by a desk, yet it is not its price, but my intent with it which was the contentious issue. My father feared my possession of a desk would lead to my continued and unsavory pursuit of knowledge. All sorts of it. I am not choosy. History. Geography. Alchemy. Mathematics, though it is not my most favored discipline. I have even begun studying the ancient tongue, taking pains to learn how to draw runes from memory. There is, of course, a drawer in the desk so I may hide my parchments and the books I filch from the Priory when I am away from my chamber. I insisted the desk would hold my hair potions and cosmetics, as well as my sewing box, and my father seemed reassured. Edda knows better, but she does not reveal my secret.

And she will not, as long as I grit my teeth when she does my braids and slathers on my face paint.

Finally finished, Edda clicks her tongue, satisfied with her efforts. "Now if only I could get you to keep your hair dressed for longer than one night, I would be satisfied. You are a rare beauty, when you allow me to style you. You may as well try to enjoy looking so lovely, for I haven't the faintest notion of who will tend you when you travel with your new husband to his kingdom, wherever it may be."

There is suddenly no air in my chamber. I struggle for breath, and fear I will have an attack, as I sometimes do when the seasons change or I have taken a chill. I am not a stupid person. How had it not occurred to me that, by gaining a husband, I would lose Edda? It is the custom in the Northlands for noble brides to take new servants from their husbands' houses. This is not a fair bargain. I have no use for a husband, but Edda is indispensable to me.

Though I would never tell her this.

"Come, child. Do not dwell on what cannot be changed. We must get you ready with all haste."

Her voice is brisk, as always, but I know she senses my sadness, as she anticipates all my emotions and has done for twenty-one years.

"Why? I am not allowed to meet the contestants until this afternoon."

"Call them suitors, child, and must I teach you everything, as though you were still a wee babe? If we hide in the minstrels' gallery, you'll be able to see them when they enter the hall to greet your father. They'll never even know you're there."

"Why bother? I do not care what they look like. Nor does it matter. Father will choose my husband, not I."

These festivities are merely performative, intended to make the princelings of our neighboring kingdoms feel petted and valued, so they do not declare war when they are not chosen as my bridegroom.

"And here I thought you were the most curious child who ever walked the lands of Vagmar. I must have been mistaken."

Oof. She knows just how to get me to do her bidding.

"Fine. If we treat it as...an intellectual exercise...I suppose there is no harm in heading up to the gallery. After all, I should be better informed as to the identities of my suitors." Whoever it is, I will have to bear his children. Worse, I shall have to suffer under him each night until I conceive.

It is not far to the minstrels' gallery, which shares the second floor of my father's hall with just two other chambers, mine own and my father's. They are reached by a staircase wending precariously from the floor below to a terrace encircling the perimeter, where the thatch of the roof meets the timber frames of the hall. Were it not for my privacy door, the occupants below would be able to look up into my chamber, should they care to do so.

I have never traveled outside Vagmar, but I have heard tales of the royal halls of our neighboring kingdoms. I know ours is modest by comparison, despite our nation's wealth. But it is still my home, and I do not wish to leave it. Especially not to become the wife of a man I do not know. The sparseness of our hall is not due to a lack of funds, but the Vagmarian character itself. We are a hard people, not fond of ostentation. If only our kingdom were less prosperous.

Then no one would want to marry me.

The minstrels' gallery is partitioned, so their music may be muted when my father wishes it, which is often, and also, so none of the minstrels fall to the floor below when they are performing. This safeguard was installed based on past and painful experience. Our musicians do tend to become inebriated when called to play for us, so the risk of such accidents is ever present.

When not in use, however–and it rarely is, as my father thinks their music to be only so much noise–it is the perfect perch from which to spy on the goings-on in the hall below. Were I not a deft hand at eavesdropping, I would only have found out about the particulars of this Handfasting Ceremony days ago, when my father called for an audience to inform me of its proceedings. That many kings and princelings would be traveling to Vagmar to compete for my troth. He told me with such enthusiasm, as though I were a girl in spring, awaiting the visit from Eostre's rabbits who deliver sweets to well-behaved children, in anticipation of the season's fertility rituals.

Had I not known of the competitive nature of this ceremony, I might have reacted in a manner that would only infuriate King Skerr. He is quick to anger, and I have learned over the years how to diffuse his temper. I did not acquire this skill to please him, but to make mine own life a little easier.

Dropping eaves is also how I learned of what truly happened to my mother, who died when I was small. But I already carry enough worries today, without the added burden of thinking of her and how my memories of her embrace are so few.

We settle ourselves behind the partition, which is a screen fashioned of tightly woven hawthorne branches, fastened to the beams that support the terrace with great iron bolts. The branches leave small openings through which we can peer down into the hall. If a minstrel was determined enough–or drunk enough–he could still topple over the partition. But for our purposes, it serves as a useful barrier between ourselves and those on whom we wish to spy. I do not need to worry about taking a fall, as I have not even quaffed a small ale yet this morn. When I broke my fast, I sipped an herbal tisane to soothe my fluttering belly.

It did not work.

But later, mayhap I will indulge in something stronger than small ale. It is not my custom to lose sobriety, though for most Vagmarians, it is a national sport. But if any day called for over imbibing, it is Handfasting Day.

My father must sit at his throne, which is positioned on a dais at the back of the hall. Unfortunately, this dais is directly below us, so I cannot see him. But I will be able to see each contestant–pardon, suitor–as they enter the hall.

The herald announces the first of our guests. "Sven Guttersson, Prince of the House of Ingeborg," he says in a booming voice, which is a touch extravagant as the hall is almost empty, save for my father, this Sven character, and a handful of servants going about their duties. His voice echoes against the timbers.

"He's not bad looking, My Princess," Edda whispers to me.

She's right. He is tall and slimly built. His fair hair is cut short and seems clean. I am not close enough to tell the color of his eyes or whether he has all–or at least most–of his teeth, but his nose is not crooked, and he has no questionable rashes on his face. As for the rest of his body, I have no way of knowing what frightening, contagious skin conditions lie beneath his finery, nor could I ever know until our wedding night, which seems grossly unfair.

A bride ought to know ahead of time if her intended has brothel pox.

"You're right, but Father will never choose him. Sven of Ingeborg has an older brother, heir to the throne, but already married. Father is most insistent I will one day be queen in whichever kingdom he chooses."

Which seems rather greedy of him, as I will already be queen in my own right of Vagmar one day.

I see the princeling bow to my father before he disappears from our sight underneath the gallery. I hear the low murmur of their voices as they exchange pleasantries. It is a short conversation, and I am sure it is because Father has already decided against him. Is it my imagination, or do Sven's shoulders seem to sag as he beats a hasty retreat out the door?

We decide to enjoy ourselves for a spell, perhaps more than we should. Edda has brought an apple, and we slice it in halves with my eating knife to enjoy as the herald bellows out the next name. Canute Rikkardsson of Toth. A kingdom with little wealth and even less territory. Father would have already conquered Toth if it did not serve his purpose to use them as willing allies when we go to war against our greatest enemy, the Kingdom of Logaland. Father will dismiss this poor boy as well, I am sure of it. He and his guests will not hear us crunching the fruit, as they are too far below us. Unfortunately, this means we also cannot hear them. But really, it is more amusing to put words in their mouths anyway. Though it seems a touch cruel, these suitors have brought our drollery upon themselves. They are too old or too young, too timid or too preening, too squalid-looking or too flamboyant in their costume.

What matters most, of course, is my intended's character, not his looks. But if I am to be bound for the rest of my earthly days to one of these characters, I do not feel it is beyond the pale to be just a little judgmental of their appearances.

The herald announces our next visitor. "Prince Rufus of Echen, son of King Nefl, known as the Fair."

"Oh, My Princess. Now, sakes' alive, isn't he a sight for starved eyes?"

"I'd no idea you had such an appetite for a handsome face."

"You'd have to be a Hel-dweller of the Frostfangs to ignore such a specimen as that."

Is Edda calling me a Hel-dweller? Hopefully, she just speaks rhetorically. This princeling is handsome, though. And yet, even from this distance, I can see he wears a haughty expression, as if he finds this whole business distasteful.

Listen, Princeling, you're not the only one. At least Rufus of Echen had some choice whether he traveled to Vagmar for the competition. I have none. Prince Rufus turns to the herald. Of course, I cannot hear what he says. Though my hearing is far more acute than the average person's, it is a great distance to the hall below, and kings and princelings are not in the habit of shouting their conversations for the benefit of lurking eavesdroppers. The herald clears his throat and bellows, "Creator of the Joust, scourge of lists everywhere, defender of maidens, protector of–"

It is at this juncture I quit listening. Rufus of Echen lost my attention at 'creator of the joust.' So it is him I have to blame for this absolute waste of a day.

As the princeling bows and presents himself, however, I hear my father laugh. This is a rare feat. His mirth is genuine, not forced. A sense of humor is never unwelcome in a spouse. Perhaps I should not discount this one entirely.

Next, the Princeling of Hausen enters the hall. Poor Harald. It is just his luck to follow on the heels of the most blindingly handsome man in Plane. Though the conversations taking place below me are only a distant murmur, I recognize this boy. Pardon, man. I know him. Or at least, I did when we were five. Harald is of an age with me, but I do not believe he has matured quite so well, though I say it myself. Last I heard, his father, the King of Hausen, was trying desperately to increase his own potency so he could sire more heirs. He is of that age, you see, when men have trouble bedding women as lustily as is their wont. He even took a nubile, younger wife in the hopes he would procreate again. Edda does not hold with the acquisition of multiple wives, though I am not so sure it is a terrible notion. If my future husband takes up with a newer model, he will not bother so much with me.

"I've heard his father eats minced bulls' testicles with his pottage every evening," hisses Edda beside me.

"And I hear Harald cannot leave the bulls alone, hence his father's desire to produce a new heir."

"No, no, it is not the bulls, but their cows."

I clap my hand over my mouth to stifle my laughter. The Kingdom of Hausen is wealthy and vast, but I do not think my father will bind me to Harald. He loves me too much, even if he can be a touch...distant.

I notice when Harald bows, his scabbard lands with a thud on the wood-planked floor of my father's hall. Even from this distance, I can see his face redden in embarrassment.

"Poor child." I can't help but feel sorry for him. But then I recall the cows he's allegedly violated, and I feel a little less pity for him.

He'd be better than this next one, though." Edda gestures toward the next contender for my hand with her pointy chin.

Harald of Hausen descends the dais, to be replaced by a chap who's seen the back end of sixty.

The herald is evidently hopelessly lost, red in the face and not knowing what to do, when the next candidate breezes past him without waiting to be announced, as though poor, wee Harald is shite on the bottom of his boot, to be scraped off on the nearest pile of straw.

He can only be Arno, King of Dervnonia. I should not be surprised. I would be his sixth wife. If I remember correctly, the others passed in less than transparent circumstances. Arno has a temper, or at least that's what my father says.

I think he is a worthless turd, but it is only my humble opinion.

"Harald is looking better and better," I mutter to Edda.

"Do not despair yet," my nurse responds, pointing at the prospect who has just ambled into the hall.

The herald can't keep up, for he hasn't announced this princeling's name either. The wind follows him in, and if I am not mistaken, a few snowflakes. It is unfortunate for all that my birthday falls in midwinter, when the weather is bleak. The roads in winter are difficult to traverse, making the journey to Vagmar arduous for many suitors. You might think this fortuitous, but if I am to be forced to marry, I would rather there be as wide a selection of grooms as possible.

It may be my imagination, but Harald of Hausen and Arno of Dervnonia seem to shrink into themselves as this stranger approaches the dais. Unlike his predecessors, this contender is surrounded by no fawning retinue of retainers.

His hair is long and black and sleek, woven into intricate braids that course down his armored back. I hear Edda suck in a breath. She must be delirious with joyful appreciation of these braids. Bands of gold and silver encircle his arms, displaying his prowess to all. These are only won in jousts or in battle from one's enemies. I would be disappointed if his have all been claimed during a joust, though it should not matter to me at all.

He is not blindingly handsome like Rufus of Echen. His stance is too menacing, his shoulders a touch too hulking, the planes of his face too stern. But for some reason, I cannot take my eyes from him.

My father must stand to greet him, and the stranger bows his respects in return. I cannot hear what he says, nor what my father responds. But I hear my father laugh. It is a forced, tentative titter, a thing I never thought to hear from him. This man makes my father nervous. There isn't a person alive, at least not one I've ever met, who can make my father sweat. Not until now.

Who could he be? Though as I said, I have never left the Kingdom of Vagmar, I am well-versed in the geography and habits of our neighbors. I know the lineage of their monarchies as well as I know mine own. It is one of the few pieces of knowledge my father saw fit for me to be instructed in. But I cannot place this man. The neighboring kings are ancient. The princelings, insipid. I would remember if one of them looked like this. Moved like that.

The stranger looks up, and his eyes meet mine. But how is that possible? Then I realize I am so taken with him, I have risen above the partition that encases the minstrels' gallery, and I am gaping at him openly. Of course he can see me. But strangely, his expression registers no surprise, as though he knew I was there all along, spying on him.

For the first time, I think–

Perhaps marriage could be not so terrible, after all.

"Come, child, it is time to head back to your chamber. We are not finished with your toilette."

"I am never finished enough for you," I grumble.

But I suspect Edda's real reason for forcing me out of the gallery is so that I will stop staring at this stranger.

2

THYRA

If I am to smile beatifically all afternoon and hold my tongue whilst men simper and smirk for me, I must have more sustenance than half an apple. Valkyrien require nothing but the blood of warriors for sustenance, but I am both human and Valkyrie. I (thank the gods) cannot rely on blood alone for nutrition. I will admit, I haven't much of an appetite, which is why I am too skinny. Edda is forever lamenting my bony elbows and pointy chin. Of course, I cannot be discovered stuffing my gullet by any potential suitor–disgraceful, Edda would say–so I sneak out to the kitchens to hunt up something to tide me over until this evening's feast.

But Edda is not here to shame me. She has gone to help our household's other retainers to prepare for this day's ceremonies. I am left to my own devices, not to mention the rumble in my stomach.

Feeling like a fool, I tiptoe out of my chamber, proceed down the rickety wooden staircase that connects the royal chambers and galleries to the hall, and scuttle against the wall until I reach the entrance. I know where every creak and groan is on these stairs, and I manage to reach the first floor in silence. I must take such pains to be unseen, not only because a princess is not supposed to have normal bodily needs, such as the requirement of sustenance, but also because an important part of this Handfasting business is that I must be presented to all the suitors at once, as though I were a succulent boar's head or a confectionary sculpture.

Something to be marveled at for one brief moment, then devoured.

Amazingly, I have managed to make it this far without being discovered. I am just about to push against the door to peer outside for onlookers before I make my mad dash to the outbuilding that holds the kitchens, when a voice stops me in my tracks.

"Do you always spy on your father's guests from the minstrels' gallery?"

The voice is lazy, almost uncaring. And yet, before I even turn from the door, I know to whom it must belong. Him. The stranger with the dark hair and even darker eyes. He speaks in dulcet tones, but his voice still fills the hall. This is a man used to giving commands with ease and having them obeyed without question.

"Quiet, or someone will hear you," I say without thinking. I often do this–speak without deliberating whether my words are the wisest course of action. But I have never before encountered quite so intimidating a stranger.

"I may be mistaken, but are you...shushing me?"

"You have no one to blame but yourself." His Vagmarian is flawless, with only the hint of an accent. I feel my cheeks grow hot as he stares at me. "Sneaking up on a body like that will get you in trouble one of these days."

I am closer to him now than I was when I observed him

from the gallery. We are only feet away from each other. This close, I can see the stubble on his jaw and how his eyes shine in the midwinter gloom. I could reach out and touch him.

I feel my cheeks grow even hotter.

"Who says it hasn't already? Do you know, I was not certain at first whether you were the Princess Thyra. Many a dim-witted maid has spied on me in her time, so you see, you are only one of dozens. But it can only be you. No attendant or retainer would be so impertinent."

"I will take that as a compliment," I say.

"If you wish," he agrees easily enough.

Too easily.

"Why are you being so agreeable?" I forget my hot cheeks, suspicion forming in my mind. This is good. I infinitely prefer feeling suspicion to embarrassment.

"Are not potential bridegrooms supposed to make themselves amenable to their ladies' desires?"

I do not like how he says the word "desires." It makes me grow hot again, and this time, all over. Not just in my cheeks. "So you are here to woo me. I thought as much." If I can manage to treat him like every other suitor, I will survive this encounter with a shred of my dignity left intact. I still have trouble believing he is royalty. There is a hint of danger in his eyes and in the way he walks. Though his eyes sparkle with amusement, there is a menace in them no one should ignore, nor will I. Most princelings are pampered and soft, not hard like this specimen. "I should counsel you, sneaking up on your intended is not the most potent form of flattery."

"Mayhap not, but I suspect this is all the compliment you need."

For the first time, I notice he is holding something

wrapped in a linen napkin. I should have observed this sooner, but this man's presence is...overpowering. It is difficult to notice anything but him. And his shoulders. And that cheeky grin. Then the smell hits me.

"I could hear your stomach growl from the top of the stairs," he says.

"Mmm. Bread." I sigh with pleasure. I cannot help myself.

"And a little butter as well. You are not the only one too hungry to wait until this evening's feast to eat."

He offers the linen bundle to me, a smug grin on his face. Hunger overwhelms reason. It has ever been a failure of mine. I reach for the bread, but I manage to stop myself before taking hold of it. I hesitate. "What must I offer in return for this bread?" For there is always a price to be paid. Nothing in our world is ever freely given. There is always an expectation of recompense.

His black eyes dance. "I am not expecting you to agree to be my bride, just for a slice of bread, if that is what you are asking. Though I am offering butter as well, so perhaps I should."

"Our dairy maids churn some of the finest butter in all of Vagmar, but it is still not worth my entire future." I keep my voice light and teasing, but I am deadly serious.

To my surprise, his expression sobers. "No woman should have to bargain for her future."

I repress a snort of derision. "Tell this to my father."

He takes a step closer to me. His eyes gleam with an intensity that almost makes me shiver–from fear or something entirely different. I know not.

"Let me be very clear, My Princess. I know you have little agency of your own in the matter, but if your father chooses me as your bridegroom, you will be...pleased. I will make certain of it."

"Is this a threat or a promise?" Again, my tongue works quicker than my mind.

"Consider it both."

He grasps my hand, turns it over, and places the bundle of bread in my palm. His fingers linger on my own, and for one deranged moment, I feel my eyes closing. My body leans into his touch. This is madness. And besides–

"Why are you so intent on marrying me? You seem..." I cannot find the words. Too virile? Too handsome? Too disdainful? "Too proud to care so about a marriage contest."

He shrugs again, a habit of his, it seems. One I am growing to dislike. "I must marry. I must have a queen. And I must sire heirs. The princess who brings with her a dowry of the northern continent's finest butter may as well be my choice. Now run along, Princess, back to your chamber. We mustn't let anyone find out you've already met your bridegroom."

"Nay, just one of many suitors."

"If it comforts you to think so, fine."

I do not feel comfortable, not in the slightest. It is not an entirely complacent sensation, how my skin flushes against my will or my body sways toward this man like I am a deranged plague dancer, after just one touch.

What is better, a marriage to Arno or Harald, with whom I know what to expect? Who I might even be able to influence for the better when I am queen? Or the prospect of pledging my troth to someone I find...

Tempting.

I turn to return up the stairs, then halt. I realize I only do so because he commanded me, and I obeyed. Furious, I turn and make my own demand. “What is your name? From which kingdom do you hail?”

But the great oaken door of our hall is already closing. He is gone, the only sign that he was ever there, a gust of snow-speckled wind twirling in the air.

3

DRENGR

I came here to marry the Princess of Vagmar. I did not care if she walked like a duck or had hairy moles on her chin. My father's dying wish was that I be the one to take her hand, and it is what I will do, for I made an oath to him, and I always honor my oaths.

But as it turns out, she does not walk like a duck. If I am not mistaken, she glides as though the rushes on the floor and the knotty planks that cover the hall's more well-trodden spaces are the smoothest of surfaces. And she has no hairy moles–at least, none I can see–though there is one fetching birthmark perched just above her lips, on the left side of her face. I found myself wanting to lick it, to see if it tasted as good as it looked on her, but I decided (wisely, I think) that such behavior should probably wait for when I have known her a little longer.

At least another several hours.

My tent is perched in a location of honor, erected on the very top of the hillside, with a perfect view of the tournament grounds. There cannot be a betrothal without a grand display of feats of arms. This spot was not bestowed on me because my kingdom is the most powerful in Plane, but rather because my greedy little valet, Davith, snagged it before any other princeling could.

At our last encampment, the bastard made me wake at dawn so we would be the first royal party processing into the capital. I'd been wakeful during our entire journey, as Vagmar is my kingdom's traditional enemy, and I could not rest for fear an ambush awaited us at each temporary encampment. Finally, on our journey's last night, I felt I could rest easier, as the King Skerr of Vagmar is no fool. He would not risk an attack against our party so close to the capital, where only he could be blamed. He possesses many terrible qualities, but stupidity is not one of them. If only it was. It would make the vows I made to my father all those years ago so much easier to fulfill.

My attendants, under Davith's terrifying supervision, have pegged the tents with lightning efficiency. Mine own is larger than most any other princeling or king's, though again, it is not because we are the wealthiest country in Plane. (Even though we are.) It is because Davith spent many sleepless nights sewing additional panels onto my already perfectly serviceable tent. He refuses to be outshone, and it is his life's most lamentable challenge that I do not care a fig for pomp and circumstance.

But today I must pretend to care. And so I have allowed Davith to place massive carved pillars with dragons' heads at the entrance of the tent. It took six men to move them from the carts and drive them into the ground. Throws from what seem to be every known animal growing fur in Plane bedeck the ground and my bed. No mere cot would do, but instead Davith had a timber frame and down mattress brought from the castle. Heavy velvet curtains are draped from the canopy to keep out the chill.

I am from the mountains of Logaland, where deep snows blanket the ground for almost half the year. There is barely a chill in the balmy air of Vagmar, but this signifies nothing, apparently. Appearances must be maintained.

Or in this case, falsified.

I have also allowed him to commission a new suit of armor, one I would not normally be caught dead wearing in battle. Also, there was no 'allowing' involved. Davith insisted. It is plated with gilt, and the helmet has dragon horns. Actually, I quite like those horns. Mayhap when this business is finished, I will have the gilt removed from the helmet and keep it.

By business, I mean winning the tournament (which, of course, I will) and then securing the hand of the Princess Thyra.

Speaking of princesses and nuptials, I feel as though I am a maiden being styled for my wedding. "Davith, if you make me wear a wreath of flowers instead of this helm, I may take issue."

"You are not cooperating, Your Grace. Stop slouching. Do not make me tarry with your costume any longer than needs must. I do have a life, you know."

"This is news to me. I thought you lived for making me appear more kingly."

"The warriors from Ostocam are known to prefer the company of other gentlemen, and I will not see their like again. They are said to be deadly handsome. The Kingdom of Ostocam is a two months' journey from Logaland. I will never have the time to travel there."

"I have heard it is because they only deem other warriors as fit companions, so you may find yourself in a bind, as you are no soldier. And it is not a costume, young Davith. It is a suit of armor."

He shrugs. "I hope to find myself in at least several binds, but I take your point. I am a lover, not a fighter. Still, I shall rely on my old standbys–charm and good looks. They've never disappointed me yet."

"If you cease polishing my armor, I will give you five months' leave to journey there." Indeed, I would relish the reprieve.

"Five months? Whatever would I need five months for?" His busy hands cease moving, and he seems nervous, as though the unthinkable has become possible. That I might have grown tired of him.

"It is two months to travel there, and so I would guess two months for the return journey as well. And you would need at least a month in Ostocam to make your leave worthwhile."

"Ahh." Relieved, he continues buffing an imaginary scratch out of my chest plate.

"Did you not hear the important bit? My deal is only good if you leave me alone."

"You're just testy because you met the princess, and you didn't find her hideous. It would be ever so much easier for you if you did. There would be no emotions involved to complicate matters."

Vagmar is our traditional foe. I am not certain how the enmity between our nations began. It was many generations ago when Vagmarians and Logalanders decided they hated each other. There was probably some dispute over a few sheep and whose field they should be grazing in, and one shepherd was a Vagmarian, the other a Logalander, as our kingdoms share a rather lengthy boundary, and you can guess what would happen from there. Of course, kings and princes and jarls would have to become involved, because though the aristocracy does not normally concern itself with the doings of peasants, when it comes to a boundary dispute that takes square footage away from one kingdom and bestows it on another, the peasants' feelings on the matter suddenly become very important.

I am aware the traditional enmity between our nations became more personal in the previous generation. I am painfully aware of this fact. It is why my father's dying wish–more of an edict, really–was that I marry the Princess of Vagmar. Her father hated mine, and I am quite sure mine own father returned the favor. Why the solution is a marriage between their children escapes me.

I had accepted that binding myself to the princess was what I must do, and I was prepared to perform my duty. Honor my oaths. I was not, however, expecting to enjoy any part of the process. The fact that I might actually rub along well with this Princess Thyra is now a possibility–emphasis on the word rub, which I would dearly like to do to her–and I am not sure how I feel about it. I was prepared to put aside any distaste I had for the marriage and to school my emotions. I had not counted on the possibility that one of those emotions would be lust.

"I wish I hadn't told you I met her."

"But you did," Davith says with relish as he swipes a comb through the pieces of hair that peek out from my helmet.

This is a step too far. "Put the comb down before I chop off the hand that holds it."

He gasps. "How could I forget! Your sword. I need to have a page fetch it from the smithy."

He moves to the tent's opening, presumably to track one down, but I am quick to block his path. He stops short with a sigh of frustration. Most people would be intimidated by having me in their way. I am a rather large fellow, though I say it myself, and I do not remember a time when I didn't have a weapon on my person or know how to wield it. I doubt my nurse let me around pointy blades when I was still in leading strings, but I cannot be sure. Davith only seems irritated, though, at having to waste precious moments trying to get around me. I summon my most menacing stance, which again, really is rather frightening. I cannot tell you how many times other warriors have decided it was an unwise decision to engage me in combat, based on this stance alone. It should manage to scare even the likes of Davith, who knows me too well.

"What did you do to my sword, Davith?" Up to this point, I have only been jesting with my valet. But if he did something with my sword of which I do not approve, he may very well lose that hand, then take a permanent vacation to Ostocam. "Tell me you did not also coat my weapon with gilt."

"Even I know there are some boundaries that should never be crossed, Your Grace. I merely asked the smithy to add a small...enhancement."

"What?" Anger churns within me, burning through my guts.

"I asked him to engrave its name on the handle."

Dragonspear. It is not the name I gave my sword. For it is not just my sword. It was my father's and his father's before him. It has been in my family since the first dragons came to Logaland. The blade has a vein of ignatum running through it, forming its core. Ignatum is an element found only in the fiery pits of the mountain volcano of Muspel, where it is said the first dragons of Logaland were born. It is an indestructible metal. Dragonspear will never bend. Never break. To be blended into the sword, ignatum must be melted at the hottest of temperatures, using only dragon's fire for its forging. As metaphors go, it's rather on the nose. Logaland will always dominate Plane because of its dragons. Her kings will never submit, never surrender.

But still, it is a most superior weapon, and I treasure it.

I do not think my father, or his fathers before him, would disapprove of Davith's decision.

Cocky bastard.

"You could have asked my permission," I say sulkily.

"And you could have said no, which is why I didn't."

I sigh. It is no use arguing. "Well, then, do I look presentable, at least?" It is not a question I can ever remember asking in my life. Nor can I think of a time when I would have cared about the answer.

If I didn't know better, I'd say I'm nervous. It's not a sensation with which I have much experience. I'm not one of those obnoxious, pretentious fellows who would boast they've never known a moment's doubt or hesitation, not in the whole of their lives. There was the time I lost my virginity to a lass who worked in one of the taverns by Old Town's gates. She did not know my identity, for I wanted to prove I could woo a maid without the benefit of my pedigree. I succeeded, to such a degree I must say, I've never again felt nervous about proving my prowess.

Then there was my first battle. I was nearly shitting bollocks, such were my nerves. I was a resounding success in this arena as well, however. Still, after hundreds of battles, I have flutters in my belly when I take command of the shield wall. Any man who no longer feels hesitation before battle, particularly when he is in command of many levies and responsible for whether other warriors live or die, is a fool.

I am many things, not all of them favorable, but a fool is not one of them.

I am not nervous about the joust. The possibility of injury is ever present, but I have won almost every tournament I ever entered, and it is not because I am the king, so others allow me victory. The princelings and kings of other nations do not care. They are not my subjects. I am just better. This is not boastfulness, just fact.

I realize I am apprehensive about paying suit to the Princess Thyra. I suspect she is not the sort to be impressed when I win the joust. That she will not fall at my feet in a delirium of appreciative joy. If only she would, then this business would be so much easier.

Davith seems to realize I no longer care about his interference and slides past me to fetch the page, so I may be reunited with my sword. I cannot let him off that easily, though. "Oh, and Davith, do try to remember to ask me first, in future, when you want to tamper with my weapons."

He grins. "Do not worry, Your Grace. Rest assured, I will not."

4

THYRA

You'd think this Handfasting spectacle would involve some conversation between myself and the applicants for my hand in marriage. But you would be mistaken. The festivities begin with a joust. It's a lovely word, joust. One thinks of heroic knights astride their gleaming steeds, their banners flying, begging ladies in the stands for their favors. But it is a muddy, bloody business, especially when the warriors from our neighboring kingdoms are involved. The peoples of the North are not exactly known for their fanciful notions of what constitutes a knightly gentleman.

Kill. Or be killed.

Rule. Or be ruled.

A man's purpose in the kingdom of Vagmar–and in all of Plane, if I am not mistaken–is to fight. He is born being expected to be a warrior. He is trained from a young age. A Vagmarian woman is also trained as a warrior, but her responsibilities only begin with the defense of the kingdom. First and foremost, she should be able to defend home and hearth when her man is away. But also, she should be ornamental when required.

Unless you are a princess.

Then your purpose is to appear ornamental but also bear as many heirs as possible to your husband, so the kingdom may be preserved. It is difficult to achieve both objectives at once. Constantly conceiving and delivering children is not an occupation which lends itself to preserving one's youthful beauty.

Vagmar is not the wealthiest kingdom of Plane. This honor belongs to Logaland. But it is prosperous. My father has outdone himself with the preparations for this festival, and the joust is no exception. The tiltyard is groomed immaculately. There are stands provided for all, even the poorest citizens of our kingdom. In the section where our nobles sit, garlands of flowers bedeck every row of benches. A miracle, it seems, when one considers it is midwinter, and flowers can only be harvested from hothouses.

The contestants, both of this joust and for my hand in marriage, are mounted before us in the tiltyard, saluting my father, who sits under a damask gold canopy on a throne-like chair fashioned by his own royal woodcarver for this very occasion. I sit to his left, lower of course, so he may appear that much grander. Mine own seat has a back, unlike the benches on which the other spectators sit, my ladies-in-waiting included.

Lyda is my favored attendant. Her father is a prominent jarl and sits on my father's council. But I do not prefer her company because of her lineage. I enjoy it because she has a sense of humor. I cannot say the same for most of my ladies, who were chosen by my father because of their ancestry, certainly not their suitability as my attendant.

"I could not bring myself to bed a single one of these

turds," Lyda hisses to me, keeping a watchful eye on my father, making sure he does not overhear.

"Why, thank you, Lyda. Your words are such a comfort to me."

"Oh, please. You know this to be true. The best you can hope for is to pop out an heir and a spare for one of these lechers, then pray you may take up with a serviceable young guardsman when your childbearing duties are finished."

"You are forgetting, adultery in a queen is usually considered treason. I'd probably lose my head, even if I did find a guardsman I fancy." Not that it is likely. If I were to have a choice in my partner, it would be someone with a more academic bent than a soldier. And yet, I suspect the stranger from the hall is more soldier than scholar, but this does not seem to bother me.

"I must say, however, Harald of Hausen's mount is quite a specimen. He must have acquired him from Logaland. Though I am surprised he mounts a horse and not a sheep," says Lyda.

I clap a hand to my mouth, stifling my snort of laughter. "I'd heard it was cows."

"No matter. What I know for certain is he does not deserve such a magnificent piece of horseflesh."

Lyda is an exceptional equestrian. I can tell she begrudges Harald his mount, and I must admit, he is fairly useless as a jouster. Come to think of it, he is not quite serviceable at any knightly or princely skill. But enough of Harald. Lyda has mentioned the Kingdom of Logaland, and my merriment evaporates like water in the southern desert kingdoms of Plane. Lyda places a comforting hand over my own. "I am sorry. I did not mean to bring up Logaland. I spoke without thinking. It is their horses, you see. I forget reason when I think of those magnificent steeds. It is positively unfair such a powerful nation, already in possession of a legion of dragons, should also breed the finest horseflesh."

I was nervous about this joust already. Not just because at its conclusion, my betrothed may be named. But because I have to sit through hours of violence and potential bloodshed, clenching my teeth in the hopes they will not form into fanged points. Praying to the gods the scratching sensation between my shoulder blades stays only a minor irritation and does not presage the eruption of my wings. Edda cinched my stays so bloody tightly, they'd likely be caught in the confines of my gunna. This sounds painful, and I do not wish to discover whether I am correct. Besides, I do not think even Edda's handiwork can contain my feathered friends for long. Nothing can. Smell blood. Grow wings. It has ever been my curse. And my senses do not distinguish from the false combat of a joust and the mortal danger of actual warfare, which a Valkyrie craves more than air.

These worries threaten to overtake me, but I find my resolve, knowing Lyda is waiting for an answer. Knowing crowds of spectators likely observe me at this very moment, wondering if I favor a particular opponent. Searching for any signs of weakness in my behavior. A frown, perhaps, or hunched shoulders. Any betrayal of my misery, and the entire capital will know of it by nightfall.

"It is no matter," I finally say. "I should be able to bear to hear its name spoken without flinching. A princess should have more control over her emotions. Though if anyone begins speaking of the old king of Logaland, I may scream."

I mean the present king's father, the one responsible for my mother's death.

"I shall not mention him, but you should be aware the new king, his son, is here. It is all anyone can talk of. Had you not been hidden away by Edda in your chamber, you would have known already."

"Why is he here?"

"I suppose he has traveled to Rhok for the same reason as all the other princelings of Plane. To secure your hand."

"But that's preposterous!" Fear grips me, opening a cold pit in my belly, for I suspect it is, in fact, possible the Logalander king has come for my hand. Logalanders always take what they want, and of course, their king would want Vagmar and all its riches.

"Is it? And here I thought the purpose of a royal marriage is to secure an alliance between kingdoms. To heal past misdeeds. To forge a brighter future for all parties involved...excepting the bride and groom, of course. They're usually miserable with these arrangements."

Lyda's violet eyes sparkle. She is, of course, wearing a gunna in a matching hue to complement them. It is one of Edda's greatest regrets I am the royal heir and not someone like Lyda, I am sure. My friend appears every inch the princess–head always tilted regally, soft brown hair never out of sorts, quick to horse, and even quicker to arms. We should switch places. Indeed, if we could, I would.

"I see your point, but my father would never allow it." Or would he? He is ever cunning and devious in his political dealings, but I'd never thought he would jeopardize my own well-being to achieve his aims. And my well-being is exactly what would be at risk if I am wed to Logaland. Vagmarian princesses who travel to that nation have a habit of winding up dead.

It is then I see him, the prince I could not take my eyes from when he stood in the hall in front of my father. Forget what I said about crude warriors and even cruder tongues. Here stands a true knight. He is in possession of a gleaming steed and polished armor. A scarlet plume of feathers stands erect atop his helmet, which he has tucked in one arm. I cannot see him well from this distance, but it does not matter. I have already seen him this morn, and he left an impression.

Something about him sets him apart, besides his looks. At first, I cannot quite place my finger on it, and then I realize what it is. He does not seem amused by the joust. Indeed, he seems bored. Dismissive, even. As though he is silently mocking all the swearing, fetid warriors surrounding him in the field.

He strides forward to pay his respects to my father and me, and I must restrain myself from gaping. Edda is not here to remind me to keep my teeth together. Only a handful of my ladies sit beside me, and all but Lyda are too busy tittering at the specimen before us to notice I act just as foolish as them for once, when encountering a handsome male.

His eyes are even blacker than I thought, if such a thing is possible. And they are pinned on me. Not in an appreciative way. Nor in a seductive manner. But as if those eyes... own me. In our world, black hair is a rarity. Black eyes, I do not think I have ever seen. I have heard stories of the people to the South, that such features are more common there. But in the cold of the North, our eyes are light and our skin even lighter.

He does not ask for my favor. Every warrior in the lists today has asked for it. It is expected, of course, as they are here for me. To impress me. To win me. As though I were a prize courser or a bag of silver. As instructed by my father, I cannot bestow my favors on just one knight. It would make the others jealous if I seem to prefer one suitor so early in the proceedings.

And this directive suited me, as I have no interest in bestowing favors on a single one of these insipid man-children. At least, not until now. If this warrior asked for my favor, I might be tempted.

I am irrationally angry he has not asked.

I peer closer at the coat of arms that decorates his shield. If I can recognize it–I am familiar with most, and those with which I am not familiar are likely not worth knowing–I will know from which kingdom he hails. And of course, his name. Then I will know for whom to cheer. Marriage is unavoidable. I have accepted this. But it may as well be to someone whose touch I might actually welcome. Whose eyes make me feel short of breath when he looks my way. Even princesses deserve to feel a little breathless sometimes.

His shield is broad and tall, but then so is he. Painted on its surface, a pair of black dragons sit on either side of a cloud, seeming to hold it up. My heart plummets to my stomach. Atop the cloud is a crown. The coronet is painted black to represent the dark metal of what I presume to be ignatum. Actually, what I know to be the indestructible element of ignatum, for I recognize this coat of arms as well as I know mine own. Though it is devoid of precious jewels, this crown is known throughout the Realm of Plane, for its adornment is unmistakable and grotesque. The coronet is encircled by fangs.

Dragon fangs.

This is the king of Logaland.

I hadn't realized until this moment the sensation I felt burning within me all morning was that of hope. Whether the mysterious warrior with whom I'd shared bread won or lost the joust, I felt certain my father would take my wishes into account and consider this man above the rest. I knew two things before this tournament began. One, the stranger made me laugh, and two, I did not recoil when I thought of him bedding me.

It was enough to get me to cooperate with the Handfasting. Enough to make me stop feeling sorry for myself. To remember I was a Princess of Vagmar, and marriage was my duty. It could be worse. For instance, I could be the princess who eventually wed Harald of Hausen or Arno of Dervnonia.

I hadn't known how precious this sense of hope was until I lost it.

There is no one in Plane whom I hate more than Drengr of Logaland, except for maybe his sire. And he is dead, so he will, sadly, never fall victim to my revenge. But this Drengr is a different matter. I swore on my mother's grave the people of Logaland would suffer for what they'd done to me, to my father, and to all of Vagmar.

I may as well start with its king.

5

DRENGR

She may not realize it, but I realize it the moment she realizes who I am, which is a complicated and pedantic means of saying...Shite, she figured it out. I'd been dreading my appearance in the lists. I'd debated going without my shield, which displays my coat of arms and is a telltale giveaway of my identity, or perhaps borrowing one of my carls'. But I have never been a coward, and I do not intend to take up the habit simply because I want the princess to like me.

I'd hoped to see her again before the tournament or at least before she discovered my identity, which I suppose was a fool's errand. To make her like me, before she detested me. The hatred would inevitably follow on the heels of her discovery, but if I could have just inspired a little regard on her part, my foot would be in the door. And once my foot is in any door, I never waste time. I crack that son of a bitch open with a sharp kick and barge in.

Sadly, I think wooing this princess will take a more nuanced approach. Subtlety is not a special talent of mine. Getting the princess to like me will take a lot of work. I'm not sure I'm cut out for it. I'm also not sure I should even bother trying. But then I remember the alternative is to break my oath to my father and keep Vagmar our eternal enemy.

My herald begins to announce me–King Drengr Dagmarsson of Logaland, son of Dagmar Oakenshanks, Master of Dragons, Lord of the Great Blade Dragonspear, Scourge of the...of the..." The herald's voice trails away. He was about to say "scourge of the people of Vagmar," which would have been in rather poor taste. It is, however, how I am traditionally announced. I find myself waiting with anticipation to see what my herald will come up with. He's a rather pompous fellow, and I'm not so sure he thinks well on his feet. Out of the corner of my eye, I see Davith gesturing from underneath the stands, on the other side of the lists. He is mouthing something to me, but he is also cupping his mouth with his hands, presumably to conceal what he is trying to tell me from prying eyes. Unfortunately, he is also hiding it from me, and I was no lip reader to begin with. I gesture for him to take his hands away from his mouth.

Ass four huh fay-vor.

Favor? I got that last bit. What in Hel does he mean?

Then I remember. Ask for her favor. It is not a thing I've ever done when competing in the lists. I never cared to. Why would I want the silly hair ribbon or lace hankie of a stupid chit whose parents were first cousins and aunt and uncle are also likely her cousins? I'd rather get a real favor later, after the joust is over, when I visit whatever local tavern is at hand. The lasses are always quick to celebrate the tourney champion, especially when he is a king who is under fifty and can still maintain an erection with relative ease.

Smart thinking, Davith. Though I don't believe this princess will care so much about the elaborate ritual of bestowing her favor upon her chosen knight as much as my valet hopes. Though she hasn't given it to anyone yet, so maybe there's still a chance she's waiting for the right warrior to come along and ask. I remember belatedly the "right warrior" is highly unlikely to be me, as I am her hated enemy. Still, it can't hurt to try, my father always said, and though he was usually talking about taking another horn of ale or challenging much larger boys to mock combat, I think his sage advice applies here. Then again, he lied. I can confirm too much ale and too many fights with older boys do indeed hurt like Hel.

I prod Holfnir, my stallion, forward. He snorts in distaste, as such an effort on his part is not usually required and most assuredly beneath his dignity. He is made for one thing and one thing only. Jousting. To be more accurate, winning at the joust. I suppose, in retrospect, he is bred for two things, for he covers most any mare in the capital when they are in season. He is sire to many of the swiftest and smartest horses in the world. Logaland is known for its prize horseflesh, and this is no idle boast. We sell our horses to all corners of Plane, and thank goodness, else I'd have to raise taxes to give a boost to the Royal Exchequer. Then I would not be so popular a monarch.

"May I beg your favor, My Princess?" I hold my lance out for her, as countless other contestants have already done today. It is the custom. If she refuses, it is not generally meant to give offense. A tournament is always held in honor of a lady, and she can only bestow her favor on one warrior. But a hush settles over the gathered crowd. For they have realized what I already realized the princess realized, long before she ever realized it.

Vagmar's princess is being asked by her mortal enemy to tie a bow on the tip of his lance. As metaphors go, it's rather on the nose. It is why most warriors love carrying such big lances, not to mention why the maidens enjoy tying their bows. It is the only opportunity they've ever had to put anything on a big tip. If you hadn't caught on yet, the lance is a giant cock, and the lady's favor is intended to signify she wouldn't mind sitting on it.

I know she hates me, but do I have shite on my face? Or a particularly heinous rash? I smell nothing foul, and I avoid brothel pox by, first, avoiding brothels, and second, always wearing a sheep's bladder sheath when I bed a woman. The look on her face is like none I've ever seen before. The green eyes narrow, the lips purse, the forehead creases. When we are better acquainted, I shall have to tell her to not frown so. She is too young to develop wrinkles.

It was her green eyes I first noticed when she peered at me–most rudely, I might add–from the minstrels' gallery in her father's hall. I could not be sure at the time she was the Princess of Vagmar, but I hoped she was. If I am being honest, the very moment mine own eyes met hers, it is what I wished. So green they pierced the gloom, were her eyes. I am no poet, and so believe me when I say her eyes slayed me. A bard could do her eyes better justice, but they'd likely be far worse under the bed furs than I am. Why waste time with flowery words, when there are more important bits to tend?

And all the rest of those bits are also quite lovely. Her hair cascades down her back, flowing as only a maiden's does. It is as red as the sun when it is setting on the eve of a placid dawn. She is a bit too tall and skinny, but then I am much too tall and run to fatness if I am not careful. Still, she is well formed, as many of the women of Vagmar are. They are trained as warriors along with their menfolk, making their breasts even more pert, their arms and legs muscled, and their waists narrow. The one mar on her beauty is perhaps her chin, which is over pointy, but I do not see this as a flaw. It is indicative of a defiant character.

She does not know it, but this stubbornness is actually quite highly desirable to me. I do not jest. For a woman with such fire in her veins is absolutely insatiable between the bed furs. This is fact, not just mine own theory. I have tested it time and time again. Were she an ugly wench, her enthusiasm for bedsport would be a welcome distraction from her lack of comeliness. But since she is quite lovely, the combination of beauty and passion is positively alluring.

I lean toward her, as far as Holfnir's ears will allow, and say in a stage whisper, "My Princess, do you have urgent need of a privy? For your face has gone all funny, as though your bowels will loose at any moment. You didn't drink any of the Dervnonian wine, did you? Filthy stuff."

She wasn't ever going to like me anyway, so I may as well demonstrate I do not care for her good opinion. Arno, the king of said kingdom, must be shooting daggers at my back, for though he is at least twenty years too old for such sport, he also competes in the lists. Even if the princess was not destined for myself–which, of course, she is–I would not wish Arno of Dervnonia as a husband for my worst enemy. And come to think of it, she is. Or at least, she thinks she is. But these are just semantics, really, to be hammered out and smoothed after we are wed.

The King of Vagmar and all the attendants present stifled gasps of outrage. Though if I am not mistaken, the pretty maiden sitting next to the princess smothers a smile. A fetching blush of rage creeps up the princess's neck and blooms onto her cheeks. If she is not careful, it will reach her hairline, where no one will be able to tell when flesh ends and hair begins. But to her credit, she composes herself, a feat I can only admire.

"Nay, Your Grace, I shall not bestow you with a favor. Not when there are other competitors more...worthy."

My cock hardens. Thank Odin for my armor. I normally welcome an erection, but now is not an opportune moment. The tourney will begin soon, and I cannot be thinking about how the Princess of Vagmar's tongue may be able to do other wicked things besides speak insults.

"You'll say differently on our wedding night, Princess."

And before she has a chance to respond–or her father has the opportunity to cleave my head in twain–I turn Holfnir and retreat to the lists.

To win at the joust, one must only be the contestant who breaks the most lances. Mine own are fashioned from Logalander oak, tipped with dragon heads forged from iron. Once, the kings of my country had spears tipped with ignatum, but it is a dear substance, and not just in price. There is only a finite amount of ignatum under Plane's surface. I am fortunate most of it lies beneath my kingdom. Again, I would not be so popular a monarch if I had to raise taxes to increase streams of revenue.

'Tis the simplest thing in the world, breaking lances, and yet extremely difficult. This is to say, most warriors find breaking lances a challenge. For the most part, I do not. Really, 'tis unfair when one thinks on it. I believe jousting to be a stupid pastime.

My contemporaries would tell you it keeps a warrior in fighting condition, so it prepares him for battle, when it comes. Nonsense, I say. Nothing prepares a warrior for battle except prior experience in battle. And standing in the shield wall, gripping your spear and shitting bollocks, waiting for your fetid enemy to slice you at the knees, is nothing like a joust. True, blood and sweat run freely during the tourney as well as in battle, but in general, tears do not. And the goal is to prevent your opponent's death, which is sometimes unavoidable, even when taking precautions. But there are rules in place, an expected code of conduct, by which we all must abide. In theory, such a code is supposed to exist to govern how battles are conducted as well, but theory rarely translates to practice. For after all, when the levies are called, it is mostly yeomen and blacksmiths, coal miners and shepherds, fighting in the shield wall. Rarely princelings and kings or even jarls and knights.

Why these nobs think fighting each other with beribboned lances prepares them to face down a disenfranchised farmer who's been forced to leave his land (often at planting or harvest time, when the weather is ripe for both war and agriculture), who hasn't had a decent supper in a fortnight and would gladly skewer their livers and fry them over the campfire, is beyond me. The fact that it might be royal liver would only enhance the flavor, more effectively than any pinch of salt.

If I sound critical of this hypothetical farmer with a penchant for sweetmeats made out of human organs, I do not mean to. I would prefer to stand in the shield wall with just such a man, rather than half these princelings present in the lists. First, because they are survivors and will not fall to pieces at the slightest hint of danger. And second, they are infinitely more amusing companions. Most princelings have no sense of humor.

I blame my parents, as one often does for various and perceived injuries and deficiencies throughout one's life. They named me Drengr, one of the most common names in existence. It means, depending on who you ask, "lad," "boy," or "warrior boy." I prefer this last one. They hoped to keep me humble. To remind me I owe allegiance to every citizen of Logaland, and not the other way round. Respect is earned. Fealty is given. A king must be deserving. This is not conjecture on my part. My father literally told me he gave me a peasant's name to help ensure I would not grow up to be an arsehole.

I'm not sure whether the lesson took, but I do know I have a preference for the company of the lowborn and not those of mine own class. But I digress. Tournaments have always been a popular means of promoting friendly competition amongst the kingdoms of Plane. Even when we have been fighting pitched battles elsewhere, Logalanders and Vagmarians make nice when jousting in the lists. At least, we pretend to.

But in recent years, the tournament has undergone changes, and not for the better, if you ask me. But no one has. Once, we took up our shields and swords–or spears or axes, depending on one's preference–and engaged in combat. Rather than broken lances, broken shields were the objective. This mode of competition was far more effective at preparing warriors for the shield wall than this foolish jousting.

It is the fault of Prince Rufus of Echen the tournaments transitioned to these nonsensical jousts. He is one of the vainest peacocks in existence, even if he is a friend. He thought it would befit his majesty if he sat atop a steed, charging down the lists, lance at the ready. He wasn't wrong, either. And where Rufus leads, others follow. He is a bloody plate of fashion. He also already knew what to do in a shield wall and didn't realize the harm he was causing to the likes of Harald of Hausen and others of his ilk. They need every opportunity for battle practice they can seize.

I will not compete for hours yet, as I am the champion

everyone hopes to defeat. This waiting business is more boring than jousting itself. At least then, I get to put Holfnir through his paces. The other warriors must work their way up to me.

It is Harald of Hausen, who likely hasn't stood in a shield wall in all his years and hasn't a virgin's chance in Hel of defeating anyone in this tourney, who opens the day. My horse could hold a spear in his mouth and probably poke the poor boy bloody before he would ever remember to raise his own lance in defense. Sven Gutterson, Prince of the House of Ingeborg, defeats him handily.

I make a point of shaking Harald's hand, clapping his shoulder, and sharing a few encouraging words after his loss. Hausen manages to stay neutral in the wars between Logaland and Vagmar, and its envoys even travel between both kingdoms as welcomed guests. This is a rare feat indeed, one which, of course, is a testament to the skill of said envoys and Harald's father. Odin help us when Harald takes over. He'll probably send his most favorite sheep on diplomatic missions. But though Harald was born five sticks shy of a broom, he is gracious in defeat.

Prince Sven of Ingeborg must then enter the lists again, to joust against the next princeling. Tal of Merne, his name is. Merne is a kingdom far to the south, though it still enjoys four seasons. Its winters are mild, its people peaceable. I do not think Tal of Merne will trouble Sven, though I do not look forward to facing the boy if he progresses through the lists.

Sven cheats, using plaster to tip his lances instead of iron, so they will break more easily. But it would apparently be unknightly to mention this, so we all just pretend he progresses through these tourneys, purely on his own merit. Even with such artifice, he is still no match for myself nor a few select others, one of whom idles next to me this very moment. Were he not a friend, I would ignore him.

"Why are you here competing? I did not think you were in the market for a wife."

If I sound annoyed, it is because I am. Rufus of Echen is more handsome than me. If I were a vainer man, this would pain me to confess. But as Davith is ever lamenting, I care not for such vanities. At least, I usually don't. But if he ruins this Handfasting for me, I'll bloody his bollocks. He is more proportionate than I, with a slim but strong build. My shoulders are rather...broad. He walks gracefully, even in bloody armor, upon legs supple like ash wands. Mine own legs are more like trunks. Very large trunks. It is not for nothing my father was known as Oakenshanks. Thankfully, the moniker was already taken, or I might be stuck with it as well.

The Princess of Vagmar may fall prey to Rufus's charms, like so many women before her. What if she begs her father to handfast Vagmar to Echen, instead of Logaland? I doubt King Skerr would, under normal circumstances, take his daughter's preference into account when deciding which marriage alliance would most benefit his kingdom. But then again, the Kingdom of Echen is not the mortal enemy of Vagmar.

"Hel no. Bite your tongue. I am not wife shopping. I am here for the usual reasons. Glory, riches, women. Note, Drengr, I did not say one woman, as in, a wife. I mean many women, preferably without pedigree, and hopefully all at once. Besides, I cannot abide a redheaded woman."

"You are aware, are you not, that you have red hair?"

"Exactly. I want no competition in my marriage, if such an event ever takes place. Everyone knows the color is most superior, and I cannot have anyone thinking my wife more comely than myself."

"I always thought it strange Wilhelm doesn't have red hair." Wilhelm is Rufus's brother, but more on him later. "Every other one of your father's natural sons does. The kingdom of Echen is littered with them."

Rufus nods contemplatively. "Red hair is common enough in the Northlands, but I will say, it is entirely possible if a child has it in Echen, he or she belongs to my father."

"In Hausen, too. Remember, your father fostered with Harald's grandsire," I add helpfully.

"True enough. If Harald had red hair, I'd worry his mother may have become overfond of my father."

It is only then I notice our conversation has an audience of one. Ulf Olafsson of Vagmar, Councillor to King Skerr. Like Rufus and myself, he stands outside the tourney field, soothing his horse, who chafes to run at the tilts as much as he does. Likely more. It is the way of steeds bred for jousting. Olafsson, also, waits on the day's proceedings, to see who he will oppose in the lists. He is a talented jouster, I must admit. On one of the rare occasions I was defeated in the lists, it was by Olaffsson. The man is a right old pain the ass. And he is the last person I wish to overhear any conversation about the Vagmarian princess. I decide to distract him.

"And for that matter, old man, what do you do in the lists? You couldn't possibly be competing for the Princess Thyra's hand."

"I would never presume to such a thing. But I am here to defend her honor, as I always shall be, no matter where she goes, no matter to which kingdom she is wed."

Harald of Hausen, even, would recognize Olafsson's

words as the threat they are intended to be. It would be unwise to goad him, as I am trying to betroth myself to his princess, but I find myself opening my mouth to retort. Maybe something about his bald head. Yes, a perfect barb about his shiny pate. No matter that it would likely not bother Olafsson in the slightest. But insulting him would make me feel better. Then a dull roar rises from the crowded audience, and all three of us turn to see what has caused their dismay.

"Who died?" Rufus asks casually. It is a nonsensical question, for neither Olafsson nor I know the answer. But a page comes streaking through the camp, wearing the livery of the House of Ingeborg–stars and a crescent moon above a baying wolf–presumably to deliver some ill-fated news of Prince Sven's injuries to the tourney masters.

"Boy, halt!" barks Olafsson before I can. As I stated, the man is a right old pain in the ass. "Is something amiss with your master?" he asks him.

The page, who cannot possibly have seen ten winters and has a wen weeping from his neck, obeys. I feel a moment's pity for him, as it cannot be easy to have to heed more than one lord at any given moment. He must deliver his news post-haste, but also cannot ignore the directive of the Vagmarian king's chief advisor.

"Aye, we fear him dead," the boy answers. Then, before we can question him further, he darts off.

Rufus sighs. "I suppose we must all go assess the situation, see if we cannot lend some aid to the House of Ingeborg."

Olafsson and I make unlikely companions as we process to the lists, Rufus walking ahead of us, churning up mud and shite with his greaves. I notice the Vagmarian wears a simple suit of armor, without benefit of his sigil displayed on his cuirass or cloak. He probably thinks I look like a prancing, preening princeling with my gleaming, obsidian-coated armor and fanciful cloak, fashioned of scarlet-hued silk. I remind myself to have a word with young Davith later. Olafsson is attired in much the same way I would be under normal circumstances. As in, if I hadn't allowed Davith free reign over my costume after he insisted he would make the Princess of Vagmar fall in love with me before she could realize it was a terrible decision.

It is a walk of about five hundred paces to the tourney field, but our cumbersome armor makes it seem more like a mile. Our progress is slow. Though Rufus, with those obscenely long and slim legs, does not seem to be as discomfited as either myself or Olafsson, as he soon outpaces us.

I must think of something to say to the old fart. After all, I want to marry his beloved princess. The gods know he will not trouble himself with speaking to me first.

"I had thought I would enjoy your milder climate, Olafsson, but the snow melts when it touches the ground and churns the earth into a right old pile of shite."

There. I thought of something to say. Davith would be proud. Or perhaps he wouldn't be. I've never been any good with small talk.

"If you mislike it so much, Your Grace, perhaps you should go home. The sooner, the better, in point of fact."

"I do not scare so easily, old man."

Hel. I'd meant not to call him old man aloud again. On second thought, I'm telling Davith nothing of this conversation. As far as I'm concerned, it never happened.

"It will take more than a few piles of turd-like mud and a foul stench in the air to make me turn tail and ride home." There is no stink in the air, just the earthy aromas of wet soil, horseflesh, and hay, but I have an admittedly difficult time reigning in my tongue once it gets going.

"Then what do you fear, Your Grace?"

Olafsson's voice drips with sarcasm, and I am sure he truly does not care to hear my answer. So of course, I must disoblige him. "I am afraid of many things, Lord Ulf. For instance, there was this one time, when I was just a lad serving as a squire to the King of Echen." This is why Rufus and I are such friends, despite our differences. "I was still a virgin, you see, but several of the kitchen maids asked me to show them what lay beneath my tunic and whether it was as impressive as it seemed. They also mentioned some whips and chains might appear if I obliged. I tell you, I shuddered, and being a virgin and only a lad, it was not just from anticipation."

"Forget I asked."

"My mother taught me never to ignore others, as it is rude, and I would hate to have you think me rude."

"Thinking you just rude would be an improvement upon what I think of you now, Your Grace."

Ignoring him, I blithely tackle my next greatest fear. In truth, I still have not completely outgrown my fear of bondage. It's all right every once in a while, but I do not spend enough time in any one woman's bed furs to acquire the level of trust necessary to commit to such an endeavor.

We have almost reached the lists. I must finish this conversation before I lose Olafsson's ear. It may be the only opportunity I have to impress him. And if you're thinking making a good impression on him at this point is nigh impossible, you haven't been paying attention. "What I fear most, however, is that your princess will never be able to overcome her hatred of my kingdom and all its inhabitants.

For you and I both know I would take better care of her than any of these fools."

I gesture to the princelings running toward Sven of Ingeborg, who lies crumpled in the middle of the tourney field. His horse, a rather bedraggled-looking bay–Ingeborg is a poor kingdom and cannot afford Logalander horseflesh–noses the boy's pallid face. His eyes are closed, but he is alive, for no dead man makes such a grimace of pain.

"No, I do not know anything of the kind. Harald of Hausen will never break her heart, for he is not capable of inspiring her love. Arno of Dervnonia may be cruel, but My Princess can handle herself. He will never bend her to his will. Indeed, if Dervnonia is My King's choice, I suspect it will be the other way 'round."

I suspect this as well. Though I've only spoken with her twice, she does seem rather formidable. Again, I feel that rush of excitement. "Come now, you know I am the best choice, and for that matter, so is Logaland. We would finally achieve lasting peace through our marriage. If the King of Vagmar is grandfather to the heirs of Logaland, it is rather difficult to make war. Surely, you must know what they say of how the Princess Thyra's mother was treated when in our capital is utter falsehood."

"I know nothing of the sort."

"She did not even die within the palace."

"Even so, it does not mean your father was not responsible."

This conversation has not gone as I'd hoped. And it is too late to try to resuscitate it, for we are finally at Sven of Ingeborg's side. Rufus has been here for more than a moment, but he only crouches by the princeling and eyes him contemplatively. I bend down to join Rufus and ask in a hushed whisper, "How goes it? Will he live?"

"Since there is absolutely nothing wrong with him but a smashed toe, I'd wager he'll be fine."

But it is not Rufus who answers me. It is the royal harridan of Vagmar, red curls flaming and dancing in the wind, green eyes blazing with an expression of pure disgust. This time, I believe this distaste is not reserved for myself alone, but for all the warriors present, particularly Prince Sven.

I'd not noticed before what the princess was wearing. I was too busy inspecting her shining hair, bright eyes, and whether she had decent breasts. She does. Did I mention? In fact, they are magnificent. Not quite large enough, given her skinny frame, but quite shapely. Her gown is a silvery color, made of a very fine silk. The hems of her sleeves and collar are embroidered in ermine. She looks elven, ethereal. But she'd look better in green, to match her eyes. When we are better acquainted, I shall have to tell her so.

It is the fashion for highborn ladies to wear ridiculously long, wide sleeves. Hers are shoved above her elbows. She kneels next to Sven, ignoring how her silken gown becomes instantly encrusted in mud. She puts her hands–elegant, long-fingered but strong, I notice–on either side of his helm. Gently, she removes it. For a moment, I think she will place his head in her lap and play up her role as Maiden of the Joust. Then she slaps him–one loud, harsh crack to the cheek.

"Easy, Princess, 'twas only the boy's second joust."

"No, it wasn't," says Rufus. "It was his fourth, at least."

"Are you sure? I held one in Innangard just last Spring, in honor of the goddess Eostre. I distinctly remember, Sven was not there."

"Yes, he was. But he did not progress beyond the third round, even with the cheating."

Where was I then? For even though I would not have yet been competing, as no one comes for me until at least the tenth round, it was my tournament. My sister Mist was the Maiden of the Joust. Then I remember there was a particularly fetching taverner's daughter plying her father's wares that morning, showing off her jugs...of ale, I mean...and I became distracted.

"He is going into a stupor. I am merely trying to prevent it," the Princess Thyra explains.

"Then here's hoping when we are wed, I never go into a stupor. I do not like your method for dealing with one."

The look she shoots me is pure venom, and I find my cock tightening again. Marriage will be funner than I thought.

"Prince Sven," the princess says in a commanding tone–one my cock can't seem to get enough of–"It is just a toe. You can still participate in the joust, if you wish."

Sven's only response is a pitiful moan. It will be difficult to continue to defend the boy if he carries on with this behavior.

"Come, Prince Sven," Olafsson says in a fatherly voice, one I hadn't realized he was capable of. He helps the boy to his feet and drapes an arm around his shoulder, offering his support–not an easy feat when they are both outfitted in heaps of armor. Sven hobbles away with the Vagmarian lord, still moaning unintelligibly.

Rufus, however, lingers.

"My Princess, you handled young Sven with admirable efficiency. It seems you have a knack for healing," he says.

The man is shameless.

Because we were raised together, I know Rufus as well as I would a brother. I recognize that suggestive tone. It is the one he's used in brothels and taverns, as well as royal halls, throughout the kingdoms of Plane. No woman is safe from its effects. But for once, his intention is not to tempt a woman under his bed furs.

It is only to infuriate me.

The Princess Thyra is pleasant enough, though brisk, when she speaks to Rufus. "I have some talent as a healer, My Prince, but sometimes the most appropriate remedy is an invigorating slap."

"I couldn't agree more," Rufus croons.

"Don't you have someplace to be, Rufus?"

"Not that I'm aware of."

He answers me, but he doesn't take his eyes off the Vagmarian princess.

I lean in to hiss in his ear, so the princess cannot hear me. "If you do not find a place to be, and quickly, I shall ensure by tonight's feast every eligible woman in Rhok thinks you have brothel pox."

Rufus only grins. He's achieved his objective, which was to goad me. He bows to the Princess Thyra and tells her he must go prepare to enter the lists. I am alone with her at last. What to say?

"Princess, you have ruined your gown."

She looks down to her lap, to where my gaze lingers. I swear, with no prurient intent whatsoever. She blanches.

"Edda will kill me."

I have no notion of who this Edda is, but if the princess is afraid of her, she must be quite fearsome. Her eyes meet mine again, a challenge in their green depths.

"You are clean enough for the both of us, Your Grace. I do believe I can see my reflection in your armor plate. Obsidian, is it? You spared no expense. I am sure the people of your country are willing to miss a few meals, just so their king can appear to best advantage when jousting."

The worst part it, I agree with her. I look a fool. But I cannot let her think she will ever have the last word in our dealings with each other.

"The people of Logaland are fortunate their king can be outfitted for a tourney without having to be taxed. And if you at all know your geography, you will be aware the plummest obsidian is mined in Logaland. It helps to keep costs down, having such a precious substance just underground."

"Yes, I had heard talk of the King of Logaland's pride in the size of his rocks, but I'd chalked it up to ugly rumor."

And then she saunters away. Damn. She still had the last word.

Not that I had a retort ready for that fantastic piece of offensiveness, anyway.

6

DRENGR

I decide to seek out Rufus's company again. Bothering him will take my mind off this Thyra and how I want to know what her tongue feels like on mine. But Rufus is of no assistance.

One glance at me, and he says, "Why so glum? She is pretty, after a fashion, and she has spirit. Besides, after you are wed, you may take a mistress, make her official, as my father did with Wilhelm's mum. Give her a suite of rooms and servants and all the rest. Treat her like a queen. Better than a queen, really, since she won't have to fulfill royal duties, and the sex will likely be funner. Hel, you could even take another wife, though I can't see why you'd want to. One's enough trouble."

"The kings of Logaland have not had multiple wives in hundreds of years. Not since Dagobert III made all four sisters from the House of Jarl Kuhn his brides because he could not choose which one was the prettiest."

I don't know why I take issue with the bit about multiple wives first. There are so very many things wrong with what Rufus has said. For instance–

"You think her only pretty, after a fashion?" I am irritated with this description, though I can't say why.

"I told you, I am not overfond of red hair in a woman."

"Rufus, you are being just a little hypocritical."

"I don't care. We'd clash when appearing together at court functions. Besides, I wouldn't want the competition. Some folks might think red hair suits her better than it does me."

I am one of those folks. Her hair is like an incandescent flame, and I am a moth who can't seem to stay away from it. I want to touch it. To feel it brushing against my skin. My cock.

Damn. If these thoughts don't cease, I will be quite uncomfortable seated atop Holfnir, my armor squeezing against me in all the wrong places.

Wilhelm Hornungr is my squire. He is a perfectly adequate one, though he will never achieve greatness. He is the younger brother of Rufus, sent by their father to learn from me. I am not sure he has acquired much knowledge. He is also, as it happens, a bastard. Something I do not hold against him, but also a circumstance of birth his father does not like mentioned in polite company. Unfortunately, his elder brother received all the looks and talent for combat, which seems doubly unfair, since Rufus is also Echen's legitimate heir. It is strange, for Wilhelm's mother was a princess from one of the Southlands kingdoms. Thisal, I believe. They are known for the beauty of their women, and Wilhelm's mother is no exception.

Have I mentioned, I would very much like to travel to Thisal one day?

But Wilhelm possesses many hidden talents.

"I found where they make the best ale in Rhok, and they only cheat you a little," he says by way of greeting. But he is holding a flagon of what I presume is the ale in question and my favorite drinking horn in the other hand, so I do not reprimand him on his rudeness.

This is Wilhelm's talent. Finding what I need. Whatever I need. When we travel, which tavern trades in the best ale, but just as often, it is something far more crucial I need him to track down, though I do not mean to underestimate the importance of ale.

How many carls guard the burh I am trying to overtake. When their shifts of duty change. Whether they are loyal to their commander, or if they can be bought rather than killed. Somehow, he always knows this information.

He also can't fight worth a damn, and so his career as a squire will be short-lived. He shall never earn his spurs, even if he is a king's natural son. He is a good lad. I shall have to find another place for him in my service.

Soon, I will enter the lists, so I've returned to my tent to prepare. I cannot count on Wilhelm to assist me much, so I've come back early, even though I wished to return to the Princess Thyra's side and taunt her a little more.

To his credit, though, Wilhelm does try. He hefts one of my lances from the racks with the intention of putting it in the moving cart, then promptly drops it.

I will have to find him that new place very soon.

Deciding to give up on the lance, he summons one of the carls over to lift it back into place.

"The Vagmarian carls are betting two to one odds against Arno of Dervnonia, so it stands to reason you will fight his opponent," he says.

"I am not surprised. Arno is a dried up piece of jerky. Do you know who he fights?"

"No, I do not. But the strange thing is, no one else does either. I've asked the household carls of every royal party here, but none of them know."

"What, he has no sigil?"

"He does, that's the even stranger part. It is a giant tree, as mighty as the Great Ash, surrounded by a serpent. An enormous black one with a flaming tongue. It's fair squeezing the life out of the poor tree."

"I'm not sure trees can strangle to death, but I take your point."

The Great Ash is the tree which props up the Nine Realms, Plane included. Its roots begin in Hel, and the tips of its branches curl around The Vales, where we all hope to rest and to feast one day.

For I do not think Hel is an amusing place.

Wilhelm shrugs. "He will show no one his face. He has not lifted the visor of his helm at all, not once this morn. It must be his first tourney, for he entered the first round, though he has defeated all with an efficiency at which I can only marvel. He was the one responsible for the Prince Sven's injury."

This does not necessarily prove the mysterious warrior's talent, as a blind, legless beggar could have likely defeated Sven, even with the cheating. But still...

"Well, marvel less and eavesdrop more." I motion for him to depart and fulfill my command. I must know the identity of this competitor. Is he a princeling seeking Thyra of Vagmar's hand, or is he merely some jarl or thane from a neighboring kingdom who wished for a day's worth of good fight and gold-gifting?

It is important to know the answer. I thought I'd identified all my rivals, and I do not speak of this foolish joust. If the mysterious stranger is here for Thyra, I must defeat him, and again, I do not speak of the lists.

I summon some of my household carls over to assist me with my armor and weapons, so Wilhelm may go on his fact-finding mission. Truth be told, it is better to have the carls' help here and have Wilhelm go play to his true strength.

I must also enlist the carls to help with Holfnir's armor. Unlike myself, he is quite pleased with Davith's ministrations. He snorts with pleasure when his silken tunic, bearing my coat of arms, is draped over him, followed by his gleaming armor. Davith spared no expense, apparently. Even Holfnir's armor is coated in obsidian.

Wilhelm returns as I am helping the carls to hoist the last of my lances into the moving cart. I can see from the look on his face he has found out nothing. He looks crestfallen. He will take his failure quite hard, even though I will not hold him to account. If my squire cannot find the information I seek, then no one can.

"Who in Hel is this bastard? I mean...sorry, Wilhelm, I meant no offense."

But Wilhelm is not troubled. "None taken, Your Grace. On my rounds, I discovered Prince Rufus has an assignation planned with the wife of Jarl Sigurd of Dervnonia, who came in King Arno's train. King Arno himself is having an attack of the gout, but still plans on jousting. He is ordering his carls to strap him into the saddle so he may stay upright. He must really hope to impress the Princess Thyra."

More likely, he hopes to curry favor with her father, the King of Vagmar. For it is he we must all impress.

Wilhelm darts ahead of our train to seek out more information. I take Holfnir's lead and turn toward the lists. If I tried to climb atop him before it is time to charge, he'd likely throw me. He does not suffer a rider for petty strolls. We follow the trundling cart, driven by one of my carls, packed with my lances. I make sure to always have at least twenty during these competitions. Luckily, timber is one of my kingdom's most prolific exports. As we approach the tourneying ground, I hear both cheers and groans of displeasure from the stands. Betting at these events is even more cutthroat than the jousting competition itself. It seems either those who wagered against Arno, or those who cast their coin against his opponent, are disappointed.

My squire returns. "King Arno has been eliminated, courtesy of our mysterious friend. He will take on my brother next, after Canute's joust, so it should be a good fight, at the very least."

Rufus and I have frequently faced each other in the lists, and though I am more often than not the victor, he is a fearsome opponent. I would rather face him in the lists, especially since, even if he does defeat me, I know he has no interest in marriage to Princess Thyra.

The herald of the House of Toth announces King Canute Rikkardsson has entered the lists. Canute is a decent jouster, though I do not expect him to progress past this round. I am able to feel charitable toward Canute, because there is not a hot piss's chance in Hel of him being chosen for Princess Thyra. He already has two wives, as well as a bevy of heirs. King Skerr cares too much for his own honor to place Thyra in a position where she will be only a spare wife and her own children have no chance of inheriting a throne.

Holfnir and I watch as Canute is handily defeated by the stranger. He has not ceased fighting since this morn, taking no respite between rounds of competition. He is indefatigable. I feel a sensation in my bowels I cannot remember experiencing in years, except when entering the shield wall.

I am nervous.

I expected I would be fighting Rufus or Ulf, which was just what I wished, since neither wants to marry the Princess. It would hurt my pride if I lose to Olafsson, but there are worse things.

Like not marrying this Thyra.

But it seems it is not Rufus or Ulf whom I will engage in combat. It is this boy stranger. I call him a boy, though he could have seen sixty winters for all I know, since he will not take off his help. But something about how he moves, with a litheness even Rufus would envy, tells me he is young. Very young. I watch in astonishment as he defeats first Ulf, then Rufus, in rapid succession. Three stampedes down the lists atop his stallion, three lances broken against their shields.

That is six splintered lances, total, if mathematical ciphers are not your talent.

He is well built for a stripling, tall and wide shouldered. He carries a shield with his sigil, which is also displayed on his cuirass. His visor is open, but from this distance, I cannot see his features. I am not a fanciful person, but I feel as though his eyes are burning with hatred for me. I cannot think why. We all stare each other down before we prod our steeds into action, but it is part of the sport. No warrior truly detests the other, at least not for reasons that have anything to do with jousting. I suspect after this night, the Jarl Sigurd of Echen will loathe Rufus, but only because he fucked his wife, and not because Rufus is a better jouster.

I could pause here and make some juvenile japes about my friend's skills with a lance, but I shall honor your intelligence and spare you.

I do not even know this boy. No one does. How could he

already hate me? I do not care to dwell on the potential answers to this question. Did I fuck his sister? His mother? His sweetheart? These are all valid reasons for him to hate me, I must admit. Oh dear gods, the boy cannot be my son, can he? I have always been so careful. The consequences of siring an illegitimate son would be dangerous. I am no Gorbel of Echen, Rufus's father, who sires bastards as often as other men take porridge to break their fast. Whoever my son is, he will have powers most can never imagine.

This is why it must be Thyra of Vagmar who births my heir. My father commanded it, and it will be done.

But even if I did bed the boy's mother at some point, he cannot be mine. I am not so old, and he is not so young. If this truly is his first tournament, I am reluctantly impressed. Though breaking lances was not yet the fashion, I was beaten bloody in my first rout.

His armor is black steel, though without the benefit of obsidian glaze. His is duller in appearance, and I am jealous, once again. First Lord Ulf, and now this stranger. It is as though they conspired to make a mockery of me.

His charger must be of Logalander stock, for he is powerfully built and clearly impatient to begin, stomping his hooves on the ground, kicking up mud. He is a bay-colored stallion, not black as midnight, like mine own Holfnir.

But still, Holfnir could be his sire. Mayhap if this is the case, the bay will have too much respect for his father to charge at us full speed.

Likely not, however. If he is his father's son, he will only wish to prove his superiority.

7

THYRA

If you do not find a place to be, and quickly, I shall ensure by tonight's feast every eligible woman in Rhok thinks you have brothel pox. I am sure the King Drengr thought he hissed softly to his friend, so I could not hear, but I am a Valkyrie. I hear the wind knock down acorns in the trees when they are two stones' throws away. Drengr sounded...jealous.

And damned if I do not feel tickled at inspiring such a man's jealousy.

I forcibly remind myself, however, that what he covets most is Vagmar, not mine own person.

I resume my seat in the stands, next to my father. I managed to tend the Prince Sven's injury without a single scratching sensation between my shoulders, nor even a pricking at my gums, where my teeth always threaten to erupt when I scent the stenches of battle and men in agony.

Of course, I should not be so quick to congratulate myself, for Sven's injury was so minor, a little girl would have born it with more circumspection.

"How fares Prince Sven?" my father asks.

I shrug. "It is only his toe. He may continue competing, if he so wishes. But I do not think he does."

My father smirks. It is a rare display of genuine mirth, even if it is at poor Sven's expense. "I remember when his father and I competed in tourneys. Of course, we did not yet break lances. Our competitions were conducted with sword and shield, with our feet on the ground, as the gods intended. Ingeborg often found himself feeling unwell, just as the tourneys were about to begin. A remarkable coincidence, that."

"Like father, like son, then."

And what of me? Like father, like daughter? I want to say no, but I am well aware I share many of my father's qualities. He may have no use for book learning, but he is clever. And calculating. He keeps his thoughts and his plans close to his chest and only shares them when the timing is right, when he knows it is to his advantage. Though it pains me to admit this, his strategies are sound. I have learned much from him.

"What have you decided to award the victor?" he asks.

"I must give him something besides dominion over my very self? It seems a touch unjust."

My father's eyes narrow. He does not enjoy my wit, particularly not when it is at his expense. I do not apologize for my words, but I deign to answer his question.

"I had a dwarf-forged cuirass commissioned for the occasion."

Actually, Edda commissioned the breastplate, after reminding me to do it countless times, finally giving up, and taking care of the matter herself. But I provided valuable input. I told her to think of something as expensive as possible, to hit my father where it would hurt most.

His royal wallet.

"I did not think you would balk at the expense, as

Vagmar must put its best foot forward in the coming days," I say in a honey-laced voice.

He swallows visibly, his throat bobbing with the effort. "An admirable choice," he says, though it sounds as if he may be strangling. But recovering himself, he asks, "And is there a particular contestant you hope to be victorious?"

Why is he being so nice to me? Does he realize he will likely never see me again after I am handfasted, so he's feeling guilty for once?

"Does it matter? If he is not of your choosing, I will not marry him, regardless."

Father has been maddeningly evasive on whom he wishes me to marry. I think it is because he hardly knows whom to choose.

"Who do you hope will be the victor?" I ask, hoping to put him on the defensive.

"I hope it is the competitor from the same house to which I plan on wedding you. It would make for less rancor amongst all the princes. It does not do to have so many disgruntled representatives from Plane's kingdoms, all under the roof of mine own hall."

"I don't suppose you would care to inform me as to the identity of this fortunate prince?"

"I'm not sure I know the answer myself."

He lies. But prodding him to share his thoughts has never worked.

The minstrels, perhaps my father's most hated enemy besides the kingdom of Logaland, trumpet furiously as King Drengr and his opponent enter the lists.

"Daughter, do you play any instruments?"

The music must remind him to ask the question. If those minstrels are not careful, they will also become my enemy.

I shake my head.

"Not even the harp? Or the...what's that silly one called, the one the troubadours are always carrying around on their shoulders?"

"The lyre?"

"Yes, that one. Well, do you play it?"

"Alas, no."

Should I explain that I did try to learn both the harp and the lyre? As well as the lute, the virginals, and a tympani drum, aided by a music master who would mutter oaths and finally quit after a year, despite his undoubtedly generous salary.

Last I heard, the music master was a court troubadour in the volcano-pitted kingdom of Arsenoa, where the ruler is rumored to put those servants who displease him in a stew. He is, from all accounts, infinitely happier.

Thankfully, that king is already married and did not travel here for my hand. I will hopefully be married to at least a marginally better spouse before he decides to put his current wife in the stew as well.

"What about languages?"

"I know Vagmarian."

"Of course you do, child. You are the bloody Princess of Vagmar. But what of the tongues of our neighboring kingdoms? Logalander? Arsenoan? Hausenese? No? Not a one of them? Didn't I also employ a master of languages for you?"

He had, but he'd gone the way of the music master, though I've heard he was not employed by a tyrannical king. He'd decided to work as a translator in the elven realm of Gob. For some reason, the elves had a sudden urge to learn the tongues of men. Once a human passes into the Realm of the Elves, he is never allowed to leave. Apparently, this did not deter the Master of Languages.

"Can you sew?"

Ah. Here is an opportunity to place myself in a better light. Every woman in Plane can use needle and thread.

"Of course."

"Do you stitch your own garments? What of shirts? Your husband will wish for you to fashion his shirts."

Damn.

"Edda schooled me in fashioning garments, Your Grace."

I do not need to add that her attempts to educate me failed.

But my father seems pacified.

We watch the tourney in companionable silence for a while. Avoiding conversation is one of the tactics we each employ to achieve a semblance of harmony with one another.

But then my father must spoil our peaceableness by asking, "Come now, even if the victor does not become your betrothed, there must be some young swain on whom you've pinned your hopes. One who you think will triumph over all. It is the custom of the maidens present at these events to choose a favorite."

Truly, he knows little of me. I sensed this already. But has he even met me? At any point in our history together, have I given him reason to believe I would do as other maidens and fawn over these knights? It is not that I do not appreciate a well-formed figure, but a jouster–especially a royal one–is the last man I would find attractive. I prefer the more studious sort.

Unbidden, an image of King Drengr's shoulders invades my thoughts. He is a warrior, not to mention my most hated enemy. I was practically weaned on stories of the evil of the rulers of Logaland.

But he is undeniably attractive and most definitely not a scholar.

Then again, most scholars are priors, and they are forsworn from marrying. Shame. But let us not dwell on how I convince myself the one type of man I would consider marrying is unavailable. I am well aware it is too convenient.

Instead of answering my father's question, I ask one of mine own. "Who is it that King Drengr fights? I do not recognize his sigil."

The opposing knight is fashioned in armor that is a somber, dull twin of King Drengr's obsidian-crusted finery.

My father replies. "I do not know. From what I understand, he is not of a royal house. Ulf tells me he hails from the village of Whittleby. He is here for the competition, not for betrothal."

Whittleby is a village in southern Vagmar. It is the Jarl Sturri who rules there. I did not know he had a son old enough for tourney competition, though perhaps this boy is newly promoted to knighthood and is only the son of a thane, or even a yeoman who was able to afford to outfit him. But I am too distracted to probe further as to this knight's identity, because I have just realized the stranger has broken a lance against King Drengr.

For once, the gods are just.

8

DRENGR

I have never enjoyed the joust, but I am most skilled at it. Did I mention? I may have, once or twice. Though this boy seems to want to murder me–and as to that, I must discover the reason–I have every confidence I will break the first lance.

And the second.

And, of course, the third.

I lean forward to murmur in Holfnir's ear. "Be ready, my friend, this will be a rare fight, if I am not mistaken."

In reply, he snorts with unmistakable pleasure. The joust is what Holfnir was made for, and he takes far more joy in it than myself. In general, he is a lazy creature, content to while away his days in the royal mews, munching oats and occasionally covering mares when required. But when he is put through his paces in the training grounds, he is as fierce as any dragon. Of course, he does not breathe fire or fly, but his spirit and intelligence are equal to my dragons', or so I like to believe.

My opponent, atop his own stallion, sits almost preternaturally still. When his squire brings him his lance, he takes it with seemingly no effort whatsoever. My herald already announced me to King Skerr and Princess Thyra earlier, but of course, he must do so again for a wider audience. It is expected. Olaf Snagtooth is as wordy as a skald, and indeed, often serves in both capacities at court. Master of Dragons, Ruler of Fire and Frost, Scourge of the Northlands. I admire his creativity. Instead of hailing me as the 'Scourge of Vagmar,' he has broadened the moniker to encompass the entire region. I have never fancied myself quite so destructive, but upon reflection, my dragons do have a tendency of laying waste to my enemies.

We all wait impatiently for Olaf to be done, but he does take an extraordinary sense of pride in his work. He finally departs the center of the lists, from where he's been addressing the stands, and I wait with more anticipation than is my wont for my opponent's herald, for here, finally, I will discover his identity. However, the boy has no herald. I might, under normal circumstances, only feel jealousy. I am embarrassed by Olaf's overbearing praise and have often wished it was not the custom of kings to have heralds in their tourney trains. It is not uncommon for lesser known warriors, or those with little experience, to be without heralds, but it is significant information, because this means the boy is not from a royal house, nor even the son of a jarl, for if he were, he would have a herald, no matter his lack of experience. It is impossible to escape heralds who announce your existence to all, just in case they forgot for a moment, if you are highborn. My curiosity about the boy grows ever more. How can a warrior, so youthful and lowborn, have claimed so many victories in just one morn and against some of the finest warriors in this realm?

I haven't time to wonder, for the horn sounds, and it is time. I see the boy and his steed hurtle towards me, and only then do I remember to prod Holfnir into action. Maybe my late start is the reason for what happens next. Perhaps it is because I have become so engrossed in puzzling out this warrior's identity, I forget where my attention should be...on the joust. Mayhap it is even visions of the Princess Thyra's breasts still dancing through my mind. All I know is,

his lance breaks against my cuirass with such force, I am launched backwards, flapping like a ragdoll against the pommel of Holfnir's saddle. I am so shocked, I do not even register any pain. Having a lance broken on yourself is a common enough occurrence for tourneyers.

But not for me.

How did this happen? I replay in my mind the image of our first round of joust. He tilted to the left, I know this much, and it caught me by surprise. Only very strong and very skilled jousters have the strength and experience to tilt in their saddle. I had not expected it of him, which was most foolish of me.

In our second bout, I am determined to be more prepared. I cannot lose to a child. As I return to the start of the list, Wilhelm approaches me, clutching my next lance. I know he must have something to tell me, for he normally leaves this duty to one of my carls, which is my preference as well. It is not exactly fitting for a king's squire to be seen dropping lances.

"My King, I have just learned from one of Arno's squires that, after fighting this warrior, he reversed his wager in the betting pool and has now chosen him as the likely victor. It is not good news," Wilhelm says mournfully.

"This would have been useful information to know before our first bout."

"Sorry, My King, but I was occupied trying to discover the lad's name."

"And did you have any success?"

"No. It seems no one knows from whence he hails. His sigil is not one any here recognize."

"You are full of good news, Wilhelm," I say as I mount Holfnir and take my next lance.

I approach the start of the lists again. The stallion snorts in anticipation, determined to be the victor in our next bout, as am I. I wait for the sound of the horn, attuned to my surroundings, prepared for battle. I notice the motes of dusty earth spiraling up from the ground, kicked up by the horses' hooves, the scent of musty sweat on Holfnir's neck, the frown on the Princess Thyra's pouty lips.

No, no, best not to notice that bit.

I wait for the horn to sound, but my opponent does not. Just before its signal, he kicks his spurs into his destrier, barreling towards me. Once again, I am thrown off my guard. I do the same to Holfnir, but moments too late. I'd thought myself better prepared for this bout, but once again, I am mistaken. Or perhaps I am not. Mayhap my opponent is simply a better jouster.

No, no. Impossible.

I am ready for the impact of his lance this time, or as ready as one can be. The anticipation of his blow is worse than the pain itself when it does come, against the right side of my chest, where I am unprotected by my shield. But I feel my arm shudder with the impact of mine own lance crashing into his. See the splinters of broken lances fill the air around us. We have both been victorious in this round it seems.

But then I am falling. It is as though it is happening to someone else, and I am merely an observer. I have never been thrown from a horse during the joust. I topple from Holfnir's saddle like a sack of potatoes, landing on the ground with a thud. Holfnir snorts in disgust. I dare not move until I have determined no bones are broken, that my armor has not cut my skin anywhere, particularly my neck. It's been known to happen in such falls, that the gorger, the piece of armor that usually protects a warrior's neck, instead severs it.

After a few moments of lying there motionless like an imbecile, I turn my neck gently to ascertain whether it is broken, or if any pieces of armor poke into the skin. It is then I notice with no small amount of satisfaction the boy is unhorsed as well. As we have knocked each other off our steeds, we must fight with blades now, on foot. My preferred method of combat. Though judging from how he lifts himself to his feet with lithe grace, despite toppling from a destrier tall as twenty hands, wearing six stones' worth of armour, it is his as well. He swaggers as he takes his sword from his squire and enters the tourney ground again, striding towards where I lay in the dirt.

I try not to grow furious. Anger, spite, personal vendettas. They have no place in battle, even if it is the false kind, fought on a tourney ground. A man who fights with his emotions is a dead man, or in this case, a defeated one. Though I think this niðing would kill me if he thought he could get away with it. Truly, he seems to loathe me, as one would a beetle he's crushed beneath his boot, whose guts won't scrape off the sole.

He struts around me, hitting his sword against his cuirass. The clang it makes sounds throughout the tourney grounds, bouncing against the stands where the spectators watch. Where the Princess Thyra sits. It is not lost on me I must make an impression during this battle, and not on her. I am certain she cares not for feats of bravery in battle. It is her father I must convince of my superiority.

And I do not speak only of battle.

"Will the great King Drengr be able to lift his own sword without one of his dragons to help him?"

The boy taunts me, and yet he has the voice of a man. Warriors often exchange insults during battle, both in tourneys and in the shield wall. Very frequently, they deal in descriptions of the smallness of one's opponent's cock and its inability to perform even the slightest sexual endeavor, but this boy seems to know just what insults will annoy me the most.

No one speaks ill of my dragons without punishment.

"Bastard," I mutter without thinking.

This is, you may have noticed, an epithet I use often, to my shame. Some offend the gods when they swear, others insult mothers everywhere, and I attack the children of natural alliances, outside the shackles of wedded bliss.

We all have our thing.

Fortunately, Wilhelm is not a sensitive soul, for as he is a bastard, I would hate for him to be offended when I spew words so unthinkingly.

But this boy seems to hesitate, his blade unsteady for the first time since we touched steel.

Have I touched a nerve?

"Who are you? From which kingdom do you hail? Who was your sire?"

I suspected the boy would ignore my questions, but I did not realize they would invigorate his efforts. He is focused again, prowling around me with a sure-footed gait.

Then the warrior feints left and brings his sword up in a quick, flashing arc. I turn from his blade, but not quickly enough. Pain stabs at the skin covering my ribs, just below my arm. I realize in shock, the stranger meant to deal me a killing blow. A warrior's plate and cuirass protect him well, but there is weakness in every suit of armor. Underneath the armpits is one such area. If a blade spears the flesh near there, it can enter the lungs, the heart. In a tourney's ground combat, the goal is to break the shields of one's opponent, not to kill them. If death was the objective, there would be few noblemen left alive in Plane.

"Have I wronged you somehow, boy? Fucked your bedwarmer, perhaps? Or mayhap I have visited your sire's court before and accidentally broke your favorite plaything? You are still young enough to play with toys, are you not?"

My words do their work, as intended. He is young and not able to contain his anger. He swings his sword wildly, not caring whether his blows are shield breakers. His only desire is to kill me.

Even if it were possible to defeat me, no one stands a chance against Dragonspear. Forged of ignatum when the Realm was barely more than mists, it has the power of generations of kings imbued in its blade. And kings of Logaland, too.

He is the most talented stripling I have ever beheld, but even his strength is no match for mine. I have trained for many more years, born the weight of both sword and shield and axe and of governing the most powerful kingdom in Plane. If I can manage to prevent him from sneaking his blade into an unprotected piece of flesh again, he is doomed.

Some warriors are strong; others are quick. With Dragonspear in my hands, I am both. I take the direct approach, hefting Dragonspear crossways, up to the left, down to the right, in a blur of strength and speed. I have never met a man yet who can match me muscle for muscle, stroke for stroke, and I am not disappointed this time. He retreats from my onslaught, barely raising his blade in time to meet each one of my blows.

Take off your helm, boy. Your hatred of me is not worth your death, I scream silently. For if he does not take off his helm, which would signal he accepts defeat, I will be forced to continue pummeling him, and this will only end in his demise. He falls, unable to continue to defend himself.

Finally, he does take it off, deciding the embarrassment of losing is preferable to a young death. It is a startling face, and as young as I'd expected. Younger, even. Milky as winter sun, with one dark eye and one green. His hair is dark, as dark as mine, which is a rarity in our northern lands, where faces are pale, and hair even paler.

But I do not have time to question the boy again, for King Skerr approaches, his ermine-trimmed robe flowing around him like a sea wave. He raises his hands to the sky in a gesture of praise.

"Well fought, young King. I thought for a moment, you would be bested, for once."

Skerr's voice is jovial, but his expression is guarded. It is no surprise. I believe the only person who hates me more than the King of Vagmar does, is his daughter.

Here is my opportunity to discover the mysterious warrior's identity. Skerr must know it, if he allowed him to participate in the tourney.

"I would like to pay tribute to my opponent, My King, as he is the fiercest I have ever faced." I hope Rufus is not somewhere close, listening. He'll be bloody furious. "But I do not know how he is called."

"Young Grinn here is a Traveler Knight from the Southlands. He fights for gold and nothing more. But he, like all other competent warriors, was welcome in our lists today."

Horseshite. This Grinn understood every word I spoke

and responded in the Logalander tongue with barely a trace of an accent. If he hailed from a kingdom in the Southlands, he would not speak my language so well. And if he, in truth, is from a neighboring kingdom, I would know of him, for no warrior with such skill stays anonymous.

He is even more of a puzzle than before, then. But at least I have a name. Grinn. I will remember it, just as he will remember mine, of this I am certain. What I am less confident in, though, is whether I will be as successful against him as I was this time, should we ever meet in battle again.

King Skerr says, "Come forward and claim your prize from the Princess of the Joust."

The Princess of the Joust is, of course, the same maiden as the Princess of Vagmar. Thyra. I tell myself the reason my breath quickens as she approaches is because of my recent exertions. That hair. Those flaming tresses would drive any man mad. When coupled with the sarcastic turn of her pouty mouth, the duo is devastating.

She stands on a wooden dais of recent and shoddy construction, so as I walk towards her, I must look up into her face. I do not mind. She bends toward me, inviting my eyes to gaze at her breasts, which she can't possibly know. With a smile as sweet as any honey I have ever tasted, she says, "I cannot tell you how much I regret spending a dwarven fortune on this cuirass."

"Especially since I shall have the royal engraver work with the smithy to etch my sigil into it. You shall always know you spent so much coin on a fantastic plate armor, only to have a dragon grace its surface. Only to have a dragon wear it, for that matter."

The expression on her face is priceless, like a goat urinated in her porridge.

This time, it is I who have the last word.

9

THYRA

It may not be the wisest course of action, but I must have some answers, and only this Drengr can give them to me. Like his obsidian armor, his tent is ridiculous and pretentious, bedecked with plumes of red ostrich feathers which are imported at a dear price from the Southlands. Truly, this king seems bent on bankrupting his people and his kingdom. But it is not for me to care, as there is not a hot piss's chance in Hel I will be marrying him, for I suspect this is his intent in traveling here. Indeed, I know for certain, as he has now told me so on numerous occasions.

I hesitate at the opening to the tent but realize if I do not act in an assertive manner, King Drengr will not take me seriously. I square my shoulders, give a dirty stare to the carls who stand guard on either side of his tent flap, and stride inside.

Inside, the tent is as lavish as its exterior. Though there is a scarred, oaken table in the corner with a Hnefatafl board at its center and a few cushions on the floor, which belie the otherwise luxurious interior. As well as a king's ransom in furs, there is a good carpet on the ground. From the

Kingdom of Thisal, by the looks of it, but I cannot accuse the Logalander king of extravagance in this. Midwinter in Vagmar is a muddy business. In the other corner lies a stand with a pitcher and ewer of water, but it is then I realize I have made a grave error. For there is a certain king holding the pitcher, pouring water over his head whilst he hangs it over the basin, careful to avoid dripping on the floor. Drengr is naked, or so close to it, the braies he wears are irrelevant. I'd thought him impressive when he stood in my father's hall, wearing only a tunic and breeches. I'd pretended I found him intolerable when he entered the lists, obsidian armor gleaming, but in truth, it was only his demeanor I found disgusting. With his figure, though, I could find no objection.

It is unfair that my most hated enemy has a muscled form the gods would envy.

I stare, unable to stop, as the cascade of water moves down his body, first in rivulets down his corded neck, then lower, over his chest, which is lightly covered in black hair, the same color as his mane. Then those same droplets of water move lower, towards his belly, and I am able to recover myself, lest I further my embarrassment by allowing this king to spy me ogling him.

But though his eyes are closed and he is occupied, not to mention uncaring about his state of undress, he must know I am there, for ever so casually, he says, "Princess, I was wondering when you would arrive. I anticipated your visit."

Then why did you not dress? I want to ask. But instead, I find myself saying–

"If you must marry, why are you so insistent it is to Vagmar? There are many eligible princesses in Plane."

"But I want you."

I snort. "It cannot be because of my personal charms. I

have few to speak of. I am, much to my father and Masters' chagrin, entirely ordinary."

"I don't think so. Your hair is red, your eyes green—quite a striking combination. Your skin is clear, though a bit freckly, and your teeth are decent. I've seen better breasts, but the curve of yours improves upon further acquaintance. If you are ordinary, then I believe ordinary is...perfectly sufficient."

"I am flattered by your words of love. Truly, you woo as well as any bard. Please, answer me truthfully. Why me?"

"It was my father's dying wish. I pledged him my oath."

"Yes, but why? Why was it so important to King Dagmar that you marry me?"

"Does it matter? You're quite an impudent little thing, aren't you? Always asking questions, like a hen who can't stop pecking. After we are wed, I shall have to take steps to correct this impertinence."

"And I shall have to sleep with a dagger under my pillow."

He laughs with a surprised bark. "If I want to improve your manners, Princess, no mere dagger will stop me."

"I'd rather marry Harald," I say. It is the worst insult I can think of. Poor Harald.

"The Hausten princeling, the one with the sheep?"

"It's cows," I say, before I can think better of it.

"I'd heard his preference was sheep, but no matter." He shrugs, indifferent to Harald's predilections, not to mention to the wholly unsuitable pool of applicants for my hand. That damnable shrug again. Does he know it accentuates the breadth of his shoulders, when he moves them in such a fashion?

I am sure he does.

Harald of Hausen is my first cousin, twice removed. Or is

it second cousin, once removed? I can never remember, but it is a small (very tiny) mark in Drengr's favor, that we are definitely not related. Vagmar and Logaland have been enemies for too many centuries for any marriage alliances.

Until now.

I try again.

"Mayhap the boy who almost defeated you, then. It is a rare warrior, indeed, who can make the great King Drengr sweat."

"Grinn is only a Traveler Knight. Something tells me he will not be your father's choice.

"How do you know his name?"

"The King Skerr introduced us after I nearly pummeled him into oblivion," he answers in a self-satisfied tone.

My father told me he did not know who the young warrior was. He lied to me. Why? But I cannot become distracted. Refusing to allow Drengr to see how much he has rattled me, I try once more.

"Then there's Prince Sven of Ingeborg. He is comely, after a fashion. I should find him a much more pleasing candidate."

"His face is fair enough, but dig under the armor, and you'll find a case of brothel pox so contagious, even your bed furs will develop a rash. But by all means, apply to your father for a marriage to the Kingdom of Ingeborg. Oh, wait, it wouldn't be to the kingdom, would it? For he is the second son. You'd be just a princess and never a queen, the rest of your days, with a fetching rash to boot."

"I am a princess, and a Princess of Vagmar, too. My father values me too highly to waste me on a second son."

"He values you as a daughter or as a bargaining tool?"

He opens his mouth to say more, then abruptly closes it.

Does he know the question he asks, rhetorically, I am sure, is the one that plagues me? He cannot...can he?

After a moment, he says, "Your people were pirates. They still would be, had Logaland not put an end to their pillaging. You value yourself rather highly, if one considers your ancestry and not just your title."

"We are–and were–traders." I correct him. "And put an end to is quite the euphemism, since your great grandsire used his dragons to burn our ships. Vagmar's fleet has never fully recovered."

"If you are waiting for a conquer of dragons to descend once again on your capital, you will be disappointed."

"A conquer?"

"Yes, it is what we call a grouping of them. Like a gaggle of geese or a murder of crows. A conquer of dragons. More than three present in the same vicinity."

"Fitting."

"If you do not wish for this marriage, merely say so. I want a bride, not a martyr."

"Do you mean this?"

"Of course not. But trust me, Princess, when I say I am your best option, even if our kingdoms are mortal enemies."

"I could overlook our kingdoms being adversaries, but it is your father's responsibility for my mother's murder I can't seem to get past."

"I am hazy on the details of what happened all those years ago between my father and your mother, as I was only a boy myself, but I do not believe her death occurred in quite the manner your father claims."

"I do not care what you believe. Nor do I care that you wish to marry me, or that it was your father's dying wish. Indeed, the fact that it was his desire makes it all the sweeter that I refuse to marry you. I will never say yes, not even if my father tries to bind me to you. You will never touch me."

"Maybe I won't, but as to the rest, you are mistaken. We will marry, Princess, and then I will take everything from you, every illusion you hold dear, until all that is left is me and the misery I offer. You will beg for it, in the end. But I will not force myself on you, unless you ask me nicely."

He insists I am mistaken, that I have somehow been lied to my entire life. That I would prefer being shackled to him, rather than staying free in Logaland. He has presented me with so many mysteries to solve, so many questions unanswered.

I know what I must do.

I must go to the library.

10

THYRA

The library at Whistletree Priory is where I have gone for solace since I was a child. For comfort. For distraction.

All of which, I need now.

In a kingdom where knowledge is not valued, where books and scrolls are even less appreciated, the Priory is indispensable. It only exists because even the kings of Vagmar have long recognized it is necessary to keep a written record of our histories.

There is another reason I enjoy coming here, though this is a recent development. I believe my attraction to a certain novitiate of the Priory occurred at roughly the same time as my father announced my imminent Handfasting.

Brother Matthias is of an age with me, or at least he appears to be. He is fae and therefore immortal. He has never shared his age with me, but it could be anywhere from twenty to two thousand summers he has seen. He is most handsome, after a fashion. He is slender and scholarly. His blue eyes are gentle, and his smile is shy. He is always clothed in the grey woolen robes of his order and would likely find the King Drengr's finery ludicrous. He came here last year to begin his novitiate. Where and how he lived before coming to Rhok are a mystery to me, which has only added to his other attractions. I must admit, my already frequent visits to the Priory became even more common.

If I must marry, it should be to someone like Matthias, who shares my interests in reading and research, who would treat with me quietly and kindly.

Until he found out I am a Valkyrie, cursed to hunt the battlegrounds of Vagmar, draining the lifeblood of warriors.

After such a discovery, it is possible he might no longer hold affection for me.

But even if I could secure such a match–and more importantly, have it approved by my father–it would never be to Brother Matthias. Even were he not pledged to the gods, he is fae, and Vagmar has no need of an alliance with his people. The fae stay out of the affairs of the kingdoms of men, and we allow them to mind their own business in turn.

Then there is the matter of his gruesome execution, should he ever break his vows of chastity.

Still, he greets me with a smile as I enter the priory gate. I sent word to him of my impending visit, knowing he would make the time in his busy schedule to meet me. Though he is cautious, he looks forward to my visits. He would not ignore me, no matter his vows. Though perhaps his enthusiasm for my visits is not as hopeful as it sounds. If he pined for me, he would be more likely to avoid me, to resist temptation.

"My Princess, I am surprised you are here this day. I did not think you would be able to leave the festivities of your Handfasting, not even for a moment, to visit we, your humble servants."

His words are proper and modest, but his lips smile, and

his eyes shine with mirth. He carries a great pile of dusty tomes and motions for me to follow him as he ascends the stairs to the tower which holds the library.

"What brings you here this day, when you should likely be in your father's hall, entertaining your suitors?"

There is no rancor in his voice to betray any jealousy, nor censure, even though I abandoned my duties to visit here. I find myself wishing he was angry, at least a little. It would mean he cares. If he were not so scholarly, not so devoted to his studies and to the Priory, perhaps he would challenge the King Drengr. He would claim me as his.

Ludicrous. I have never wanted to be fought over, like a choice morsel between two hounds. And yet, what if...? What if Matthias was willing to abandon all, to sacrifice all, to put his very life at risk to be with me?

It is only a small chamber, this library, but it is everything to me. Located at the top of the Priory's southern tower, it is a lovely room. I think it is because the matrons and monks who serve as its guardians have been left to their own devices, as no lords or other pompous officials have taken any interest in the business of intellectual pursuits. More fool them. Wooden beams crisscross the rounded ceiling of the tower, traveling down the limestone-coated walls to where shelves encircle the entire tower.

"I must take leave of you, My Princess, though I wish it wasn't so. The Prime Matron has instructed me to spend the afternoon researching a matter which concerns her."

I wonder what the overbearing Prime Matron wishes to know. How many tithes the Priory collected each year before she took over its leadership? Whether she could squeeze more from the people of Rhok, so she may afford some new plate for her dining table or luxurious cloth for her habit? Matthias is an intellectual, unlike so many of the men of Vagmar. It is why I was drawn to him. So why do I now find myself irritated he uses his skills as an excuse to leave my side?

"Matthias, wait..."

He turns, a wary expression on his face, as though he does not wish to hear what I have to say. As if he knows what it is I wish to say. At least one of us does. Matthias, let us run away together. There are other kingdoms where we could hide. We could live together, be happy. Let us leave, this very moment.

But is this what I want? Would Matthias even leave the Priory, if he could? I am not sure I want to know the answer.

"You do know my father's choice of groom will be announced this eve, at my betrothal feast, do you not? And tomorrow is the ceremony. Then the next day, I depart. I will never return to Vagmar...at least, it is unlikely."

A false cheer imbues his voice. "I do know, My Princess. All of Vagmar rejoices at your good fortune, those of us in the Priory perhaps most of all. I bid you good day, My Princess, and wish you safe travels to wherever your destination lies, and a long and happy life, blessed with many children."

This is what he is supposed to say, though at least his happiness seems feigned. I can take some solace in that fact. What was I hoping? That he would snatch me to him and kiss me? He'd have to drop the pile of books he carries, which he would likely never do. That he would tell me he loves me and promise to do whatever he must to keep me by his side?

I sigh in resignation. Brother Matthias, and any chance of running away with him, is a lost cause. I did not come here only for him, though. Indeed, if I am honest with myself, seeing him was the least of my reasons.

Today I am not here to borrow (or snatch) a manuscript, but rather, I just want to sit in the gloom and breathe in the scent of old parchment. I want to feel the dust motes alight on my skin. Only then will I be able to think. Should I go through with this marriage? Can I, even? Will I be able to bear heirs to the man whose father was responsible for mine own mother's murder?

"How fares My Princess on this blessed morn?" An elderly gentleman shambles into the chamber, clutching an armful of scrolls. It is Old Nasmell, a patient of many years in the convalescent ward of the Priory. He is mad but quite harmless. And he turns a blind eye when I snatch books. Sometimes he even sets them aside for me, in anticipation of my stolen visits. Though it goes without saying, he is an invaluable companion.

I try not to pout like a child when I reply. "I wish I was better, dear Nasmell. It seems I shall be marrying soon and leaving Vagmar. I do not wish to leave my home, but I desire even less to marry."

Especially not to Drengr of Logaland, but this, I keep to myself.

Nasmell seems more upset than I would have thought. He sets the scrolls down on the nearest table and takes my hands. The gesture surprises me. Though I fancy ourselves as friends, it is not exactly customary for an invalid of the Priory to be so familiar with a princess. I am not upset, though, for I see how flustered he is. Tears swim in his rheumy blue eyes.

"You mustn't go, My Princess."

His palms tighten; his strength is greater than I'd expected. I do not fear him, though. He does not mean to hurt me, and even if he did, he could not succeed. Even when not transformed, I possess strength normal women do not. I think he only wishes to keep me with him in the Priory. I hadn't realized he was so attached.

"You mustn't bind yourself to Logaland. It cannot come to pass, this marriage. You will set in motion a series of events that cannot be changed, not without great sacrifice." His face greys; his lips quiver. Sweat beads his brow, and it smells old, old like the parchment with which he surrounds himself.

"Whatever do you mean, Nasmell?"

But he abruptly drops my hands and stumbles out the door, shaking and muttering to himself.

Were I to interpret his fears, I would say the sacrifice he speaks of is mine, in binding myself to Logaland. And the series of events that cannot be changed is this marriage, which I cannot avoid. What I said to Drengr in his tent was all bluster. We both know I cannot disobey my father and convincing him to choose another princeling is a laughable notion.

I'd not realized Nasmell cared so for me, and I am touched. I shall have to be certain to visit him again before I leave and promise him I will write. Slightly deranged he may be, but he is a man of great knowledge and knows his letters well. He will be an invaluable correspondent when I am gone from here, in no small part because he does not filter his words and will tell me all the news of Vagmar, even the information I should perhaps not know. And if I shouldn't be privy to it, Old Nasmell definitely should not be, which will make having the knowledge all the sweeter.

Speaking of, just how did he know it is to Logaland I will be promised?

I look down to the scrolls he left on the battered study table. I reach for the one closest to me, as sniffing parchment is, after all, for what I came. It is a map, I discover as I unfold it, a map of the entire Realm of Plane. My eyes travel to the boundaries of Vagmar first, of their own volition. Sometimes I forget, as I am so rarely able to travel to the sea, but Vagmar is a nation of islands. When the Great Sorceress, Queen Maeve, created the Realm of Plane, she fashioned the rocks and the trees and the seas much as she'd remembered them from her ancient homeland.

In the Old World, the Realm of Hjartagard, the sons of Vagmar were feared above all other princes, for they ruled the seas. By rights, in the Realm of Plane, we should still take precedence over all other kingdoms, both those of Men and of Monster. But something happened in the Quickening of Maeve's world that even she could not anticipate.

The Kingdom of Logaland was established in the mountains, where its people were most comfortable, but unbeknownst to Maeve, she awakened the veins of ignatum that lay deep beneath Logaland's peaks. Dragon eggs can only incubate in fire heated by volcanic lava containing ignatum. The Rise of Plane caused the Volcano of Muspel, long dormant, to erupt.

Dragon eggs, which had not hatched in centuries, began to stir. The Great Sorceress had not intended for dragons to rise from Muspel. Though Plane was created as a haven for the Monsters of Hjartagard, even Queen Maeve did not wish for dragons to rise again. In ancient times, they laid waste to the Realm of Hjartagard. There is no reigning in the fury of a dragon when it is provoked. No controlling it.

Though it seems King Drengr has found a way.

I hate him for this ability, as I burn to know how he does it. But I wonder, would it be better if he did not have dominion over them? If they left the confines of the boundaries of Logaland? I think not. Dragons destroy whatever is in their path, and they are rather indiscriminate about it.

Perhaps it would not just be Vagmar who'd been forced to submit to the dragons, but all of Plane, if they did not heed the Logalander kings and them alone.

One of the matrons strides in and tells me my presence is requested at court. My father wishes for an audience. I dread our meeting, even more than I usually might. And I can tell you, I never look to our little confabulations with anticipation. For there is only one subject he would wish to discuss with me before this eve's feast.

My marriage to Drengr of Logaland.

I STRIDE INTO THE HALL, discordant voices greeting me as I enter. It is my father and Ulf Olafsson, arguing. They are so caught up in their disagreement, they both ignore my arrival. Without knowing the subject of their discord, I decide I support Ulf's position.

"There is a clear choice for this betrothal, and it has little to do with his victory in the tourney."

My heart plummets to my belly. It is Ulf speaking, and he seems to support the alliance to Drengr of Logaland. Nevermind. This time, I support my father.

Ulf began service as a thane in my father's household. He was not a jarl with his own holdings, nor was he even one of the higher-ranking courtiers in our hall. But he has become my father's chief advisor. He is indispensable. When one considers his origins–I sound pompous when I say this, but I only speak truth–his rise has been remarkable. He began his career as a yeoman farmer of honorable standing. His family's holdings are a day's ride from my father's great hall. Just as he married and his wife fell pregnant with their first child, the levies were called, Vagmar's banners were raised, and we set off to war against Logaland.

Well, not we, per se. I was three and unable to assist the campaign. Though I am sure even then, my wings and fangs would have sprouted at the scent of bloodshed and the sounds of battle, if only given the opportunity.

At the Battle of Devil's Bridge, so named because this structure connects our territories to the lands of the Kingdom of Logaland, which are separated by the River Ignis, he held the Logalanders' army single-handedly from crossing the bridge while his levy waited for reinforcements. He planted himself on the Vagmarian side of the bridge and took on several Logalanders at once as they crossed the narrow ramp. Had the river been more shallow at this particular juncture, or the bridge less narrow, he might not have managed it. But armed with only an axe–which is still his preferred weapon, though he is now a thane and entitled to carry a sword–he held an entire enemy kingdom at bay.

It goes without saying, I am sure, that Ulf is a rather large fellow and quite vicious when provoked. Most of the time, however, he is as gentle in his demeanor as a spring lamb. My father's first act after the Battle of Devil's Bridge was won was to knight Ulf, there next to the pile of bloody Logalander corpses he'd left in his wake.

He has never regretted his decision, as Ulf has proven to be even more intelligent than he is dangerous. His counsel is sound and can always be trusted. This has been a comfort to me many times, but since he is currently attempting to convince my father to marry me to Drengr of Logaland, I am less than pleased.

"It is as I expected. It stands to reason, a man who commands dragons also will defeat all his foes in these games of war. But I still hate the thought of it," my father says.

I am absurdly pleased he cares. At least I will know, if this betrothal to Logaland does proceed, he had some qualms of conscience over my future happiness. Then my father continues–

"If it were not for the fear of Logaland's might, I would prefer to marry Thyra to Hausen. They are one of the wealthiest kingdoms in Plane. Even if Logaland is the most powerful, it is with Hausen we have so many trade agreements. Imagine the imports of grain and oil and wine, not to mention the timber and iron ore. We would pay a fraction of the current prices, were she married to Hausen."

I did not think it possible, but my heart plummets lower. Somewhere to around my knees, I believe. It is not me he cares about, but his coffers. This does not surprise me, but it still wounds me.

"Whoever marries Thyra will rule Vagmar," he continues, "as well as their own kingdom. I must be careful whom I choose as a son-in-law. There is little monetary advantage for Drengr to ally himself with Vagmar."

The solution to my father's woes seems simple, and yet, it is something of which he never took advantage. I walk closer to my father and Ulf, announcing my presence by asking, "Father, why did you never remarry? You would have more children, mayhap sons who could lead Vagmar." I decide it would not be a suitable time to bring up this foolish law we have in Vagmar that only men can inherit titles, including the one of monarch.

"I could not, after your mother died."

He is a man of few words, and yet still, his answer touches me. For one so distant, so consumed with battle and legacy, the tenderness he so clearly still feels for my mother, after all these years, is heartwarming.

"Then if only you'd had more children with Mother. Sons, of course."

I wish this for both my father and myself. For him, so his cares would be fewer. For me, so I would not have to marry the one man living I hate above all others.

"We did," he says softly. "Did I never tell you? Several babes were born to your mother and me, before you were born. But only you survived."

His answer wounds me. I know he loved my mother. It is perhaps one of his only redeeming qualities. No matter how distant he may be as a father, how hard as a ruler, I know he is capable of great love. He forgave my mother her failures, apparently, which is not easy to do, when a kingdom demands heirs. Many a princeling more forgiving than mine own father has discarded his wife because she was not able to produce sons. That he never castigated her for it, that he never set me aside, speaks to a deep attachment to her.

As difficult as it is, though, I must remember why I am here, standing in this hall.

"Why did you bother with all this pomp and circumstance, if you knew all along you would wed me to King Drengr?" I ask.

"I didn't want him to think he had the advantage going into our negotiations. Your bride price is the highest in Plane. I was not about to undercut our advantage."

"And so I am just supposed to walk blindly into wedded bliss with the son of the man responsible for my mother's death? With the kingdom responsible for Vagmar's near destruction?"

"Foolish girl. You do not think I would wed you to our mortal enemy without an ulterior motive, do you?"

I appreciate his insult, for I am restored to my normal state of resentment towards my father.

"Drengr believes I offer you to him willingly, that all our enmities will be forgiven once you are wed. This is what I wish him to believe. In truth, you have one responsibility, and one only. You are to learn how to destroy him and report back to me."

Of course. It sounds so simple, Father. But aloud, I say, "And just how am I to accomplish such a feat?"

"Feign attraction to him. Get close to him. It is how you will learn his weaknesses."

As my father says this, his eyes bore into mine own. He cannot speak all his thoughts aloud, for Ulf does not know my secret, but there is an unspoken command hovering in the air between us.

You are a Valkyrie. Kill him if you must.

Before I can protest, Ulf speaks. "But Your Grace, you ask too much of the Princess. She has not been trained in the arts of deception. She is no spy. How can you expect her to feign happiness whilst plotting against her husband? I feel uneasy with this deception. It would be better to handfast her to a different kingdom, one where you truly do wish for an alliance."

Yes, thank you, Ulf. I quite agree.

Though perhaps not to Harald the cow-fucker.

My father surprises me with a compliment. "Thyra is a quick learner. I will leave it to you to school her in all the training she requires to equip herself for her duties." And with this pronouncement, he leaves us.

"Ulf, how am I to..." How to ask such a question of this man, more a father to me than mine own? "How am I to bear his heirs but also plot his destruction? It is nonsensical." What I mean is, how can I, a virgin, lie with Drengr, then betray him?

"I do not know, My Princess." He runs his palm over his head in vexation, though he ceased to have hair growing there long ago. "Treachery is no more in my nature than it is in yours."

"This is not helpful, Ulf."

He laughs ruefully. "I do not know why your father expects me to be able to school you in deceit. For once, he may have overestimated my talents." He looks contemplative. "Or perhaps he has underestimated me, in this case," he murmurs.

"What do you mean?" I'm not sure he meant to speak the words aloud, but I must know the answer.

"I have served your father for these last three decades, and he has never asked me to lie. Or steal. Or cheat. I mislike he asks it of me now."

"Where will we do this training? You cannot teach me how to commit treason in front of crowds. My father's hall is a busy place, and Drengr is bound to discover what we are doing."

"I have thought on this, and I believe I have the answer. When Elfgiva left us, she abandoned her tower. Though we may have to share it with some mice and the odd bat or two, I think it will serve our purposes well. We only have three days to prepare you."

Elfgiva was our court völva when my mother was still alive, but she is gone now.

"Please don't remind me." I feel as though I could be given a thousand days of training and never be ready for what my father asks of me.

11

DRENGR

It must be said, I find the Princess Thyra no less attractive this evening than I found her by daylight. Indeed, the soft lighting of the hall's torches only seems to enhance the flame-like qualities of her hair, the sheen in her green eyes. She has changed out of the gown she wore during the tournament, which she would have done, as it was covered in mud, but also, I suspect, because it is the custom of ladies to change into different attire for evenings. Idiotic, if you ask me.

But no one has.

Still, I cannot complain, for she is wearing green velvet now, with lace trimmings of butter yellow at her neck, sleeves, and hem. Green is her color. Perhaps I shall make her wear it always after we are wed.

I am, of course, seated next to the Princess, as I expected. King Skerr is no fool. Through numerous diplomatic missions and even the odd personal missive or two–a thing I am not in the habit of penning–I have made my intention of marrying Thyra clear. I think my last letter went something along the lines of–

. . .

Dearest King Skerr,

You and I both know I shall make war on you if you do not give me your daughter's hand in marriage. Her Handfasting day approaches, as you know I know. Give her to me, or I will set my dragons on you.

Regards,
Drengr

What? I do not have time for pleasant talking.

On my other side sits King Skerr, who has announced our imminent Handfasting. He gave direction the first course of the feast should begin as he made the announcement, which was clever on his part. The news had a better chance of being received without violence by all the princelings present if they had a little food in their bellies. He is a gracious host at least. We are not kept from our dinners.

No one seemed surprised I was his choice. Harald of Hausen pouted a little, and Arno of Dervnonia looked quite sullen, but they were wise enough to keep their own council. I try to think of a topic on which to converse with Skerr, but upon reflection, I'd much prefer to torture the Princess Thyra.

I turn to look at her, to lean in to talk to her, but I realize my mistake. We are so close, our sleeves touch when we reach for our shared wine goblet at once. I feel the warmth of her body, not to mention the fury emanating from her. My cock hardens, and I almost forget the subject on which I was about to goad her.

Almost.

"You look enchanting in the green velvet, Princess. It brings out the color of your eyes. Perhaps I will command you to always wear green, once we are wed."

I am only half joking, as I truly do enjoy seeing her in the color. I'd rather see her without it, naked. But I shall have to wait a bit.

Thyra only says, "Excuse me," in a most demure fashion and moves to rise. "I must have words with one of my ladies. I will return shortly."

I am surprised for a moment by her graciousness, but only until I realize she has upended the goblet we were sharing, so it leaks Dervnonian wine into my lap.

I am left with the Thane Ulf Olafsson for company, who stands behind us, ewer of wine at the ready. He is royal cupbearer for the evening. This is not as much of a demotion as it sounds. As he is not royal, he cannot sit atop the dais, but Skerr's choice of him as cupbearer signifies his importance. The Vagmarian king cannot be without Olafsson for a moment, not even for the space of time a feast takes, and so has made him cupbearer, rather than relegate him to one of the dining tables below the dais. He is wearing a disapproving frown, as though someone took a piss in the trout platter. There is nothing wrong with the trout. It is grilled to perfection, then braised with a garlic and cream sauce, dashed with a tiny bit of lemon juice, which is quite dear, as citrus fruits must be imported from the Southlands. I can only presume he wears this unattractive expression because of his distaste for...me.

Ignoring the fact that my lap is growing increasingly wet, as I have not yet righted the goblet (I do not want to draw anyone's attention to Thyra's little victory), I decide Ulf is the next likely victim for my taunting, now the Princess has disappeared. There is no chance he did not notice the wine drenching my tunic. I notice he is in no hurry to right the goblet and refresh it. Something tells me this shirking of duty is intentional. I turn to him, trying to ignore that my balls are shrinking as the sour Dervnonian rot turns cold in my lap. "Listen, old man." There I am, calling him old man again, though I've sworn not to do it. "Either you believe I will care for her, or you do not. There is no in between. It is not training with sword sticks in the yard or casting a line in the carp pond. No accolades for effort."

"I believe you will care for her." He looks as though he's going to regurgitate his dinner or have a fainting fit, like a fish gasping for air on the dockside, but at least he's said the words.

"And what is it that convinced you I will protect her? My charming personality? My skills at the joust? Or is it my ability to ignore the Dervnonian piss on my tunic, which, by the by, was made from silk weaved in the Kingdom of Eastnor, by moths that can only be fed on the nectar of Parvat hibiscus, which can only be harvested from the so-named mountain peak, which is the highest in the Eastlands." Though I am out of breath, I must add, "It blooms for just one day, at the Summer Solstice."

I had not wanted to wear this tunic, but Davith insisted, saying the Princess would be impressed. I am pleased now to be wearing it, as complaining of its ruination is excellent ammunition to use against both Olafsson and the Princess Thyra.

"Allow me to make myself clear, King Drengr. I trust you no more this day than I did yesterday, and I certainly did not trust you at all then. I know you will not mistreat My Princess, because I will cleave your rotted brain in twain if you ever hurt her. I do not care if you have the might of dragons at your disposal; they cannot always be there to guard you. Indeed, they are not now, are they?"

His voice has taken on a sinister tone, one I'm not sure I like.

If anyone could figure out how to circumvent my dragons and assassinate me, I'd put my wager on Ulf Olafsson.

And don't you dare ever repeat those words. We shall pretend such an admission never occurred.

12

THYRA

"At least consummation will not be all that difficult. It would be much more of a chore with Harald of Hausen, believe me."

I sought out Lyda's company for reassurance, for distraction, perhaps a bit of a jape at Drengr's expense. She sits at one of the tables closest to the royal dais, reserved for my ladies and a number of the jarls visiting from the territories of Vagmar. The princelings from the other kingdoms represented at this feast all sit atop the dais, with my father and myself.

"How can you say such a thing? I loathe Drengr of Logaland. I cannot imagine lying with him."

"Yes, you can. You'd have to be a Hel-dweller of the Frostfangs not to be able to imagine bedsport with that man. And do not lie to me. Your mind hates him, but your body does not."

I do not appreciate being compared to a demon of the Apocalypse, particularly since they are said to be immune to lust. I am about to tell Lyda so when I hear a commotion erupt on the dais.

"A betrothal is as binding as a marriage, or at least, it should be. But you would not be the first princeling to winkle out of an arrangement if you were to find a more tempting offer."

It is Ulf speaking, making no attempt to lower his voice. He holds a wine ewer in a menacing fashion, as though it were a mace. He is causing embarrassment to our House, but I cannot seem to care. I just want Drengr to suffer.

Drengr raises himself from his seat, and I note with no small amount of satisfaction, a wine stain covers a sizeable portion of the middle of his tunic. If only urine were as red as Dervnonian wine, everyone would think he'd pissed himself.

"First, I am no princeling, which you should remember. Second, you impugn my honor. And third, I am graciously giving you the opportunity to apologize, before I ram my fist in your face."

Ulf barks with laughter and claps Drengr of Logaland on the shoulder.

"I do heartily apologize. I shall call you kingling instead."

King Drengr laughs as well. What is happening? How is it that Ulf and this Drengr seem to be...bonding? Ulf has always been my champion, my ally and defender against my father, and at times, even Edda. He is supposed to loathe Drengr of Logaland.

My father has chosen him as my groom, though it is for reasons of deceit. My most trusted advisor and friend is warming up to him, and my dearest friend thinks he will be good in bed.

Is no one on my side?

I resign myself to return to the dais, but I feel a gentle touch on my arm, just above my elbow. I turn to see

Matthias, gentle expression firmly in place, clutching a large piece of parchment. My heart blazes with triumph for one wild moment. He is here. He will do it. He will challenge Drengr, defy my father with me, tell the world he loves me. Of course, he's never told me he loves me, not even in private, but this is neither here nor there.

"Brother Matthias, what do you do here? You never come to the hall, especially not during a crowded feast."

"I could not be sure I would see you again if I did not seek you out. In the course of my research today, I found something I thought you would appreciate. It is a map of Logaland, complete with its capital, its forests, mountains, and rivers, its provinces and their capitals. Even the names and locations of the larger villages. I wanted to give it to you, so you may acquaint yourself with your new home. Think of it as my parting gift."

"How did you know I would be wed to Logaland? My father did not make the announcement until only moments ago."

Perhaps thank you should have been my first words, but I am irritated. Did everyone but me know Drengr was my fate?

"My Princess, everyone speaks of it. Though I do not often venture outside the Priory gates, there are many visitors in Rhok who wish to pay their respects to our gods, to seek blessings on their travels while in a foreign land. They talk of nothing but this Drengr's pursuit of you."

Matthias's eyes slide to the dais where Drengr sits, sprawled indelicately, as though he sits at a campfire and not a royal feast in his honor. But his own eyes are alert, like a hawk's, and fastened on Matthias. He does not look pleased.

I feel a little thrill of pleasure. Though I cannot use

Matthias in the manner I'd intended–fleeing, marriage, perhaps some fucking–I can employ the novitiate's presence to good use still. I belatedly thank Matthias, grasp the parchment, and return to the dais, trying not to grin, for then I will give the game away.

"Who is that?" Drengr asks casually.

Too casually.

I do not care if he is jealous, and if he is, it can only be because he already views me as his own property, not because of any of my personal charms. But I do enjoy it when he is discomposed.

"It is Brother Matthias, from the Priory. We are... friends."

I allow the word to linger suggestively in the air, hoping he is questioning some of his heretofore most treasured assumptions. First, that I am indeed a maid, which my father promised to all my suitors. Second, that I am not impressed with men who are all might and no mind, that I prefer a more scholarly sort.

"How friendly are you? Will you be sad to leave him, as you will be to leave this other friend of yours, with whom you were just conversing? She is one of your attendants, is she not?"

He must have been observing me closely, to know such information. Perhaps he is more perceptive than he seems. I will have to be more circumspect.

"Oh, no, the relationship I have with Lyda is quite... different...from the one I share with Matthias," I purr.

"What did he give you then?"

"A token of his...appreciation. It is a map."

"Ah, yes, nothing says 'I'd tup you well in the bed furs' like the gift of a dusty old piece of parchment."

"Truly, you are crude. Are you sure you are a king?"

"It is a thing my mother often wondered as well when I was a child, fearing I was a changeling, such was my behavior. But rest assured, I am my father's son. There is no denying it."

His voice has taken on a more serious tone, more contemplative. He is not teasing me anymore, but lost in some thoughts of his own. This will not do. I'd meant to goad him, to make him lose his control. His smirk is ever present when we are together, his nerves never rattled. I wish to change this.

"I did wonder, as Drengr is a rather common name. Perhaps your mother was trying to tell your father something."

He does not even blink. My words did not so much as sting, let alone bite.

Ignoring my insult, he asks, "What is the map of? How to get under a woman's skirts and find all her pertinent bits? For I doubt Brother Matthias would be able to do so, without benefit of a guide."

"As he is bound to the Priory, and by his oath he must avoid getting under anyone's skirts, or risk execution. But I am sure if he wished, he could get in a woman's bed furs easily enough, no map required."

If I am not mistaken, the king next to me growls, a bit like a distempered wolf or a crabby bear.

"As it happens," I continue, "the map is of Logaland. It is quite detailed. Truly, I hope you have no map quite so fine of Vagmar in your kingdom, else you must know all our secrets."

"We have dragons. Knowing our enemies' secrets is of little import. Though now you mention it, I'd like to know yours, Princess."

"I am an open book, My King. Or an easily read map, if you will. Ask me a question, and I shall answer honestly."

Unless the question is, Are you secretly a Valkyrie? If somehow this is what he wishes to know, I shall have to lie.

"Do you want to fuck this Brother Matthias?"

He asks the question in a low whisper, so no one else can hear. Still, my ears burn.

"How dare you," I hiss.

"You promised to tell the truth."

"I did no such thing. Promises are for children and oath-breakers. But if you must know, I...I...I do not know."

For that is the truth of it.

He sighs theatrically.

"I am sorry to be the one to tell you this, Princess, but if you are not sure whether you want a good fucking from a man, the answer is likely no, you do not."

"Brother Matthias and I have a relationship that is not based on physical desires, but the powers of the mind. He is a great researcher, and I have learned much from him."

Even to mine own ears, I sound pathetic.

"And do you want to fuck me, Princess?"

"No."

I do not even have to think about my answer. It does not matter whether it is the truth or not. It would be self-ruination to admit to any lustful feelings for this man.

"You are lying. Your truth telling a moment ago was admirable, but now I am disappointed."

How would I even know if I wanted to...fuck...a man, as Drengr so crudely calls it? There must be some telltale signs one would wish for it. I think of how my breath hitches and my heart beats faster when I see this Drengr in the hall or on the tourney grounds. How when he is nearby, my body knows before my eyes even hunt him down. If he is there, he is the first person I see. And then, the only one I think of.

If ever a woman wanted to fuck a man, I suppose this is how she would behave.

Hel.

"EDDA, do you wish me to be more…regnal? More like, say… Lyda?"

I am sitting uncharacteristically still whilst she brushes my hair before bed, not that sleep will come this night. I am hoping to leave her with an impression of good behavior before I depart for Logaland. Call it a parting gift.

"Heavens no, child. Lyda Björnsson is far too well pleased with herself for my taste."

I am not sure this is a compliment. Am I lacking in esteem for my own person?

"But if you tended a maid like Lyda, you would never know a moment's agitation."

"And what makes you think this would please me? I'd grow bored within the hour. I like a challenge, my girl, and you provide a new one every day."

Suddenly, I begin to cry. It is too much. The last time I cried was when my mother died. Prior to her murder, I'm not sure I ever cried. Maybe a few sniffles when I scraped my knees in the training yard, but I am sure my father and Edda would have put those sniffles to rest with a sharp word before they ever had the chance to develop into real tears.

Without a word, Edda envelops me in her arms. She seems to know exactly why I weep.

"There, there, child. We knew this day would come. And

Logaland, for all its fearsomeness, is our closest neighbor. There will be opportunities to visit, I am sure of it."

"Edda, that is the biggest whopper you've ever told me, and on my seventh birthday, you said if I climbed down from the whistletree at the Priory, Father would find me a unicorn."

"Well, you climbed down, didn't you? And I'm sure he would have done, if unicorns actually existed. Now you listen, My Princess. Servants talk, and there are plenty from Logaland traipsing around here. If they did not think well of their king, I would hear of it. And I have not heard a negative word pass any Logalanders' lips. He may not allow you to travel back to Vagmar, but I am sure he would not say no to a visit from your old nurse from time to time."

My sobs ebb, as Edda intended.

Suppressing a hiccup, I say, "You will write, though, won't you? I shall write to you every day."

"Heavens no! You know I won't. I haven't the time for it, nor the inclination. I never learned my letters well. But if you write to me, I will read every word, and employ Old Nasmell at the Priory to help me with the ones I cannot make out for myself."

At least she is honest.

But will Drengr even allow me to send letters to Edda or to anyone in Vagmar, for that matter? Will I be able to receive any? Though I hold out little hope for chatty letters from my father, and Edda will not write, I hope Ulf will, and perhaps Lyda and some of my other attendants, though I care only for Lyda's missives. The other ladies pen a boring letter, it must be said.

Somehow, our marriage contract was drawn up with all haste, almost as though it had already been devised before the King Drengr ever traveled here, before I even knew he wanted to wed me. Almost as though my father and Drengr colluded in this arrangement, without my knowledge. The contract clearly states I am not allowed to bring any of my attendants from Vagmar to my new home. No Edda, no Lyda. Hel, I'd even take some of my more boring ladies, if it meant having some Vagmarian company, people who I already know and with whom I can converse. I am not adept with the Logalander tongue, at least not the spoken language. It is Drengr's belief I will become more acclimated to my new home if I am surrounded by Logalander folk to serve me. My father agreed to this codicil readily enough. Further down the agreement, which Ulf allowed me to read once my father left us before the feast, there is quite a detailed codicil regarding Logaland's export of timber and horses to Vagmar at a reduced expense.

I am sure my father thought this bargain well worth the price of my loneliness.

13

THYRA

Elfgiva's tower was built in the northeasterly corner of our palisade, the great wall that surrounds Rhok. She insisted upon its construction when she came to my father's court in my mother's train when they were wed, saying she could not cast her runes or look into her fires amidst the business of a great hall. This made perfect sense to my parents. It is common knowledge völvas cannot conduct their work without the benefit of some solitude.

Also, many of a völva's incantations require newts' tails, bats' wings, and all manner of slippery creatures' offal to secure their efficacy, so my parents thought it wise to acquiesce to Elfgiva's wishes.

It has been abandoned for many years now, and it shows. Elfgiva, despite her oddities, always kept her little tower room neat and tidy. There was not an apothecary jar or stewed rabbit's brain out of place. It was always swept and dusted, with fresh rushes thrown down frequently. In truth, more often than they are replaced in my father's hall. I believe I have mentioned he is a rather stingy fellow. But now cobwebs stretch across the tower's only window, and the tapestries that covered the walls are moth-eaten. Bird droppings cover the rafters and drip down the timber support pillars. I see evidence of their nesting on the wooden beams.

"I wish I had the time to employ a runes master to work with you before your departure, so you could write in a coded language to send information to us. The old tongue of Vagmar is one no one in Logaland would likely be able to decipher. But even you, My Princess, could not learn a different language in a matter of days," Ulf says.

It is a worry I share, one I have fretted over much, though as any fond parent would, Ulf gives me too much credit. I can read and write most any tongue if I take the time to study it, but speaking them–with actual people–is another matter entirely. Though the old tongue of Vagmar is a dead language, and so perhaps there is hope for me. I would not have to attempt to converse in it in polite company. And I have studied it in the Priory, though not enough for any competence in the subject.

"Gathering the intelligence my father requires will be difficult, but even more challenging, how will I send him the information I collect about Drengr, his dragons, and his kingdom?"

Though it is a nonsensical question. Even if my letters are allowed to flow freely to Vagmar, I must assume they are being read by someone in Drengr's Council or even Drengr himself.

"I have given some thought on the matter, and I think I have found a solution."

Ulf goes to the corner of the tower and with a flourish removes an oil cloth from an object in the corner. Not an object, but a...creature. It is a raven. A beautiful, enormous one, with feathers so dark they ripple with blue and purple when the pale sunlight beaming through the small tower window hits them. Once he realizes he is no longer covered, he sets to pecking delicately at his feathers.

"Hug," he (I assume the creature is male, which perhaps I should not do) croaks.

"It is the only word he knows," Ulf explains. I was correct, he is a boy, which makes perfect sense, as it is only men who preen so fastidiously, everyone knows. "I named him Huggin, after one of the Great God's ravens, and I believe he is trying to pronounce his own name. Perhaps you will teach it to him better."

For what I believe is the first time, I experience a surge of love uncomplicated by any other worrisome emotion when I listen to this bird croak. I love Edda, but I fear her, though please do not tell her. I love Ulf, but I never wish to disappoint him. I...think?...I love my father. Yes, I do. Of course I do. At least, I esteem him. I will think on this subject later. An image of the King Drengr enters my mind, unbidden. Whatever I feel for him, it is not love. Indeed, it is mostly hatred, combined with perhaps just a touch of curiosity. But lust is another matter entirely. I know I feel it when I am near him. Lust is a damned nuisance.

Nothing about Hug, which he will forever be known as from this moment, no matter Ulf wishes for me to teach him his full moniker, is complicated. I love him instantly, and he is going to love me. I will make him. I will carry mealworms in my pockets at all times and bribe him with shiny treasures, which ravens do so love. I believe in my trousseau I am taking a case of silver spoons. Those will do nicely. There is only one problem.

"He is a stunning bird, but what am I to do with him? How will he help us in our mission?"

"This raven is trained to carry messages, as though he were a pigeon kept in a dovecote. Huggin can carry the secret missives you pen to us here, in Rhok. Pretend he is your treasured pet and send him in the mornings, before the household is awake. No one will be suspicious of a raven flying through the sky. It is a pigeon they would question."

There will be no pretending about it. Hug does not yet know it, nor does Ulf, but this raven is already treasured by me. And yet...

"Ulf, I had no notion you are able to train birds."

"Alas, I do not. Huggin belonged to Elfgiva, who trained him to carry her missives. She was a great correspondent with the Priories at Echen. She always maintained ravens are smarter than pigeons, even if they can be less agreeable. He has roosted in this tower for years, since Elfgiva departed."

Departed is a euphemism for how we describe the manner of Elfgiva's leaving, for no one quite knows where she went or if she instead died. Somehow I can't picture it, though. Death comes for us all, but I suspect Elfgiva would have desired a more dramatic ending than simply... dissipating.

Ulf strokes Hug's feathers as he says, hesitating, "My Princess, are you sure you can go through with this? What your father asks of you, it is not...not..."

He cannot finish, for to do so would be a betrayal of his king. He does not fear being accused of treachery, nor even of hanging from a noose, but he cannot bring himself to say a word against the man to whom he is oathbound.

"I know you must betray this Drengr," he continues, "and I will aid you and My King in any way I can, for I am sworn to you, and gladly, but I do believe he will treat kindly with you. I thought you would feel reassured if I told you...I do not think he will ever harm you."

Why thank you, Ulf, it makes me feel ever so much better that the man I must destroy might actually not be so horrific.

Our court völva is also the Prime Matron of the Priory. A völva is a witch, of sorts. She is a runesayer. A prophetess. And a völva is almost always a woman, for it is a rare man who can set aside earthly cares and shoulder the burden of spiritual well-being for an entire kingdom. Or at least, so the theory goes.

Many völvas are full of shite and only take on the job because they are afforded a relatively pampered, rent-free existence once in the position.

The current placeholder is one such fraud. I admit to having a biased opinion of her, because she does not let me take scrolls from the library. I am forced to sneak them from Old Nasmell, who is always a willing co-conspirator. She is disappointingly fond of pomp and circumstance and the observance of proper etiquette. Her predecessor in the role, Elfgiva, was far more satisfying, just what a völva should be. She would wander the streets of Rhok when the moon was full, muttering incantations. Rather than enjoying the comforts of the Priory, she made her home in the turret I visited yesterday. It is in the farthest tower of our burh, the defensive palisade which surrounds the capital. She shared her abode with one blue-tongued lizard from the Southlands. She always kept the fire going, saying it was on account of his thin skin, but I suspect his well-being was a convenient excuse, as even only partially sane witches desire some creature comforts. Elfgiva also kept a poisonous wood viper from the Forest of Dale, who somehow never bit her but managed to infect more than several warriors with its venom. Fortunately, she possessed an antidote, which she was suspiciously out of only once, when the viper's victim happened to be her sister's former lover, who'd set the sister aside and taken up with another woman. And she had a cat, who was–blessedly–quite ordinary.

I loved Elfgiva, as did my mother. She died when my mother did, or at least, that is what her sister said. I have my doubts. I think she decided it would no longer be amusing to serve as court völva to the Kingdom of Vagmar if my mother wasn't here. I can't say I blame her.

As much as I dislike the current court völva, I am happy it is she, and not Elfgiva, who handfasts me to Drengr of Logaland. It is somehow more fitting for a völva whom I dislike to bind me to a husband I also dislike. I would have more trouble holding my courage if I could not remain dispassionate.

Only a völva is allowed to perform the Handfasting, because they are augurs of prophecy, and it is best to keep the gods on your side when setting out in marriage. Especially when two enemy nations are also being joined.

And especially when the bride and groom in question also detest each other. At least, I know I hate Drengr. It is possible he does not loathe me in return. In fact, it seems as though I amuse him, even if his amusement is at my expense. I do not intend to question him on the matter, however. Whether our hatred is mutual or he merely feels ambivalence towards me, it is not my concern. It is irrelevant.

Or at least, so I tell myself.

I may as well be honest, though. He is deadly handsome, emphasis on the word deadly.

My father's instructions are clear. I must pretend to be falling for Drengr, so he is off guard and will share sensitive information with me, which I can then pass along to my father. I must smile when I wish to scowl. Laugh when I'd rather scream. Sink my fangs into him if he discovers my treachery. Oh, and pretend to enjoy Drengr's touch, when I only want to shrink from it.

According to Lyda and I am fairly certain, every other woman in existence, I will not have to pretend. I hope they are wrong. For if I cannot control my emotions when in his presence, he will discover my intentions, and I have no doubt such a revelation will result in my death. The King of Logaland will be responsible for my murder, as his father once was for my mother's. And I couldn't even really blame him for killing me. A treasonous queen, bent on his destruction, would be a liability, to say the least. One he'd need to eliminate. I may have the venom of a Valkyrie in my veins, but I am not immortal.

"We are gathered here to unite two kingdoms," the counterfeit court völva intones. I would tell you her name, but I do not know it. When anyone asks, she frostily replies, You will refer to me as Prime Matron. "To forge a new alliance and to bind two souls together."

I repress a snort of laughter, rather unsuccessfully. It is ludicrous to speak of political alliance and the unification of souls in the same sentence, but here we are.

The Logalander king and I stand outside my father's hall, in the chill of the morning air. It is an overcast day, as many are in Vagmar. Still, I am pleased, for it is fittingly dismal weather. A trellis constructed with wands of hazelwood stands before the hall, erected by someone who clearly is a romantic optimist. Edda, most likely, with some of the carls' assistance. It is almost the season of Yule, and there is no greenery with which to bedeck it except holly and ivy. Shame. I had always loved this time of year, especially the decorating bit.

Now, I will look forward to the season with resentment each year.

This morning, Drengr wears an even more impressive tunic than the one in which he was attired at yesterday's feast. It is pale blue, with cloth of gold weaved into its neckline, hem, and sleeves. His hair has been freshly braided and gleams like a raven's feathers, though there is no sunlight. Someone shaved him, though I think I prefer it when he has a hint of a beard. Nevermind. I did not just think such a thing. I do not care what the status of his facial hair is. Whether he has it or not, it is no concern of mine.

I look rather well too, though I say it myself. I submitted to Edda's ministrations this morning, mostly because I was too distraught to put up any fight.

He grasps my hands as the Prime Matron speaks, and though I should not be surprised, for such a gesture is customary, I find myself tingling, as though I've been burned. But not in a painful way, which is nonsense, as of course burning hurts. His touch is warm and dry and reassuring, and I want to drop his hands and run for the hills. He stares into my eyes. Or at least, he tries. I keep averting my gaze from his. I do not want to see the smirking, knowing expression there, the one always lurking in the depths of his dark eyes. It is a look that makes me feel as though I am naked. As though he knows exactly what I would look like naked, even though he's never seen me in such a state. As though he's definitely imagined it, numerous times.

Has his imagination done me justice? More importantly, has his imagination enjoyed what it produced? I should not care.

"Do you enter this Handfasting under your own will, Princess Thyra of Vagmar, without the threats or coercion of any other person?"

Is her question a jape? Of course I have been forced into this alliance. Take your pick by whom. My father, Ulf, Drengr himself. It is not as though I had a choice in the matter. At least my father had the grace not to try to pretend I did. He informed me Drengr and Logaland were his choice, and he was to be obeyed. Ulf tried to soften the blow, which I appreciate, but he has not protested the match, not once. And as for Drengr, he is deluded enough to think I will come to want him. To acquiesce to this marriage, in both mind and body. To want his touch.

It is at this juncture I try to ignore the tingling sensation in my hands, where his hold mine.

I try very hard.

If my skin burns where he touches it, what will it feel like when he touches me in...other places? The body is covered in a great deal of skin, and there are many places to be touched. Caressed.

Kissed.

Dear gods, I am an imbecile.

I feel a gentle pressure on my hands, and realize Drengr is squeezing them. In commiseration, perhaps, or as a reminder to answer the bloody woman's question. Either way, I do not appreciate his considerate gesture.

"Yes, I do."

It is the only answer I can give.

I notice, though, the Court Völva does not pose this question to Drengr as well. However, she does pose him a question that is perhaps even more challenging, I must admit.

"Do you swear to pledge your life to this woman, to give yours up to protect hers?"

"I do."

He utters his vow so easily. So casually. I wonder at his duplicity. He cannot possibly mean it.

Satisfied with Drengr's answer, the Prime Matron says more loudly, "Do any here object to the vows about to be spoken?"

Yes, I do. I scream it silently.

I hope Harald of Hausen will speak up. I know he was disappointed he wasn't chosen, the poor lamb, and perhaps he thinks if he makes a claim he is a better candidate for my hand, this farce of a betrothal ceremony will end. I look over to him, but he is not paying attention to the völva or anyone else for that matter. I follow the direction of his gaze and see he is paying attention to a hawk who just landed in one of the boughs of a neighboring pine.

I could accomplish quite a bit as Queen of Hausen. Harald would probably allow me to do anything I wished. Change the country's name. Import a never ending supply of citrus fruits from the Southlands and pass the bill to our taxpayers. Make all his household carls my personal sexual thralls. He would never bat an eyelash.

He'd be too busy staring at hawks in boughs.

I jest, of course. I do wish to be queen of a kingdom. I am not ashamed to admit it. I have been prepared since birth to be the queen regnant of some kingdom or other of Plane, as well as monarch in mine own country. I have always known I would never love my husband, that he would be a pawn in the game of rule as much as me. But I hoped to improve the kingdom I was sent to, to make a difference. To be accepted by its people.

I am not sure Drengr will allow me to make any improvements. To actually serve in all the capacities of queenship, not just bearing royal heirs. His is a strong personality, and there will likely be no room for my assistance in governing, nor my advice.

Harald does not speak, and I know then I am doomed. No one speaks out against this handfasting, and why would they? Even amongst the princelings present, the ones who stayed after the joust, even after they'd been discarded in favor of Drengr, none speaks against our betrothal. It profits all of Plane if its two most powerful kingdoms are no longer adversaries.

If only this were the truth. If only I went to Logaland with a clear conscience, with a directive from my father to try to make the best of a difficult situation, and not to lie to my husband.

If only people could put aside their enmity as easily as kingdoms.

14

DRENGR

The Princess of Vagmar looks as though she's been hit in the head with Thor's hammer. Like someone told her a favorite horse died, just before the ceremony began. What is adorable, is she probably thinks she's being quite stoic about the whole business. That I cannot tell she is about ready to turn on her heels and flee from this Handfasting like the very hounds of Hel are pursuing her.

She does look quite lovely, though. She wears a garland of flowers on the crown of her head. Someone must have forced the blooms in a windowsill inside the hall, as it is not the time of year for chamomile or hyssop or lavender. Her maids must have chosen the chamomile to match her gown, which is white, and made of the finest lambswool. Panels of silk in a matching color cover the bodice and sleeves. Cloth of gold dots the hemlines. The hyssop and lavender match her purple cloak, long a color of royalty, which is trimmed with ermine and fastened with a gold broach in the shape of the Hanrok, a sea serpent, the symbol of the House of

Vagmar, as they were pirates–a thing Thyra denies, but which is entirely accurate.

Should I feel insulted she chose to adorn herself with a representation of her own kingdom's sigil, rather than mine own? I suppose not, I acknowledge. This Handfasting is a binding of two kingdoms, long at war, and it is fitting she should represent Vagmar during the ceremony.

But after we are wed, she will accessorize herself with dragons and dragons alone.

The color purple suits her, though I prefer it when she wears green. It is a violet hue she wore the day of the joust, and she looked quite lovely then. Perhaps I will also allow this color to be a part of her wardrobe. I jest, of course. Something tells me there will be no telling the Princess Thyra what to include in her closet and what to leave out.

The sun peaks through the clouds as the Prime Matron begins her chattering. I confess, I do not pay attention. I lift my face to it, enjoying the meager rays while I can. Sunshine is fleeting in Logaland, summer even moreso. But though the harvests have all been brought in and the air chills, this midwinter season is my favorite. I am descended from dragon masters, and dragons make their own warmth. The leaves have turned; the wheat has gone to the mills; the hay is stored for the coming winter. The stags hunt for does in the forest, often so intent on their purpose, they make easy targets for my arrows. I am no trophy collector, but if Logalanders did not hunt for their sustenance, they would oft go hungry. Our harvests are poor, even in the most fortuitous of years.

In Vagmar, no one ever goes hungry. It has not escaped my notice a valuable trading network may develop from a marriage with this princess. My people will never needs hunt for their dinner again if we can import grain from Vagmar.

And what would the people of Vagmar receive in return? For nothing is given without something expected in return, even if the two kingdoms are united by marriage.

The end of war. It is the obvious answer. Though it may not seem a fair bargain, as war is often mutually destructive, even to the victor. But this is a different case.

We have dragons.

Vagmar does not.

I am content, though I know Thyra is not. I do not mind. She will realize, in time, marriage to me was the wisest course of action. And ultimately, the most pleasurable. But it is too soon to convince her. She will come to these conclusions on her own, eventually.

Though I am distracted, I realize a heavy silence has filled the air. Those lords and ladies congregated have gone quiet, as has the Matron, as though she expects an answer. It cannot be from me, as little is required from my mouth during this ceremony. It is the responsibility of the bride to do most of the talking.

I do not know what she is supposed to say, for I was not paying attention to the question, but clearly, she must make an answer. I squeeze her palms gently. Irritation flashes in her eyes, so quickly I might be mistaken. It is gone before I can be sure. But my gesture has done its work, for she responds finally with, "Yes, I do."

I take this as a positive sign, as No is never an appropriate answer during a Handfasting, nor during a marriage ceremony, for that matter. I have not thought much on our impending marriage. I was too consumed with ensuring our betrothal first. But I wonder now if she will look forward to that day more than this one, once she has come to know me better.

I suppose her level of enthusiasm is entirely up to me and how hard I work to convince her she will be happy. My tongue is no good with sweet words, but it has other uses, ones she will come to appreciate, in time.

Then the Prime Matron asks if anyone objects to our betrothal. I eye those congregated darkly, daring them to challenge this Handfasting. Wisely, none of them do. I'd wondered, almost hoped, Harald of Hausen would take issue with our betrothal, as he is so besotted with the Princess Thyra, but he does not. His attention is taken by a hawk ripping a rabbit's innards to bits on the bough of a scrubby pine. Typical. But I shall not complain. I did not want to hurt poor Harald's feelings. As I've mentioned, Hausen is an ally of Logaland's, and also, I can be a considerate person, when I so choose.

Take for example how I squeezed the Princess's Thyra's palms to remind her to respond to the Prime Matron's question. However, she was most unappreciative.

It could be taken as an ill omen the hawk has chosen to take its grisly meal within sight of the lords and ladies assembled for our Handfasting, but I will choose to believe it is fortuitous. The hawk secured its quarry, as I have secured mine own. So what if a hawk prefers rabbits, and I have hunted a princess?

We've both found success this day, which is cause for celebration.

CAUSE FOR CELEBRATION did not mean yet another feast, but here we are. I'd been thinking more along the lines of getting the Princess Thyra alone for a bit, and showing her my tongue is good for things besides insults. Our Handfasting must be celebrated, Vagmar must show its wealth and generosity, and Thyra must be given a grand farewell.

For we leave on the morrow, and if anyone tries to delay us, I will cleave them in twain. It occurs to me Thyra would be the most likely culprit for impeding our journey. I will not cleave her in twain, of course, but I may be sharper with my tongue than I'd hoped to have to be in our first days alone together.

Unfortunately, I do not speak of all the talented things I can do with my tongue, but rather the sharp words it also speaks, meant to insult and to wound.

We are assembled on the dais much the same as we were several days ago, when we feasted after the tourney, and our betrothal was announced. The hall is less crowded, as many jarls and princelings have departed for their own kingdoms, but some remain. Harald of Hausen, for one, though I cannot understand why he desires the punishment. He sits to the other side of Thyra, which is perhaps a seating arrangement orchestrated by her father or by Ulf, to remind me they have given the princess to me, but they can take her away, give her elsewhere just as easily.

Fools.

Once something is mine, it is mine forever. Only if I choose to relinquish it does it no longer belong to me. I protect it, nurture it. Cherish it. Granted, Thyra is no thing, no object to be used or discarded at my pleasure. But she is mine now, and I am not giving her up.

Also, she is not a heifer to be traded at market. I am angry on her behalf. Not too furious, however, as it was necessary to barter with her father for her hand, so I suppose I treated her like a piece of livestock as much as the other men in her life. I promised all manner of things to King Skerr, all of which were worth sacrificing to secure this marriage.

Timber from our forests and our other most valuable export, our horses. And of course, a vow not to set my dragons on Vagmar for the amount of time an heir with any Vagmarian blood sits the Dragon Throne. Since this is also what my father wished, I was content to make this concession part of our agreement. And timber and good horseflesh are as thick upon the ground in my kingdom as flies settling on an overripe piece of fruit.

Thyra does not seem to be full of the spirit she demonstrated at the previous feast. She stares listlessly at her platter, on which I have placed the finest cuts of roasted pheasant. I notice Harald of Hausen, who is not her feast partner, still felt the compulsion to share with her and has placed some succulent bits of tripe next to the pheasant. Of course Harald would like tripe. Truly, I did Thyra a favor by rescuing her from poor, dim Harald. I just hope she sees this, in time.

She only pushes the food around with her eating knife, and though she stares into the platter, I know she does not see it. Her gaze and her thoughts are on the future and whether she will be able to bear it. I find myself vaguely discomfited, almost as though I care whether she is happy. Some part of me wants to put a smile on her face. But since I know this to be impossible, a frown will do.

"Eat up, Princess. I do not want a skeleton for a wife. If I had, I'd have found myself a Hel corpse, fully decomposed."

My silken tongue has worked its magic. She abruptly drops her eating knife in her plate and scowls. Her dazzling green eyes no longer hold that mournful, yet wistful, faraway look in them. She turns to me, an angry blush reddening her freckled cheeks.

"Do me a favor, when you travel to Hel for this corpse bride, stay there. Set up house. Hel is where you belong, after all."

She is so clever with her tongue, almost as talented as myself. I wonder, can her tongue also perform other feats, under the bed furs? Likely not. She is, after all, inexperienced. I shall have to teach her all manner of skills, a task I look forward to, more than I'd anticipated before making Thyra's acquaintance.

I have done such a thorough job enraging her, I decide to try for smiles next. I may fail, but one never knows until one tries, as my father always said. He was usually talking about how much ale he thought he could consume in one go, but his wisdom is still applicable to this situation.

"Would you like to hear a joke, Princess? Did you ever hear the one about a völva, a giant, and a unicorn? The unicorn walks into a tavern and happens upon..." But I cease talking, for she stops paying me any mind, her attention caught by a commotion at the entrance.

Several carls are heaving open the great door. It must be King Skerr or another nobleman, for if it were anyone else, they would simply enter through one of the smaller doors. It is what I do, though it is not mete. I do not wait for the great door to open in any hall, not because I wish to point out I do not stand on ceremony, but because I haven't the patience to wait to get inside from the chill air while carls huff with exertion, trying to get it open.

It is King Skerr, who looks diminutive standing in the grandness of the entryway, but also because he is joined by the Thane Ulf Olafsson, who dwarfs most men–myself excluded, of course.

Thyra looks at her father contemplatively, sadly even. "I wonder..." she murmurs, and I am sure she does not realize she said the words aloud.

So of course, I must make her aware. "Wonder what?" I ask brightly.

"I did not say anything."

But her flush betrays her. When she lies, her neck turns crimson. When she is angry, her cheeks go red. I can't wait to discover which bits of skin blush when she is naked and excited.

Does she wonder where her father was? Doubtful. He is a king and rather busy. I am called from dinner too often to count. Then suddenly, I know the answer–

"I know what you wonder, but we do not need to speak of it, if you do not wish."

I lie. I wish her to speak, to voice her thoughts aloud, and I will do whatever it takes, say what vulgar things I must, to get her to continue talking.

"Do you think you know me so well already, then, My King?" Her voice is scornful, but her expression betrays her pain.

"You wonder if he would have forced you to wed me, had you protested. You did not oppose his command, because you did not want to find out whether he would take your wishes into account. You did not want to discover he loves you so little, that he would wed you to a beast without your consent."

Tears well in her eyes, but she blinks rapidly, and they are soon replaced by a gleam of fury. Good. Her anger is for what I hoped. I have no patience for a woman's tears. The compulsion to end her crying has nothing to do with the funny little ache I feel in my chest when I see them glistening in her moss green eyes.

"You know everything there is to know about me, is that it then?"

"I know your neck blushes when you lie, your face flames when you are angry, as it does now, and I cannot wait to find out what other bits turn pink when you are excited. I know your feelings are hurt or you are scared when you turn tetchy. I know you must be a great thinker. Either this, or you are intent on getting wrinkles whilst still a maiden, because your brow is always furrowed in contemplation. And though in this I am not certain, I am fairly confident you will make a decent queen, as the most important requirement is a willingness to sacrifice yourself for the greater good of the kingdom. The gods know you do not wish to marry me, that you are terrified, but you do so anyway, to save the people of Vagmar."

"I am not terrified," is all she can respond.

"Oh yes, you are, Princess, and you should be. For I will make you want me, when all you want is to hate me. You will crave my touch and wonder where I am when I am gone from you. You will come to hate yourself for it, before you accept it is the way of things."

"You are rather full of yourself."

I lean in closer, whisper wickedly, "Tell me you don't want me."

"I don't want you," she says without batting an eyelash.

I bark with laughter. "Gods, this marriage business will be funner than I thought." I've pondered this many a time, but never voiced it aloud.

"I'm glad one of us believes so."

I want more than anything to wipe that smirk off her face, to diffuse the sarcasm in her voice.

"Why do you not visit me in my tent later, after the fires are out? Tomorrow, you become mine. We may not yet be married, but by day's end, we will reach my kingdom, and then there is no escaping from me. We could consummate this union early."

Her pretty pink mouth parts in surprise. Hel, I want those lips wrapped round my cock. But her eyes...they shine with a desire she likely doesn't even know she betrays. Only for a moment, though, and then her habitual scowl is back in place. In fairness, I do not know if it is her custom to wear a perpetual frown, or if she only adorns it for me.

I suspect it is the latter.

15

THYRA

The kingdoms of Logaland and Vagmar are neighbors, which has always made our enmity doubly difficult. Only a river serves as our border. Despite the seas of Vagmar and the mountains of Logaland, neither our mother maker, the Great Sorceress and Queen, Maeve, nor any of the early kings of Plane, decided a more substantial marker would be more suitable to serve as our border. I was not there, as this was many hundreds of years ago, but had I been, I would have advised a different course of action to the queen.

I wouldn't, really. I do not think the Great Sorceress has ever been contradicted, nor would I wish to be the first to endeavor such an act of lunacy.

My teeth chatter, and it is not because I am still distressed from parting with my father earlier this morn. It was a rather frosty farewell, though I was much more upset when I said my good-byes to Ulf. As for Edda, I still cannot speak of her, nor think of her, but the memories keep intruding. I said my farewells to her yester eve, then cried myself to sleep. Or would have done, had I slept.

I realize I have not thought once on Matthias, nor shed a tear for him. Did I ever truly love him? Perhaps not. I know a huge part of his draw was that my father would disapprove of my tender feelings for him. It did not hurt that he was also unattainable, promised to the gods, with no intention of ever risking his life or his position of rank in the Priory to run away with me.

"We are not even near the border yet, Princess. You shall have to fashion some warmer garments or grow a thicker layer of skin," King Drengr says.

And why is he paying such bloody close attention to me, he notices even the slightest shiver?

"Logaland is no farther north than Vagmar. Why is it so bloody cold?" I ask through gritted teeth and what I suspect are blue lips. I wear a cap and cloak lined with sealskin, trimmed with otter fur, and still, I feel as though I am naked in the midst of a blizzard.

"The mountains. Have you never taken a geography lesson, Princess?"

Though we are still in Vagmar, as we approach Logaland, the elevation steepens. The snow sticks to the ground.

And my teeth chatter.

"I have read many tomes on geography in the library at Whistletree Priory. I am well aware of your kingdom's mountainous terrain. But reading of it and experiencing it are two entirely different matters."

"If you wish, you can ride pillion with me, Princess. You'll be warmer."

"No, thank you."

I ignore how his laughter sounds like the richness of burnt umber.

I sense the flutter of wings behind me before I feel the gentle touch of claws, but I do not start. In the last few days,

I have become used to my raven's habits. Indeed, we have grown rather attached. For my part, I am not surprised, as I can be rather foolish about animals. It is why Edda was always able to coax me into good behavior with visits to Elfgiva's tower, where there were many creatures, when I was a child. And if such bribery did not work, the story about seeing a unicorn did the trick.

"Hug. Hug," my raven croaks as he alights on my shoulder.

It is more surprising, though also quite endearing, that Huggin has also become attached to me. He has no need of his cage to keep him by my side and flies freely in the sky above us, always following me.

"Who is this?"

I may have forgotten to inform Drengr he would be accompanying us. Also, withholding the information may have been intentional.

"'Tis my raven. Did you not know I had a pet? I thought for sure I had mentioned it."

"No, Princess, you did not."

"His name is Huggin."

"You think very well of him, I take it, if you have given him the same name as one of the Great God's ravens."

Of course, I did not name the bird, but rather than attempt to explain how I acquired him, which would end poorly, I decide to distract Drengr, asking, "Where is your other horse, the one who looks as though he'd like to devour us all whole?"

"He prefers apples, but he might not say no to a nibble of tender Vagmarian princess. Holfnir is not for travel. Not only would he consider it beneath his dignity, but he is not built for it. He is bred to carry a knight wearing four stones' worth of armor, and to be able to charge at a full canter while doing so. Such duties require a great deal of strength, which he possesses, but very little endurance. The poor boy would tire of carrying me long before we ever reached the capital. This is Prunella."

"A girl horse? I'd not thought warrior kings deigned to ride mares."

"Females spook less easily and do not tire as quickly as males. They are often smarter, too."

"Do we still speak of horses?"

He only laughs in response, and damned if I don't feel flushed when I hear the sound. I do not care for this reaction to his mirth. Prunella snorts good-naturedly, as though she can understand the praise in Drengr's words. My words were meant to wound, but it seems they missed their target.

"By all the gods, child, keep your teeth together. Don't you ever know when to quit?"

Edda. It can't be. And yet there she is, riding on a placid donkey, her wimple starched a crisp white and disapproving frown securely in place, as though she were in the midst of a tea party and not the murk and muck of Logaland Forest.

"But...how?" It is all I can manage.

She appears triumphant. "For once, I have rendered you speechless. That young man of yours seemed to think you would not wish to be parted from my services. He sent word to me last night to be ready to leave at first light. I must admit, I didn't know quite what to do. I am ever so comfortable and established in your father's hall. But needs must, I suppose. I can't have you looking like a half-wild fairy on your wedding day."

"I will take everything from you, every illusion you hold dear, until all that is left is me, and the misery I offer. You will beg for it, in the end."

And yet, here is my nurse, tutting at me and smelling of

butterscotch. I want to cry with joy. I want to find Drengr and slice him with the dragon fang he wears round his neck.

But most of all, I want to understand him.

I am tempted to engage him in more conversation, to know him more deeply, but there is a sudden hush in the forest. The noises one does not normally notice until they are absent–the birds chirping, the boughs of the trees swaying in the breeze, the rustle of squirrels and rabbits in the dense thickets of undergrowth–it all stops. And so do the train of warriors and their horses. The carts ground to a halt as well, their wheels creaking eerily in the stillness. Drengr's men seem to know something is out there.

Or someone.

I do not know what I prefer–a human enemy, who has no advantage over me but would reveal my secret if I were to fight back–or beastly foes, ones with fangs and claws and a grudge against humans which carried over from their centuries of persecution in the Realm of Hjartagard.

Then an ear-splintering shriek splinters the air around us, and we are surrounded. I feel and hear the beat of great wings all around us, like the sounds Huggin's make when he flies, but much more ominous. More smothering. The raven alights from my shoulder with a caw of distress, but I haven't the chance to see where he flees. I can only hope he finds shelter from what is coming, for I know with certainty that we face battle.

I know what these creatures are, for I am one of them. Valkyrien. Yes, they are women, or have the look of them. Though they are not human, they have the same likeness–until one notices their feathered, giant, raven-black wings and their fangs. And of course, their fury. Though anger is a common enough trait in women. We come by it honestly. The wind their wings generate kicks up dust from the ground and pine needles from the trees, and I must close my eyes against their onslaught.

"What are they?" I shout to the king. I think this is a nice touch, even if I say it myself. By feigning ignorance of their existence, perhaps he will be fooled, and not notice mine own teeth sharpen when I hear the creatures' cries, despite my best efforts to halt their eruption.

"Valkyrien. They do not make women their quarry, but nonetheless, you and Edda will go with the guards and take cover." He summons over some of his carls and gives instructions to protect us.

This is exactly what I hoped he would say, for it would not do if I run into any other Valkyrien with whom I am acquainted. We may have met at one point, on some bloody battlefield or other. But I cannot appear too eager to escape the coming onslaught, even if my shoulder blades twitch with the effort of containing my wings and my voice sounds somewhat garbled because of my sprouting fangs as I say, "I am a warrior, Your Grace. I will stand and fight with you. The guards need only look after Edda. And I thought Valkyrien only take those who have been slain in battle, those they wish to honor in Odin's great feasting halls."

I have little talent for telling lies, even if my very existence is one. But I am impressing myself with these deceptions. Valkyrien have a rather precious reputation in the old realm of Hjartagard. There, they were mythologized as demi-goddesses of the battlefield, angels who deliver heroes to the halls of their fathers. Such stories are utter tripe, of course, and probably circulated by the Valkyrien themselves to conceal their evil doings.

I would say more to Drengr, to convince him I wish to stand by his side and fight, but I will do as I am bid, for I am intent on being a dutiful queen. It does not seem an opportune moment, however, as he unsheathes his blade and prepares to slay my sisters. My false sisters, that is. I have nothing in common with these creatures who revel in their bloodthirst.

But even as Drengr lowers his helm and clangs his sword against his chest, he answers me–

"No, Princess. These creatures are cursed by Odin, doomed to hunt living warriors to satisfy the appetite of the Great Serpent. I would feel sorry for them, if they were not about to try to take my men. I will not have them take you, as well."

And without another word of explanation, or even a backward glance, he is gone, racing to join his men in the thick of battle, where so many of the Valkyrien congregate. They hover above the ground, beating their wings, seeming to taunt the warriors below, who have their spears pointed toward them.

I know this protectiveness is not because he cares for me, but rather, because as he already explained, he's committed too much effort and silver to this marriage to have me die now.

If only he knew, there is no danger of me dying today.

From a distance, a Valkyrie looks beautiful. Majestic, even, with raven-feathered wings beating through the sky, as long as their own bodies. Perhaps even longer. Their locks are long and flowing. Some wear war helmets, but others are bareheaded. They do not carry shield or weapon, and one would be tempted to wonder how they can inspire such fear in otherwise courageous warriors, until one is closer, and sees a Valkyrie for what she truly is.

They are ghastly. Nothing like the beautiful legends which are a vestige of the old world. Their eyes seep blood. Their teeth are sharp and protruding, like a hound's.

Though their mouths are luscious, pouty and wine red. All of them have grey eyes. This is one of the differences between myself and a creature who is born a Valkyrie and not turned. Mine own eyes are green and remain so, even when the bloodlust is upon me.

When they close their jaws on one of their victims, their irises disappear, leaving only round, ghost-like orbs in their wake. Once they have stolen the flesh from their victims, the irises return. How do I know this? You may ask. I cannot see mine own eyes when I sink my fangs into a victim. But my suspicions of what mine own eyes do are confirmed because these Valkyrien set to attacking the warriors who surround us with gusto. I cannot decide if they are more eerie with or without the center of their eyes. I conclude it matters little, as either way, they are terrifying.

Correction. We are terrifying.

I am terrifying, I tell myself.

It is a useful reminder, for then the screaming begins, and their sound is unbearable. I want to run and hide, even as my heartbeat quickens with excitement when I scent the blood of the Valkyrien's first victims. I want to cover my ears, but one of the guards has taken my hand and is dragging me into the dense undergrowth. I push against him. It is a natural reaction. I cannot help it. I know he is only trying to help, but I am not used to being manhandled. Then, suddenly, I am pushing against only air. A Valkyrie's shrill scream shatters against my ears. The beat of wings in the air above me is almost as loud as those screams. I watch in horror as the carl is plucked from the ground by the fanged monster. Her wings beat more heavily with the effort of carrying her burden. Once they are twenty feet or so above the ground, she opens her mouth wide, revealing her fangs, and sinks them into his neck. Even from this distance, I hear his death gurgles.

She tosses the carl aside, and he falls back to the ground with a sickly thud. Blood from his neck oozes around him. He is dead, his eyes open, still, and glassy. I am grateful for it. Were he only injured, he would suffer in agony for some time, only succumbing when his life's blood was drained.

There is also a more pertinent and practical reason to be thankful he is already dead. Were he still alive, the willful beast inside me would awaken fully. I would have no control over her. With his agony on display only steps from me, I would sink mine own fangs into him without thinking and without hesitation.

The Valkyrie looks straight at me, a sickly grin on her pale face. It is as though she knows me. That smile tells me she has found her quarry. The one she searches for is ...

Me.

16

THYRA

It is entirely possible we know each other. There are often hordes of Valkyrien on a bloody battlefield. We may have feasted next to each other a time or two. But I cannot be certain. We tend to have eyes...and fangs...only for our victims. She may indeed know me, but I do not recollect her.

And yet, she is here for me. The expression on her ghost white face is one of not just recognition, but also...triumph. But how could such a thing be possible? Though I detest our connection, we are sisters in battle. Co-conspirators in foul deeds. There is no specific code I know of to govern our actions, but to my knowledge, no Valkyrie has ever attacked another, not even a half-blood. Though to be fair, I am the only half-blood I know of.

And as Drengr said, Valkyrien usually only attack warriors, avoiding women. It is perhaps not the time to point out many fine warriors are women. Besides, this Valkyrie could not know me as the Princess of Vagmar and future Queen of Logaland. When on the battlefield, I look much like any other she-monster, though my eyes are green.

And I doubt any other Valkyrie is paying attention to my eye color. And yet, she looks for all the world as though she has found her quarry.

My suspicions are confirmed when, with an exultant cry, she dives for me, her wings beating with such great force I am blown backward, knocked unsteady, unable to flee. Worse, unable to keep up my pretense any longer. I shall have to transform. To match my foe fang for fang, blow for blow, bite for bite. Drengr will discover my secret. Hel, after this day, the entire realm will know of it. But I refuse to allow this hag to get the better of me, to kill me, just to conceal my true identity. The transformation I usually work so hard to repress is upon me. My wings begin tearing at the fabric of my gunna. My fangs stick like pins in my lower lip. I hear a growl, and realize I've made it. Dear gods, I hate this.

Then Drengr's squire is there, Wilhelm, I believe is his name. No taller than myself and perhaps even scrawnier, he seems to be under the deluded notion he can save Edda and myself from these dreaded creatures. Wilhelm swipes at the Valkyrie with his sword, which seems about ten sizes too large for him. By what I can only assume is sheer luck, he manages to catch one of her wings with the blade. She retreats with a shriek, though she seems more annoyed than frightened. But his haphazard defense has given us a moment to run. He shouts to me, "You must come with me, My Princess. I will lead you to safety."

Without really pondering whether it is the right decision, I take Edda's hand and follow the boy. I do not wish to hurt his feelings and disabuse him of his heroical notions. Besides, my options are limited. Pretend to be rescued or do the rescuing and ruin my reputation and all my father's tenderly laid plans.

"There is a cave over yonder, beyond this grove of pines. It belongs to a brown she-bear, but it is not yet the season for hibernation. She will still be in her feeding grounds," Wilhelm shouts to us.

"And how do you know this?" I cannot help but ask. The boy's explanation is rather detailed. I must know if he is mad or just strange.

"I find things, My Princess. It is what I do."

"Yes, but how do you know this particular thing?" And most importantly, how can he be certain we are not awakening the bear from her slumber?

He hesitates, but seems resigned to answering my question. Our pace has slowed, the noises of battle have receded. He is able to take more time to respond. "Once, when we were traveling, I had to take a piss." He blushes. "I mislike going in front of the others, so I went a ways into the woods. Suffice it to say, we crossed each other's paths, and somehow, I escaped unscathed, though I confess, I never did make it to finding a private spot to go. I went right there, on the spot. Pissed my breeches."

This information is quite unnecessary for me to know, particularly since it confirms my suspicion that Wilhelm is not well-equipped to be our rescuer. We run through the tangle of undergrowth, trying to avoid the brambles that snatch at our clothes and dashing around tree trunks that seemed determined to bring us to a halt. Then I feel the wind again, and the dust kick up against my skin. She is back. I hear her cry again, this time exultant. The sound comes from above us. I look up, and my new friend is there, flying above the trees. At least they provide her with an impediment as well. But once she finds an opening in the canopy of trees, she will dive, and she will have me.

As I watch, an arrow hisses through the air, missing the

Valkyrie by only inches. It is then I hear the cries of war. It is Drengr, joined by some of his warrior carls, running through the forest, loosing arrows as they plunge toward the Valkyrie who has me in her sights. The creature circles higher in the sky, but one of Drengr's arrows grazes the tip of a wing, sending one shining black feather floating to earth. She retreats even further, hurtling out of our sight.

For one ridiculous moment, I pause to admire how well my betrothed looks when he looses an arrow. Though he is fully clothed, I imagine the muscles of his arms rippling as he draws his bow. Did I just call him my betrothed? I did not mean to.

Edda finally speaks, before I can ponder further the ramifications of mine own thoughts. "Stop staring, My Princess, like a boiled trout. She will be back and likely bring some of her friends. Boy, take us to this cave of yours."

No matter that Wilhelm is a squire, and therefore must be of a noble house, likely royal, given he is squire to a king, he instantly heeds Edda's command, as most people do. We continue pressing through the thickets, more sure-footed, now we know Drengr and his warriors have bought us some time. The cave is soon in view, surrounded by the winter skeletons of berry bushes, which must be convenient for the bear when she awakens from her slumber in spring. It is no great distance from the road, though when we were fleeing for our lives, it seemed like miles.

As we crouch to enter, I hear the shrill cries of the Valkyrien in the distance, mingled with the muffled shouts of warriors. Thank the gods we are not so close to the fighting, or I might not be able to check my transformation nor my bloodlust.

The gloom of the cave envelops us, but I welcome its darkness, as it will help to conceal us. Then again, Valkyrien have excellent night vision. Again, I know this from personal experience. But perhaps they will pass by this cave when they are searching for us. I can at least hope, even if it is foolish. I will also hope this she-bear Wilhelm speaks of is truly gone from here, stuffing her belly with fodder somewhere before she nods off for the winter. The air in the cave smells like a privy, but one that has not been used in some time. This is reassuring. The stench of bear is overpowering, and we would know if she was near. I think I'd rather take my chances with the she-bear than exit the cave and face my new friend again. Not that I'm frightened. I am sure I am more than her match. I just do not wish to reveal myself.

My reticence has nothing to do with her fangs, which a blind mole could see are longer and sharper than mine own, or with her talons, which are filed to vicious points.

We sit in silence for what seems like hours, though it can only be a few moments. The sounds of clanging steel and the shrieks of the Valkyrien are distant, yet deafening. I want to help Drengr and his men somehow, not because of any tender feeling for him, but because it seems the right thing to do, particularly since it seems these Valkyrien are here to capture me, or worse, kill me.

Wilhelm must sense my torment, for he says mournfully, "Do not be offended, My Princess, but I suspect you would be about as useful in the thick of battle as myself."

And as long as this boy–and his master, for that matter–believe this, I am safe.

"You should not deal so harshly with yourself, young man," Edda says briskly. "Without you, we might be meat for these beasts by now."

I always forget how kind Edda actually is, as she is always so bossy with me. My nurse knows full well I am a Valkyrie and am more than capable of defending our party.

She and my father are the only ones who know my mother was bit by one when she was pregnant with me, and further, that a Valkyrie's power–and her curse–were passed to me.

"I do not know why My King keeps me serving as a squire. I have no skill in battle and even less with the joust. Were I him, I'd have sent me back to Echen by now."

"You are from Echen, then? To which House do you belong?" As I suspected, he must be of noble, if not royal, blood.

"The House of Hornungr, My Princess."

Hornungr is the surname given to baseborn children. I am surprised, both because I'd suspected a grander lineage for a king's squire, and because I cannot envision any king willingly taking a bastard child into such high service. Drengr is the most powerful king in our realm, though it pains me to admit it. Hundreds of lads must vie for the honor of serving as his squire. Why did he choose this Wilhelm?

As if sensing my question, he explains. "I am the natural son of the King of Echen. The Prince Rufus is my brother." He pauses for a moment, contemplative, and adds, "Half-brother, I suppose, though to his credit, he never reminds me of it. The King Drengr would have no one but me as his squire, as he was once squire to our father and has many fond memories of those days. I think he wanted to return the favor, though he must regret his decision. Still, he never calls me to account, as much as he should."

I do not like to think of Drengr as a generous master, as one who excuses this Wilhelm's deficiencies, simply because he feels an affinity for his father and his elder brother, which I still cannot understand, for the Prince Rufus of Echen is obnoxious.

But I am unable to contemplate the vagaries of Drengr's

character and the possibility he may be decent in some regard, for the man himself appears at the entrance to the cave, heaving with exertion and carrying a torch, his bow strung across his back, his great sword clutched at his side. Sweat beads his brow, and for once, his braids are out of place. But what concerns me most is the blood that covers the front of his tunic.

It concerns my fangs as well, for they'd finally retracted, but at the sight and smell of the blood on Drengr's tunic, they threaten to poke through my poor beleaguered gumholes again. Thank goodness it smells old, not fresh, or I might not be able to stop myself from licking his tunic clean.

The King Drengr might then have a few questions.

Following the direction of my gaze, he looks down at himself and frowns. "It is not mine," he says hurriedly. "Now come, we must make haste. It will be nightfall soon, and the Valkyrien will have the advantage of us then. Their eyesight is still keen in the darkness."

I feign a surprised expression. "But we are miles yet from your capital. How will we protect ourselves if they are so skilled at attacking in darkness?"

"There is nothing for it but to erect our tents under the cover of pines and have many sentries on duty. The carls have already set to making camp. No one will sleep this night, but we will be better prepared than we were this afternoon. I have sent a messenger to Innangard, to raise a levy of household carls for protection."

"But then the capital will be unprotected," Wilhelm says. He is clever, even if he has no skill in warfare.

Drengr shrugs his massive shoulders. "There is nothing for it," he says again.

We make our way quietly through the woods, following

Drengr. All of us, with the exception of Drengr, scan the skies above us, searching for the enemy. I hear a gentle flutter of wings above me, and for a moment I tense in fear, thinking my wayward sisters have returned. Only for a moment, though. My body seems to recognize who it is before my mind, for my shoulders relax of their own accord.

Huggin.

I am a terrible bird parent. I forgot all about him in the midst of such chaos. He alights on my shoulder gently, but one of his talons digs into my cloak, ever so slightly, to remind me of my neglect.

"You are a very clever bird," I coo, but my praise does not seem to pacify him.

He caws in my ear. "Hug."

"When we reach our destination, I will give you one," I say.

Drengr glances backward, his expression bemused.

"What?" I say defensively.

He smirks. "Nothing, I just did not know you could speak in such gentle tones."

"My tone is selective, My King, based on its recipient."

He barks with laughter, but stops abruptly, realizing his mistake.

"Let me guess. Valkyrien have excellent hearing, as well as sight." I say in a whisper, though of course I already know the answer.

"They do," he whispers back.

"Then shut up."

He turns around with that ever present smirk in place, inviting me to examine the hard, muscled planes of his broad back. He still wears only his tunic, whilst I shiver in a fur cloak. It seems most unfair, and I worry for the thousandth time I will not be able to cope with the frigid temperatures of Logaland.

As I've already owned, serving as a spy whilst in Logaland is not a vocation for which I am made. My expression betrays me, always. What I am feeling. What I am thinking. And so when we reach the temporary encampment, I try to suppress my amazement. It would not do for Drengr to detect I am impressed. His carls have erected over twenty tents, though not in orderly rows, as they would for sleeping. They have fashioned their small, simple tents in a circle, so they serve as a protective palisade of Drengr's much more opulent tent. Though I notice no one has gone to the trouble of erecting his dragon totems or draping the tent with the tapestries that bedecked it when it sat on Rhok's hillside during the tourney.

Drengr gives orders to Wilhelm to check in with the commander of carls, to see if he has any duties for him. He then turns to Edda and tells her he wishes to speak to her mistress–that would be me–alone. Edda curtsies and leaves me without even a backward glance of apology. I try not to stare after her, open-mouthed. She obeyed Drengr without a word of disagreement.

Drengr motions for me to follow him into the tent. I tell Huggin it is time for bed and fetch a dried mealworm from my pocket to reward him for staying with me. Just days ago, I would have scoffed if someone told me I would be carrying around tiny, crunchy, dead things in my pocket to tempt my pet bird. But now, it is already second nature. He will bed down for the night in a comfortable bough, I have no doubt. He alights from my shoulder with a jubilant squawk of Hug.

I notice Drengr's pallet has been unbundled, but otherwise, there is nothing inside the tent. No table for Hnefatafl, no richly embroidered rug on the ground to protect his precious person from the dirt. He seems unbothered by the sparseness of his arrangements, and I cannot figure him out. When in Rhok, he was groomed immaculately, his tent richly outfitted. I was irritated with myself for finding him so attractive, in spite of his overfondness for finery.

Though I remember that first morn, before the tourney began and I did not yet know his identity, he was dressed like any common crofter. He could have been mistook for a yeoman, but never a king. He is a puzzle.

I am nervous to be alone with him, which is strange, for it is I who burst into this tent when it was still erected in Rhok, so I could give him a piece of my mind. I babble. "When the Great Sorceress created our Realm, she truly did not need to include such creatures as these Valkyrien. Nor trolls," I add for good measure. And I mean what I say. Were it not for the Valkyrien, I would be a perfectly ordinary and only adequate princess, which has ever been my goal. There are many other creatures, as well, of which I am not overfond. For instance, I mislike wood sprites. They are always trying to lead tired travelers off their paths to drown in bogs. But Queen Maeve insisted all beings, whether they are man, monster, or beast, have a choice to do good or to do evil, and they should be given the opportunity to exercise this choice, not be hunted to extinction simply because they are fanged and fearsome-looking.

I think, though, the Valkyrien prove to be an exception to this optimistic rule.

Drengr only nods in acknowledgement of my words, not even glancing at me as he unrolls a parchment onto his pallet and crouches down to examine it. Why did he insist on seeing me, alone, if he only wishes to ignore me? I try again.

"The carl who tried to save Edda and myself, I hope he

did not have a wife and children. He was very brave." I speak truth. I do not only talk to fill the empty silence.

At these words, Drengr seems to finally notice I still stand before him. "I am sorry Otho is dead," he says. "He has a mother living and two siblings. They live near the city's twelfth gate. I will write to them myself and send my condolences with his commander."

Then he stands and shrugs off his bloody tunic. One moment, he is clothed, the next he is not, his bare chest exposed. It is as though he forgets I am there again. I try not to gawk. I do. I try quite hard and fail. How can I not take a peek? Even if he were not so fine a specimen, I would want to have a look. He is, after all, my intended. I have a vested interest in examining him.

Whether in his armor or in a fine tunic, he seemed well-formed. Unclothed, he does not disappoint. Some might say he is too broad of chest and shoulder, but it suits him. There is a light sprinkle of black hair covering his chest, traveling in a narrow line down his navel. I cannot see where the trail of hair ends, as his breeches halt my gaze from descending further. I suspect I know where it ends, however, as I am not so ignorant of male anatomy, despite being a virgin.

I am thankful, for some men are hairy as dwarves. His arms are muscled and powerful, no surprise there, but what is a bit shocking is the number of tattoos he has roping around his arms and chest. When he turns to take a clean tunic from his pallet, one which a carl must have laid by, I see his back also is covered in ink. Dragons seem to be the theme of these tattoos, which of course, is not a surprise. I have never been overfond of tattoos. In the kingdom of Vagmar, they are quite popular amongst our warriors, men and women alike. It is a tradition of sorts to be inked when one makes any kind of conquest in battle. Ulf has his favorite stenciler into his quarters each time he kills a foe. It is an unattractive habit of his, quite out of character with his usual mildness.

I associate tattoos with boastfulness, and so I am not surprised my betrothed is covered in them. What does shock me, however, is how attractive I find them.

"You are hurt." I almost didn't see the gash on the back of his ribs, for they are covered in dark ink. And why does the sight of his wound bother me so?

My fangs don't even twitch, nor do my shoulder blades itch. My concern is apparently genuine. I did not lie when I told Rufus of Echen I have a talent for healing. It is one of life's great ironies–the scent of blood makes me hungry, but if I can control this urge, I often have some success with suturing wounds. And yet I always...always...must tamp down my bloodlust when tending to the injured.

Until now.

I will ponder the ramifications of this absence of bloodlust at a later date, however.

"'Tis a scratch, no more. I did not lie. Most of the blood on this tunic is not mine own."

It feels wrong to be so relieved, for no matter what, the blood belongs to someone. But it is hard to feel any sympathy for the Valkyrien, if these stains indeed belong to one of them. Cursed we may be, but when I think of how Edda could have been harmed, or how the guardsman Otho, who was only doing his duty, was plucked from the ground and devoured, as though he were a lamb in the field, I feel no remorse.

And when I contemplate the image of Drengr facing one of these creatures, I do not even pause to think on whom I would choose. Drengr.

I know him not. And yet, I cannot abide the idea of him

succumbing to the fangs of the Valkyrien. It might be in Vagmar's best interest if he'd fallen to their clutches, but it does not seem a fitting end for so great a king. And he is, indeed, great. I can admit that. My father fears him. His men revere him. Dragons heed him.

"Still, I think I should examine the wound, to see if you require any stitching. At the very least, it should be cleaned. I will fetch my satchel from the cart. If you remember, I did tell you I have some talent for healing."

"Actually, you told Rufus, but I was present for the conversation. And you will not be going to the cart. I will summon one of the carls to fetch it. Is it in your trunk?" I nod, and he opens the tent flap. I hear him murmuring some instructions, then he is back, crossing over to his pallet to once again study the map. He is back to ignoring me.

I am surprised he did not balk at me examining his wound. Most men act as though they are too tough for such ministrations. In reality, we all know it is because they fear the pain of treatment.

I stand mutely while I wait for the carl to arrive with my satchel. I think it rather rude Drengr ignores me, and worse, does not offer me a place to sit. Though of course, the only seat in the tent is either on the ground or on the pallet next to him. I'd crush the map, but worse, I'd be far too close to him. Too intimate. We will not share a bed until we are wed, this I have vowed.

The unforeseen consequence of my good intentions is that he must take off his fresh tunic, which he does, in anticipation of my ministrations, with a casualness I can only admire. He returns to his examination of the parchment. I must again see his naked upper half in all its glory. Worse, I must touch it, once my satchel of healing herbs and unguents arrives.

Suddenly, Drengr glides to the tent's entrance again and brushes aside its flap. A carl–I assume it is a carl, though I can only see his arm–wordlessly hands Drengr my satchel. I realize in amazement Drengr heard his approach, sensed it, even when I could not. Such senses are preternatural, either gods given or honed and refined through many years of training. I should know, for I possess them as well. And yet, he heard the carl when I could not. I try, unsuccessfully, to repress a shudder of apprehension. A man with such skills is no man to cross, and yet this is exactly what I have been commanded to do.

Drengr offers me the satchel, which I accept gratefully. I am as familiar with the contents within my healer's satchel as I am with mine own mind. Though of late, my mind has not been so reliable. It cannot make any progress discerning my betrothed's character. The satchel is a comforting presence, a balm to the nervousness, the uncertainty I feel in Drengr's presence.

Particularly when he is shirtless.

He sits on the pallet, and I have no choice but to join him. I move behind him, so I may have access to his wound. As he insisted, it is–thankfully–only a minor injury, a shallow tear to the flesh, but still, it could become infected. I decide a thorough cleansing with essence of lavender, followed by a stitch or two is the best course of action. When I am finished cleaning the wound, I will apply a poultice of birch bark mushroom paste, to protect against infection.

No one ever taught me how to be a healer. Perhaps this is inaccurate. The books in Whistletree Priory's library were my teacher. I have few skills, besides being able to sprout fangs and wings and talons and sever warriors' arteries cleanly. Neither nature nor inclination blessed me with any abilities of the musical, artistic, or literary variety. As I've already mentioned, I never took to battlecraft. I have even less interest in embroidery. As for beautifying myself, I am hopeless, and thank the gods for Edda, without whom I would perpetually look like a bog hag at court functions.

Do not repeat to her I praised her abilities.

But I found I have a talent for healing, for discerning which treatments are efficacious and which should be ignored. For instance, the great philosopher Sorel, who penned many of the texts I have read on healing, believed the feces of bats make for a better poultice to treat infection, rather than birch bark mushrooms.

I respectfully and humbly disagree.

Once again, I cast about for something to say as I rummage in my satchel for the bottle that contains the essence of lavender, for my bone needle and silk thread. It is the King Drengr's fault I feel the compulsion to babble so. No woman could stare at such a specimen overlong and not become a foolish puddle. But also, I must needs speak with him about today's events.

"You said the Valkyrien rarely attack women, but if I am not mistaken, the one who killed Otho was not interested in making him her prey, but rather, she was trying to get to me."

I think of the wild, feral gleam in her eyes and barely repress a shudder. There was a hunger in the Valkyrie's gaze, one I suspect had little to do with her appetite for flesh, and more with her discovery of my hiding spot under the tangle of brambles. I felt as though she was searching for me, specifically.

Drengr seems pensive and does not even flinch as I use a dropper to insert a generous portion of the cleansing essence in his wound. "The Valkyrien have never attacked a war band of Logaland. They know better. I have seen them many times on the battlefield, gnawing at the wounds of those about to die, to hurry their deaths and carry them to the gods, but they have never attacked my men. Nor do they usually separate, to attack alone, without assistance from their sisters. They would not wish to face my vengeance."

So, even the Valkyrien fear my betrothed. Why am I not surprised?

"What are you saying? That they were searching for me? Whatever for?"

This time, I do not feign my ignorance. Even if they know me to be both the Princess of Vagmar and a fellow Valkyrie, they should have no reason to target me.

"I cannot be certain, though I have some theories. What I do know, however, is that you will not be out of my sight again for the remainder of this journey."

"That sounds like a threat."

"Think of it more as a promise. I've invested far too much in this betrothal to have you be devoured."

"How touching. You make it sound as if I were chattel." It is merely an observation. I am not angry, for it is only truth he speaks.

Drengr shrugs. "You would accuse me of such unfeelingness, even if I waxed poetic about your beauty and said every word you speak sounds like sylvan bells."

"Do you, then?"

"Do I, what?"

"Think me beautiful?"

I hate myself for asking the question. I hate even more that I care so much about hearing his answer. Who knew I possessed such vanity? And where was it hiding, all those years Edda berated me for not taking enough pride in my appearance?

He scoffs. Though if I am not mistaken, his cheeks also redden. The sun is setting, and so I cannot be certain.

"You must know that you are."

"I've heard rumors, but most are unconfirmed."

"Your hair is a rather furious shade of red, but it...suits you. It goes with your green eyes, I suppose. And you have a fair few freckles, which have never held much charm for me, but your skin is good. It is...it shines."

I am sorry I asked. I must end this conversation before we are both blushing.

"Turn around, My King, and be still. It is time to stitch you, and I have never had much skill with a needle, not even when stitching flesh, which I confess I am better with than an ell of fine cloth."

"There is no need for haste. Remember, we will not be parting this evening."

"What about when I have to make my ablutions? Will you not give me a moment's privacy?"

"I take it 'ablutions' is a polite word for answering the calls of nature, but the answer is no. Either myself or one of my carls will be supervising, though we will avert our eyes."

"Ablutions are not just to do with bodily functions, Your Grace. I do, also, from time to time, wash." I finish my stitching, set the needle aside for cleaning later, and begin slathering the mushroom paste over the now-closed wound.

"I believe you think you are making a point, but I must disabuse you of some rarified notions to which you seem to cling. Every fiber of your being, from the tips of those pretty fire curls to the edges of your toenails, belongs to me. If I say you should wash yourself under my watchful eye, then you shall do so."

"You said you would never force yourself on me."

"And I meant it. But this is another matter entirely. This

is your safety we speak of. Your very life. Not a tumble between the bed furs."

He has a crude way with words, especially for a king. You'd think he'd be more cultivated.

"I will leave you now, so you may perform these ablutions of which you speak. You see? I am not unreasonable. There are guards posted just outside my tent, and so no harm will come to you, at least not in the space of time it takes me to confer with my commander and send Wilhelm to fetch Edda back to you. I am sure you need her assistance with your...ablutions." He is smirking again. How is it when I am so furious, he is merely amused, seemingly at my expense?

"And where will you sleep tonight? You cannot possibly expect we will share this pallet."

His grin only widens. "I have every expectation of it, but never fear, Princess. I will have no prurient intent. I have no intention of sleeping this night or taking any other pleasure in the darkness."

As promised, Edda returns to me, only moments after Drengr departs. And damn him for always keeping his word. At least I have a target for my frustration. "Edda, how could you just abandon me, without a second thought? Drengr commanded, and you obeyed. Who are you, and what have you done with my maid? The Edda I know would have much to say on the matter if she did not agree with her orders, even if they do come from a king."

"But I did not disagree, My Princess. He is your betrothed, and his request–or command, if you like–was not unreasonable."

"Think you I should be alone with him? We are not yet wed."

She snorts. "You are as good as. And if you think my presence alone would protect you from him if he wishes to make free with you, you are mistaken. But do you know, I do not think he would attempt to violate you. Though I know little of him, he does not seem...unjust."

"Of course he's unjust," I nearly spit as I say the words. "His father killed my mother, or did you forget?"

"I have not forgotten, and you would do well to remember, he is not his father."

I open my mouth to speak again. To rail against her as well as Drengr but find I have nothing to say, no response for Edda's fine piece of logic.

17

DRENGR

I do not wish to stray far from my tent, from the Princess Thyra's side this night, but there is something I must do before I can return to her, something of great importance.

I find Wilhelm seated with some of my lesser squires and a boy I recognize vaguely as one of my pages. They take their meal together, without benefit of a fire, as commanded. We cannot risk attracting the attention of the Valkyrien again. It is simple enough fare–hard brown bread, boiled bacon, and junket cheese–but it is plentiful. I clap a hand to his shoulder and tell him I must speak with him, motioning for him to follow me, away from his companions.

My carls made our encampment in a grove of pine, with the vague hope the trees' evergreen needles would conceal us better than the deciduous trees' bare branches. We stand underneath the cover of one, where the final rays of the setting sun leech through its boughs. "Today you showed a courage I'd not thought you capable of, if I am being completely honest," I say.

He blushes. "In truth, My King, I did not know I had such bravery in me either."

"How did you find this cave in which to conceal them?"

He blushes again. He reddens too easily in general, perhaps the only trait he inherited from his flame-haired sire.

"Everyone knows you seek privacy when you have a piss. 'Tis no secret. I am guessing you strayed off our path at some point, during the course of one of our journeys through these woods?" I say.

He stares at the ground, his face aflame, and nods mutely.

"You saved my betrothed, as well as her maid. They would not be here, were it not for you. Allow me to reward you in some way. I would give you your spurs, but–"

"No, My King, this would be no reward," he blurts out.

I laugh, forgiving his interruption. "As I was about to say, I do not think your spurs are what you wish for. What would you think if, instead, I offer you a permanent position in my household? Do you think your sire would object?"

"No, My King, he'd be ever so happy to be rid of me. He doesn't know what to do with me either. What type of duty did you have in mind?"

"That of my steward. The current placeholder has long wished to retire and has only stayed in the position for my benefit. You would be the perfect candidate."

I worried he would think the position beneath his dignity. He is, after all, the son of a king, no matter he is baseborn. But Wilhelm's face lights up with joy.

"The job of steward is a culmination of all the talents I actually do possess, My King. I could wish for no better means of employment. My father will be most pleased. And my brother Rufus, as well. Our father told him it would be he I serve as squire, upon my return to Echen."

Now for a much more challenging problem to solve. Figuring out what to do with Wilhelm was easy, but knowing what to do with the Princess Thyra is proving to be ever much more difficult.

Since meeting her, I have acquired an enemy–the mysterious warrior I encountered at the joust–whose identity I still do not know. Since becoming betrothed to her, I have been harassed by Valkyrien, costing the lives of several courageous and loyal carls. Generally speaking, no one picks a fight with me. I am the Dragon King of Logaland. It is considered unwise to get on my bad side. And yet, it has happened twice in less than a week. The one change in my life?

Thyra.

I do not know what role she plays in these troubles, nor if she is even the cause, but I will find out.

I do know I must needs dismiss her maid, for the princess and I must have a private word. When I enter the tent, both Thyra and her maid sit on the pallet whilst Edda brushes the princess's hair. There is little light left in the space, only what shines in from the gap in the tent flap, but her hair still glows like fire. I want to reach out and touch it, to see if it is as soft as it looks. To be burned by its flame. I want to be the one brushing it.

Edda leaves without a word of protest when I dismiss her, which seems like it is out of character for her. I know Thyra to be frightened of her, and I do not think my betrothed spooks easily.

The Princess Thyra wears a cross expression, and though I am used to such treatment by this point in our acquaintance, I cannot fathom what I did. "What? I must needs speak with you alone."

"She is my maid to dismiss, not yours," she retorts.

"Fair enough. Next time I must see you privately, I will ask you to dismiss her instead."

Her face falls in disappointment, and I have to stifle my laughter. She was looking forward to a disagreement, which I knew. I'd rather pass my time with her more pleasantly.

I gesture to the brush her maid left on the pallet, next to her. "May I?"

She looks at the brush as though it has suddenly turned into a viper, but she is too brave to resist the challenge.

"If you wish," she says primly, turning from me so I may have access to her glorious mane of hair, with a gesture supercilious enough to convey it makes no difference to her whether it is her maid or myself who brushes her hair. Soon enough, she will learn how grievously she's miscalculated. "Have you any experience with brushing hair?"

"Think you these braids appear with only magic? Davith is a fine valet, but even he finds my hair tiresome."

I touch the boar-bristled brush to her scalp and slowly drag it downwards. When it snags on a snarl, somewhere near the nape of her neck, I place my fingers on her scalp to hold it steady while I untangle her hair. I may or may not massage her scalp ever so slightly, a thing I know women enjoy. She may wish she was the exception, but she isn't.

"What did you need to speak to me about?" Her voice is a register higher than it usually is, and strained. She enjoys what I am doing, more than she would ever admit. I can say with absolute certainty, however, she is still not having as good a time as I am.

"Hmm? Oh, nothing. I just wanted to be alone with you, to prepare you for our evening together." I want her to stop talking, so I can just enjoy what I am doing, feeling her hair run through my fingers.

She turns to me, resentment on her features again. Her face is only inches from mine.

I want to kiss her. No surprise there. I've wanted to kiss her since the first moment I saw her, spying on me from the minstrels' gallery in her father's hall.

I had thought, even accepted, that she would not welcome it. That I would have to be patient with her, until she eventually would come to the realization I am no ogre. But hers is not the expression of someone who thinks me an ogre. Her eyes are heavy-lidded, her pouty lips parted. Though she likely does not realize it, she leans toward me. She is ready to be kissed.

I oblige. Setting the brush down, I take her face in my hands. It is a fine-boned thing, and my palms cover each side of her face. There is no fear in her eyes, no wariness. She has forgotten to keep her guard up. The only thing I see in her gaze is...curiosity.

I touch my lips to hers, gently at first. Her mouth opens hesitantly, though willingly. I should not be so intoxicated by her innocence, but I am, damn it. She melts into me, pressing closer, her lips parting further, to take more. I flick the tip of my tongue against her lips, testing, waiting to see if she will open her mouth to me.

Then suddenly, she is forcing her tongue into my mouth, battling mine own, as though our lips are at war with each other.

It seems Thyra has remembered herself, recalled she detests me, and does not wish to be burdened with actual desire for her betrothed.

"Princess, when we do consummate our union, your act should probably be a bit more...believable."

Her frown is adorable.

"You feign too much enthusiasm," I explain helpfully. "You are a virgin, are you not? I was told by your father...and Olafsson and Edda and I believe even your cook, to be careful with you. Virgins have never held any charms for me, and so I will not be upset if you are no maid. I prefer an experienced partner. But if you are an innocent, you had better go slower. If I get too excited, I will forget to be gentle."

"Is it so hard to believe I desire you?" Her lips are pouty, red, and swollen, her voice husky. It is a nice touch. She has an unexpected talent for playacting.

"Frankly, yes. You've made your hatred of me abundantly clear. And though I've never been burdened with a lack of esteem for my own person, even I am not handsome and charming enough to woo you so quickly, from hatred to lust so potent your stockings threaten to incinerate. I wonder, do you imagine it is this Matthias you are kissing, so you may pretend to enjoy it?"

I am being cruel, but I am annoyed. She wanted my kiss, enjoyed it, then suddenly, she acted false.

"Would you be jealous if I said yes?"

"Would you like me to be?"

"Do not flatter yourself, My King."

"If I had a reason for jealousy, perhaps I might be. But you have no true feelings for this Matthias. Even if you did hold some tenderness for him, I could make you forget him."

Would make her. For in truth, I feel wildly envious. She would rather kiss this boy, have his touch, then submit to me.

"How dare you? I was in love with Matthias."

Does she even know she said was, not am?

"You only think you loved him. It was a matter of convenience for you. A defiance of your father, to be sure, but also, safe. You could never marry him. He would not risk his life for you."

"Do not presume to know what I think. What I feel."

"A thing you will discover, Princess, is I do dare, and quite frequently, too."

"And would you?"

"Would I what?"

"Risk your life for me," she says ever so quietly, as though even she can't believe she dared ask the question.

"Princess, you are mine now, no matter we are not yet wed. If I were not willing to die for you, I would not have handfasted myself to you. I am the Dragon of Logaland. I do not swear false oaths." I rise, enjoying the little moue of disappointment that crosses her features, which I am sure she does not know she betrays. "I will send Edda back to you, so you may share the pallet. I will not force my presence upon you."

I leave, satisfied. She will think of me this night, when she tries to sleep. It will not be worry over the Valkyrien's return that keeps her awake, but instead, an abiding fear that when she kissed me, she liked it.

18

THYRA

I did not sleep well last night, but then, I had known I wouldn't. I shared a cold pallet with my maid with only one fur and no fire for warmth. Even had I not been cold and worried the Valkyrien would discover our location, I still would not have slept. Edda snores. But also...

Damn Drengr of Logaland, and damn his lips.

The king rides next to me with a disconcerting placidity, echoed by his palfrey, as though he'd not been kissing me most passionately just hours ago. I do not know why he insists on being by my side at all times. When I rose in the morning and left the tent to make water and wash, he was there, waiting for me. Thankfully, he did not insist on watching over me while I had a pee and scoured my teeth clean, but he did send several carls to stand guard from a goodly distance away while Edda accompanied me into the cover of the trees.

I wonder where he spent the night, whether he was comfortable, if he was warm. "Where did you sleep last night?" I curse myself for asking, but I burn to know the answer. I had not expected such a demonstration of decency from him last night, when he left the tent and invited Edda back in to share the pallet with me.

"Yesterday, fanged Valkyrien attacked my train of household guards, and most importantly, my betrothed. I did not sleep, Princess."

I regret asking the question, as I knew I would. Now I feel terrible for depriving him of his slumber. "I did not sleep either, My King." I feel it is important he knows this.

"Yes, I can tell. You are fair bedraggled. We will soon cross Devil's Bridge and enter the Sisters Forest, which means we are only a league from the capital. We no longer need to worry about the Valkyrien, because I can summon my dragons."

Does he know how obnoxious he sounds? But aloud, I ask instead, "How can you know we enter a new forest?" The trees we pass look much the same. Birch. Willow, when we are near water. I have a fondness for both, given their healing properties. There is also a great deal of pine, which is no surprise, given it is Logaland's greatest export.

"I suppose because it is my ancestors who so named it. They did not wish to have their willow and ash and pine associated with any of Vagmar's. Besides, the river serves as a boundary between the forests, as well as our kingdoms.

"Here on the mountain road, the River Ignis, which serves as the boundary between Logaland and Vagmar, slows its speed, as there are many rocks and bends around which it must wend. This is why it has always been the location of the river crossing, so the bridge would not be knocked down when the winter snows melt and a raging flood of water comes down from the mountains and turns the River Ignis into a torrent."

"Yes, but how will we know we have reached it?"

He gives me a slow, lazy smile. "Trust me, Princess. Even

without the forest, without the river, you would know when we reach Logaland."

Drengr was correct, a thing I am growing to hate. I would know when we cross into Logaland, even if blindfolded. It is not because our palfreys and wagons must file into a narrow queue to cross the river, or that it is suddenly colder, or because the pines grow thicker, though they do, hovering over the narrow road like somber sentinels, blocking the meager afternoon light. Nor is it even the mountains in the distance, though they are a dead giveaway of our location, as Vagmar has none. Its plains are as flat as Edda's expression when I wake up too late for primping.

No, it is the dragon flying overhead, almost as if it has come to greet us. First, I sense a great shadow blocking the pale sun before I ever apprehend there is an object obstructing the light, casting the darkness. The trees ripple around us, their higher branches cracking against each other. The wind ruffles against my face, blowing my hair into an unruly mess, blocking my eyes. It is only when I've swiped the tangle away that I see it.

It turns in slow, meandering circles, and I think I see the exact spot where the imaginary line of border must exist between our kingdoms, for the beast turns at the exact same point each time it circuits the piece of sky above us.

The scales of its belly are a creamy white, and then I realize its entire body is this color. When it turns in the sky to return to us, with a lazy flick of its tail, the sunlight catches it, and the scales shine with a golden gleam.

It is, and it truly pains me to say this, beautiful.

"Ah, 'tis Drusila. She is come to greet us." Drengr speaks with the affection of an overfond, indulgent father. A tone I have never heard from mine own.

I try very hard not to be jealous of the dragon.

She–for 'it' is apparently a girl–is enormous. It is my first, not to mention a foolish, thought. Of course she is enormous. Larger than my father's hall. Taller than the mast on his grandest battleship.

"You should close your mouth, Princess, before flies settle."

"She is huge," I say stupidly.

But Drengr nods in agreement. "Only her mother, Bathuba, is larger. Female dragons are, in general, larger than males."

"Really?" I do not want to have any curiosity for these beasts. They are the scourge of my kingdom, the doom of my ancestors.

And yet...

"Why are she-dragons bigger?" I can't help but ask.

"They are the ones who give birth."

"But I thought they laid eggs. Surely, unless these eggs are the size of a longship, they would not necessitate the mothers being larger."

"Ahh, but they are the ones who incubate the eggs. The more substantial a she-dragon's girth, the better she will keep her younglings warm. A mother's love and the heat of ignatum are how dragons are made."

I sigh. It seems, like princesses, even fearsome she-dragons are prized mostly for their breeding capabilities.

"Why is it called the Sisters Forest?"

"You ask many questions, Princess." Though he does not seem perturbed and answers, "King Dagobert, the third of his name, had four wives, who happened to be sisters. This was many hundreds of years ago, in the Age of Binding, and so you see how the forest has grown from those same saplings the queens planted. One of the sisters tried to stage a coup to put her own son on the throne, even though he was not the heir, as he was one of the younger children. She did not succeed, suffice it to say, and Dagobert–understandably–named the forest for the three who stayed loyal."

This fourth wife committed treason and was punished by not being remembered when the king named the forest. I wonder what else happened to her? Just how vengeful are the kings of Logaland when they encounter treachery?

It is important I know the answer to these questions, for I also plan deceit and treason.

The Age of Binding was the second age of our Realm, so named because it was a period when the kingdoms of men and the societies of other creatures Maeve brought into our world forged alliances and pacts, as well as enmities. Many of the treaties and alliances made in this Age last to this day, as well as, of course, the same hostilities.

Take Vagmar and Logaland, for instance.

I do not yet know what our age will be called. I know it began when the many centuries of peace Plane enjoyed ended, and so too, did the Age of Binding, with the sudden destruction of Vagmar by the dragons of Logaland. That is the thing about ages, though. No one knows what they will be called until after they are over.

As long as ours is not known for Drengr or how wonderful he is, I will be content with what our descendants choose to call it.

As we push onward, Drusila flying overhead, almost as though she is keeping us company, I glimpse the gleaming spires and towers of Innangard rising above the trees. Even further in the distance, Mount Muspel dwarfs the capital's buildings. I am not sure which is more impressive. The mountain, even from this distance, is hulking and somber and stolid, yet also ethereal. The snow atop its cratered peak makes it appear almost purple. Its coldness is deceptive, for underneath the mountain, the liquid fire of Muspel churns, never ceasing. The volcano erupted only once, when our Realm was first created, but it will erupt again one day, which I am sure is the reason Drengr's ancestors moved their capital here, to this location in the midst of the forest.

As we press closer, I can only marvel at the city's construction. It is the work of hundreds, if not thousands of years. The great wall that surrounds it must be the height of twelve men. It is constructed of stone, not timber, as our palisade is in Rhok. I'd expected the royal capital to be grand, given Logaland's wealth, but I'd also thought most of Innangard would be constructed of timber, given its proliferance in this kingdom. This defense is indestructible, virtually unscalable. Mount Muspel was the work of Queen Maeve, with assistance from the gods and the ignatum that lurks underneath it. But this city is even more impressive, after a fashion, for it was built without the benefit of any magic.

Several miles from the capital, the path widens to an avenue, its packed dirt changing to paving stones. The cobbles are worn smooth by the traffic of many people and horses and cartwheels.

"Is it a market day?" I ask in wonder. I have never seen so many people and carts and animals at one city gate. And there are eleven more of them, at intervals within the palisade.

Drengr smirks, as he is so wont to do. "No, Princess. Innangard is the largest city in the Northlands. We tend to draw crowds, even on our quiet days. Though in fairness, we have precious few such days in the capital. Thor's Day is for the hay and livestock markets, Freya's Day for our horses. Odin's Day is reserved for dairy products. I tell you, you haven't really tasted cheese until you've tried a wheel of

Logalander junket. I swear, our farmers must sing to their cows."

A hawker crying his wares approaches our train, shouting, "Get your meat pasties here! Finest pies in Innangard!"

The vendor realizes it is the king to whom he is squawking and hastily drops to one knee. Other passersby notice what the pie vendor has done and follow suit. I can see why few travelers recognize their king, since we fly no banners, and no herald has announced our arrival at the gate. Drengr looks rather unkingly as well, still wearing the simple tunic he donned yester eve after discarding the blood-spattered one. Is a king's return always treated so casually in Logaland?

Then again, there can't be much that shocks these people. Drusila the she-dragon still flies overhead, lazily beating her wings to keep pace with our horses, doubling back when she gets too far ahead of our train. The people of Innangard ignore her, as though such a sight is an everyday occurrence. Of course it is.

She opens her giant, fanged mouth and emits a shriek of what I can only describe as glee when she flies over the city's palisade, as though she is the herald announcing Drengr's return and her cry, her trumpet. I hear answering shouts and crane my neck toward the distant sounds. High above the city, other dragons circle in the air. They are too far away for me to perceive the color of their scales or whether any are as huge as Drusila, but I count three of them.

Including Drusila, this makes four dragons. One such creature is sufficient to lay waste to the kingdoms of Plane. Drengr has four of them.

"Two of them are not in the skies." It is as though he reads my thoughts. "One of the younger she-dragons,

Sigbertha, is nesting, and mine own Harig is likely hunting his dinner. His appetite is never satiated."

Mine own Harig. I must inquire further about this particular dragon, but first, I must try to process...

Six dragons. Six indestructible, fire-breathing, earth-shaking creatures who do Drengr's bidding. The Realm of Plane is fortunate Logaland has only ever taken issue with its neighbor Vagmar, for if the Logalanders chose, they could conquer the other kingdoms as well.

What is my father thinking, that he could ever hope to destroy this man, his kingdom?

It is impossible.

Drengr's fortress lies at the end of a wide and straight avenue of smooth cobbles. It is evident this is the city's main thoroughfare, not only because of its size and its destination, but because many shoppes lie either side of it. All manner of merchants and other vendors have established their services here. Drapers, tailors, greengrocers, bakers. My stomach rumbles at the wafting scent of dough in the ovens, warning me I must find sustenance soon. Though hunger–human hunger, that is–is a rare enough occurrence for me, I am rather irritable when it does happen.

We have very little of these wares in Rhok. They are mostly supplied by traveling pedlars. I should quit being surprised by the disparities in our capitals, but I cannot help myself.

As we progress down the avenue, passersby bow to their king, and to myself, I notice. They must have known their king would be returning with his future queen. I am not surprised, for I believe I was the only person involved in the marriage negotiations who was unaware of their end result until the Handfasting Ceremony actually began. They stare at me, making no attempt to disguise their curiosity, and I wonder if I have dirt on my face. Or is it the raven perched on my shoulder, muttering Hug to all and sundry which disconcerts them so? My red hair mayhap? It is a thing often admired but also feared in equal measure. Red hair is said to be the mark of witchery. If only. Better to be a witch than a Valkyrie. With supernatural powers, I could magic myself out of this betrothal.

But where would I go?

We pass through the inner gate, which leads to a vast courtyard directly in front of the fortress. I marvel at its size, its construction, its turrets. The only turret I have ever seen is Elfgiva's, and it is not nearly as impressive. Indeed, if Elfgiva's old lair is a turret, these monstrous domes are towers.

Once inside the courtyard, household carls come out to meet us. The entire business of unloading baggage carts and returning horses to the stables is conducted with startling efficiency. Even in the inner walls of his fortress, though, warriors and servants alike bow to him.

Drengr nods acknowledgement of his people's obeisance or waves occasionally, and I wonder if I should do the same. I am not yet their queen, only their king's betrothed. I look to Drengr, realizing I do so for reassurance, for guidance.

But he is gone.

19

DRENGR

I have missed my sister, though I will not give her the satisfaction of telling her. She would tell you she'd make a better monarch than myself, and she'd be correct in some respects. She has a temper, though, and it is one she cannot master. I have tried to explain to her patience and understanding and equanimity are as important qualities in a leader as a talent for battle strategy and the ability to grasp an innate sense of people's natures upon meeting them. Both of these, she possesses, which is why she is the commander of Logaland's army, as well as my chancellor. You may call this nepotism, but I prefer to think of it as common sense.

I've decided I'm going to keep the Princess Thyra confused, so I take my leave of her after we pass through the inner gate, quickly and dismissively. I do not look at her, and I am barely civil when I take my leave of her. If she is kept guessing as to how I will treat with her, she will find it more difficult to try to take advantage of me, which of course, is her ultimate aim.

I am not a complete ogre. I gave instructions to Davith to take her to her chambers and to see to her needs.

I go to my solar after sending a page to fetch Mist to me. It is a chamber above my hall, where no one but my closest associates are allowed. It connects to my private sleeping quarters. I am pleased to be home, though I know my troubles with the Princess Thyra are only beginning.

"Your betrothed seems to have you rattled, Brother. I look forward to meeting her," Mist says by way of greeting. She has glided into the solar like a wraith, or more aptly, like her namesake. She is the only person I know who can sneak up on me unawares.

"You will this evening, at our betrothal feast, unless you decide to descend into the kitchens."

Mist has the grace to blush. She has been seeing the cook, which is a euphemism for conducting illicit assignations with him. I do not care if she takes up with someone before marriage. In Logaland, we do not prize virginity in our maidens like the Vagmarians or Dervnonians. When one thinks on it, this insistence on a maiden's virginity is rather bizarre. Chasteness after marriage seems a much more important quality in a royal bride. It is important to know the next king is actually your descendant and not someone else's...such as the cook's. Mist will marry one day, as soon as she bloody well agrees to wed one of our neighboring kingdom's princes. But she must have a care. She has a habit of making her paramours fall in love with her.

I am not sure why. At three and twenty years, she is only two years younger than myself. I am in my prime at five and twenty, but she is growing long in the tooth. It is not I who passed this judgment; it is just the way of things. My current mistress is two and thirty, and she is still stupendous looking. Maidens are old before their time, with the cares of childbearing and early marriage, and yet they usually outlive their bridegrooms when they become crones. It is their vengeance against the fools they married, I am convinced.

Mist and I resemble each other greatly. Her hair is dark and straight as an arrow, like mine own and like our father's.

"There was a boy at the tournament. He is a stranger to me. But he seemed to loathe me." I cannot forget how Grinn stared at me, hatred in his eyes. I do not frighten easily, but his soulless gaze was unnerving.

"I'm shocked," Mist says.

"Hasn't anyone ever told you sarcasm is an unattractive trait?"

"Our cook does not think so."

"I need to find out his true identity. I'll bet my left bollock Grinn of the Southlands is not his true name, nor is he just a Traveler Knight."

Mist sobers, instantly transforming into chancellor.

"I will send two of our couriers out, one to Rhok to sniff out answers and one to the Southlands, from where this stranger alleges to hail."

'Courier' is a euphemism for spy. But if any of our agents are caught, they claim to be couriers carrying marked dispatches, making them protected envoys under the laws of Plane. Many years ago all of our Realm's kingdoms agreed to a treaty protecting marked messengers. All signatories agreed it is wise to protect the envoys of other kingdoms if it ensured the safety of their own in turn.

Reassured Mist will do as she has promised, as she always does, I turn to even more important matters. "Think you Thyra's father set her to spy on us?"

"Undoubtedly," Mist says. "But what information does he

hope to gain? This is the bit I need to know. If he just wants to know how many levies I can call, or where the ignatum veins are hiding, this is inconsequential. The answer to the first is–many, more than he could ever hope to summon, and as to the second, it matters little if Thyra discovers the source of our ignatum, for it is impossible to mine without the aid of dragons."

"Speaking of dragons, you do not think she can ferret out how we use them in battle, do you?"

"Only if you or I tell her, and I am never quite that drunk or that stupid. And you are not blinded by lust for her. Then again, you haven't met her yet. You may be quite taken with her. However, she's mine."

"So I gathered. But what worries me is, how intelligent is she? If she is clever enough, she could destroy us."

"She is quite clever, but treachery does not come easily to her. I fear her father has set her a task in which she is doomed for failure."

"The poor lamb. I have no doubt King Skerr gave her the strictest of instructions to be duplicitous."

"You should have seen her during our Handfasting. She thought she was putting on such a brave face, but I feared she'd spill her guts at any moment. And then later, when I kissed her, she seemed for one blessed moment to enjoy it, before acting like a tavern wench, and one with little talent, mind."

Mist holds up a hand to stop me. "Please, Brother, I do not need to know anything about her kisses. But I will say, if her father gave her instructions to get close to you, to spy, it makes sense she would think she must feign attraction to you."

"But it is no pretense. She does desire me."

"All men believe women pine for them, but I must

disabuse you of such a notion. We do, on occasion, dislike you."

"Oh, she dislikes me. But she also desires me. I am sure she is fair confused."

"On that note, I will leave you. She may be confused, but methinks you are deluded. I will see you this evening. I must go prepare for the feast."

As she saunters out the door to descend the stairs to the hall below, she turns and asks, "By the by, do you happen to know what color gown the princess will wear to the feast? I do not wish to wear the same color and take away from her presence. It is her celebration, not mine own."

I shrug. "I did not tell her about the feast. As I said, I want to keep her confused. Keep her guessing, so I may discover her father's intentions."

However, I make a note to fetch a page when my sister departs, to inform Thyra's maids she should be dressed in green this eve.

"If that is your objective, you are likely succeeding. But have a care, Brother. She may murder you before she ever learns how to deceive you."

20

THYRA

I have known Drengr to be both irritating and charming, infuriating and humorous. Sometimes in turns, and sometimes all at once.

But he has never ignored me.

If I didn't know better, I would say I feel...diminished. As though I have actually enjoyed the time I've spent in Drengr's company. It is not possible. More importantly, it cannot be so. The fate of my kingdom, as well as of my own life, depends on my continued hatred of the man.

"My Princess, My King has given me instructions to show you to your quarters and to make certain you have every comfort. If you and your maid would follow me."

It is Davith, Drengr's valet, with whom I am not yet acquainted, but I observed him in service to his master when we made camp. He seems kindly enough. Merry, even, with an open, broad countenance and blue eyes that seem to sparkle with wit.

Davith is not a quiet, unobtrusive servant. Indeed, he is rather chatty. As we walk through the inner courtyard of

Drengr's fortress, he keeps up a steady stream of conversation. "I also organize the household, though it seems I will have more assistance, since young Master Wilhelm has been appointed steward. Our old steward was...well...old, and not of much service."

"I am so pleased for the lad," Edda says.

I think she developed quite a fondness for Wilhelm when he risked his own life to save ours. First Drengr promotes his squire to the more permanent and exalted position of steward, presumably for his service to us, then he decides to ignore me. Strange.

The hall of Drengr's fortress is a simple affair, when compared with the elaborate architecture of its exterior. It is spacious, but still a hall, much like any other, including mine own father's. It is only sensible to lay down rushes in a hall instead of stones, or worse, carpets. There is so much traffic, so many spills. Not to mention, there is always dog shite everywhere. Even as we stride through the hall, I watch a silky-furred hound streak in, presumably from the kitchens, chasing a cat. Or what I think is a cat–the little form moves so quickly, it is blurry. But I have a fondness for cats, and there is no mistaking its four legs and shriek of outrage.

I assume we will ascend the staircase in the corner, but I am mistaken. Davith says, "The queen's quarters have always been on the first floor, so she does not have to climb stairs." We exit the hall through a small door, opposite the wall to which the staircase is affixed. I notice there are guards on either side of it. We enter into a gallery of sorts, which is much smaller and more narrow than the hall.

Davith gestures airily to the cupboards that line the walls. "This is a closet of sorts for you."

Of sorts? I notice in shock the cupboards and drawers are already teeming with gowns and veils, stockings and slippers. They could not have belonged to Drengr's mother, for they are in the first stare of current fashion. I want to rage against the presence of these garments. This is Drengr's doing. He knew he would be returning with me, was so certain of himself, he had a wardrobe fashioned for me. How did he know my measurements? It is a stupid question. He probably knew where every one of my freckles and moles are before he ever arrived in Rhok, even the ones hidden by my clothes.

"No one but those to whom you give permission are allowed to enter. Edda and your other maids will stow your belongings in here. And speaking of maids, we must appoint a Mother of Maidens. She will help you find the most appropriate ladies for your Court," Davith says.

"I know what 'appropriate' means. My intended owes their fathers favors, or their lineage is purer than mountain snows."

"Who hurt you, darling? A maiden as youthful as yourself should not already be so jaded. The most appropriate ladies will be the ones you find enjoyable, serviceable companions. But the Mother of Maidens is a necessary addition to your court. Young ladies do tend to misbehave, and your companions' behavior is a reflection on you, as well as the King Drengr. And even if he doesn't care about etiquette, the rest of the kingdom does. The Mother will maintain a strict code of conduct."

"Edda would be perfect for the job."

"She would, but there would be less time for her to attend you. And I see how much you rely on her company."

"Are you saying I would be unable to manage both

responsibilities, young Davith?" Edda says hotly. "I will have you know, it was only I who served the Princess Thyra for many years, and she was ever a difficult child."

Why, thank you, Edda.

Since my fifteenth year, I have also had a troupe of ladies-in-waiting, Lyda my most favored. But even Lyda is rather useless for anything but companionship. It is true that Edda has had to shoulder the bulk of responsibility in serving me. Not to mention, raising me.

I am again forcibly reminded how much I owe Drengr for allowing Edda to accompany me into Logaland. And yet, in return, I shall betray him. It is not a fair bargain, but then, life is so rarely fair.

Now, if anyone could manage both my ladies-in-waiting and still make time to spend with me, it would be Edda, but I take Davith's point. And speaking of fairness, it would not be just to add so much to Edda's already significant responsibilities. Also, it is important to fill my court with Logalander women, which is why Drengr insisted I bring none of my own retainers from Vagmar in the marriage contract. It seems like a cruel caveat, but it is a commonplace codicil in such agreements. It is a coveted privilege to serve royalty, one to be bestowed on loyal subjects. In this case, native Logalanders instead of Vagmarian imports.

I say to Davith, "I sense you have someone in mind for the position."

"I do. Mistress Flomilda Larsdottir. She was Drengr's nurse, as Edda was to you, and still a valued household retainer. She has a pension and a house in Town, but she is bored. She is firm, but fair, and will organize your ladies."

This Mistress Flomilda sounds like Edda. I suspect the two ladies will be a match for each other. They may get on each other's nerves, and often. In fact, judging from Edda's frown and snort of derision, which she does little to conceal, their enmity is almost guaranteed.

It is an added bonus.

At the end of the gallery is another door, and again, two guards are posted on either side of it. My security will be assured, at least. Or are the guards stationed there to keep me from fleeing?

They open the door for us, and Davith leads us into an exquisite chamber. The floors are tiled with gleaming white pavers that have darker colored veins of grey and peach running through them, likely from stone mined in the mountains. The walls are also stone, though they appear to be a pumice-like texture, whitewashed to match the floors. Most extravagantly, there are windows on the far side of my room, where there is an exterior wall. Glass is a substance as dear as ignatum. Whoever built this chamber spared no expense. Benches of carved stone are placed underneath the windows, three benches for three windows, and I cannot wait to curl up in one of them with a book.

But are there books in Logaland?

I am touched, because there is already a perch for Huggin in the corner of the chamber, though for now, he is content to rest on my shoulder. In just several days, I have become so used to his presence, I barely notice he is there.

Except when he shouts Hug in my ear or feels dissatisfied, and so digs his talons into my flesh.

What captivates me most is a bathing pool in the center of the chamber, an exquisite basin of hollowed, sanded ignatum. I am forcibly reminded of the disparities in our kingdoms. Vagmar is also a wealthy nation, but we have put all our funds into building our military, mostly to defend ourselves against Drengr and his ancestors. His dragons make a powerful army unnecessary, and so the royal coin has gone to improving the capital. My father's hall looks like a pauper's when compared with the finery of Drengr's fortress. Still...

"However did you manage to put such a magnificent pool in the center of the room?" I can see there are taps for filling it, coming right out of the ground. I have heard of indoor plumbing before, but never believed I would see it, particularly not so fine an example.

"I cannot claim responsibility," Davith replies. "It was the work of Drengr's ancestors, many centuries ago. As you know, ignatum is a rare substance, and we take pains to conserve it."

What he does not voice aloud is how it is a precious resource because without it, the dragons of Logaland would be no more.

"How is the water piped in?" And most importantly, when will I be able to try this piece of magnificence?

"Come, I will show you. You haven't seen the best part."

Davith motions for me to follow him, ushering me to a small door in the corner. I hadn't noticed it, which is no surprise, as it blends seamlessly into the paneled wall. He pulls on the sconce beside it, and the door opens. Clever. Almost too clever. How many of these hidden doors are in this keep?

The space beyond the door is shrouded in darkness. I feel a moment's unease, then realize such a response is ludicrous. Of all the Logalanders I have encountered, Davith has been the most pleasant. Unless he is an absolute master of deceit, I doubt he intends to lead me into the gloom so he can do me harm.

Still, I am relieved when he lifts the torch from the wall sconce and walks ahead of me, illuminating the space. It is a rickety wooden staircase, too narrow for us to descend together. I notice the stairs also go upwards.

"Those lead to the king's quarters, which are just above you. But your surprise lies below, just outside."

Of course my chamber connects to Drengr's. How else would I fulfill my new obligations? At least Davith is sensitive enough to understand the ascending staircase is nothing to be excited over. The descending stairs had best have a most excellent surprise at the end of them.

Davith does not disappoint. He opens the door at the bottom with a flourish, to reveal a courtyard that can only be described as...

Fit for a queen.

The hedge is bare, but I see wrens and chickadees darting through the thickets. I hear their song. It is not an entirely orderly garden. The fountain has not been doing its job in quite some time, it seems. The shallow pool from which it rises is a bit sludgy in appearance, the perfect haven for newts and frogs and all manner of slippery creatures. Their chirping will be a comfort to me come spring, when the first of the peeper frogs shrieks his mating call, long before the earth is ready for seed.

"This was once a fountain, much enjoyed by My Queen, the King's mother, but it has been allowed to fall untended for some time." Davith seems sheepish as he explains.

"It is no matter. I think it perfect, just as it is. But you must tell me what this is."

In spite of myself, I am curious to know more. In the far corner of the garden, the air steams, betraying a source of heat. Since I suspect even the summer months will feel like winter to me in this country, I am eager to find an outdoor source of warmth.

It is I who lead now and Davith who follows as I stride

through the garden. I have a sneaking suspicion of what I might find. Though Drengr cannot credit it, I do know a good deal about Logaland's geography. I know there are veritable oceans of hot springs underneath it, and they have long been treasured as a source of winter warmth and comfort by its people. Hot pools of spring water bubble up from the ground throughout Logaland, but they proliferate most right underneath Innangard.

If, in fact, there is a hot spring in this garden, I will have a very difficult time in my quest to maintain my hatred of all things Logalander.

"You've found the best part of the entire garden," Davith tells me. "In my opinion, the best part of the city of Innangard. The capital was moved from the valley below Mount Muspel when these springs were discovered. Logalanders are a hardy people, but even we could not object to having a constant source of warmth at our disposal, to give us comfort in the winter months. There are pipes running underground from this pool, which is how the water for your bath is sourced. Now, may I suggest you spend the afternoon resting? You have quite an evening ahead of you." He turns to ascend the stairs again, to return to my chamber, and I follow without question.

I'm not married yet, and so the bedding ceremony can't be tonight. What could he possibly mean? Davith must take in my confusion, for he explains. "The betrothal feast. Jarls and their families from all over the kingdom have travelled here to celebrate your Handfasting."

"But we already had a betrothal feast, before we set out on our journey."

"That was a Vagmarian feast," he explains, enunciating carefully, as though he is speaking to a child. We have arrived back in my chamber, and he closes the door. "I may as well tell you, My Princess, though it pains me to grieve you, Vagmarians wouldn't know a party if it bit them in the arse. Better to find out now, than to be caught off guard later this evening. Besides, the people of Logaland wish to celebrate the arrival of their new queen. They would be quite affronted if we did not provide them with such an opportunity."

"I'm not unpacked yet. Even with Edda's assistance, I shall never be ready with proper attire for a feast."

I feel mildly panicked. Even I have the good sense to know I must look my best for such an occasion. Edda will need hours with my hair and face paint, and the clothes in my trousseau must be emptied out of their trunks and aired before they are fit to be worn.

Davith only smiles. "I think you'll find you are well prepared for this evening. You need only rest and leave everything to me."

He claps his hands together, and on cue, a gaggle of maids march into my chamber. They are all dressed alike, in a violet-hued gunna with an under-kirtle of darker purple. Each bodice is emblazoned with the crest of the House of Logaland–two serpentine dragons, separated by a cloud, which seems to wear a crown of fangs. Stupid, if you ask me, though no one has. Clouds don't wear crowns, neither do dragons. But as crests go, it's rather on the nose. There is no misinterpreting its meaning or hoping it's merely symbolic. They conquer through their dragons.

I realize these are my maids, and their livery is proof to all they belong to my house.

"Who chose their livery?" I cannot help but ask.

"I did," Davith replies. "I hope I did not overstep, a habit I am prone to, I must confess. I did perceive you have a fondness for the color purple, and so I sent word ahead of us for your chambermaids to be liveried accordingly."

Had I been the one choosing their dresses, I would have fashioned exactly the same garments. Though perhaps that is not strictly accurate, for I'd choose a different sigil. Davith's taste is impeccable. I cannot say the same for mine own. Edda would most certainly agree.

"I couldn't have chosen better, Davith, and truer words were never spoken. My maid Edda despairs of me."

"Then you and His Grace are a pair, My Princess, for there is no force in the Nine Realms that could make him care about his appearance. Those handsome features are absolutely wasted on him."

"But how can you say so? He was dressed the finest of any king or princeling present at the tourney. The garments he wore to both nights of feasting were the first stare of fashion. And his braids are so intricate, it is as though they are stitched by fairy hands."

"I will say, he is quite proud of those braids, but as for the rest, it was all my doing. I am so pleased you noticed. It is nice to be recognized for one's efforts. All My King could do to show his appreciation was grumble at me night and day."

I am unable to question Davith further, for he turns to the maids and introduces each one. "Helg will be in charge of your bathing and dressing. She is from the village of Bythwaite and thanks the goddesses each day she was sent to the capital to go into service."

The rosy-cheeked maid curtsies and asks, "Would you be liking your bath now, My Princess, or after a rest?"

My muscles lighten at the very mention of a bath. After so much travel, not to mention an attack of Valkyrien, they scream for a soak in hot water.

"Oh, now, please. Then I can rest cleanly in my bed. I must ask, though, why is it you were so happy to leave your village?"

I cannot imagine feeling pleased about leaving the only home I have ever known, particularly since I just have, and it was a rather traumatic experience, even without the assistance of my fellow Valkyrien.

The girl blushes to the roots of her hair, and I realize I've made her uncomfortable. In Vagmar, I had only one maid, Edda, and I have often felt I am more her servant than the other way around. Here, I already have three chambermaids at my disposal, liveried beautifully. Once again, I am forcefully reminded of how powerful a kingdom Logaland is. As if I needed a reminder.

Helg looks to Davith, who nods encouragement. After taking a fortifying breath, she says, "My father is a pig farmer, My Princess. A good soul, he is, but I did not want to keep working with the pigs, or gods forbid, marry a pig farmer, chosen for me by him."

I know exactly how this girl feels. Though instantly, I feel terrible, for I would never wish to be a pig farmer's daughter, rather than a princess. Then again, the pig farmer husband doesn't sound so bad at the moment. He wouldn't have the burden of carrying my undying hatred for the last fifteen years.

Drengr probably smells better, though.

He does smell quite nice, like woodsmoke and pine forest–though this could just be because we have mostly been out of doors since I met him–and trunk cedar, which Davith probably stores his clothes in.

"I am pleased, Helg, you decided animal husbandry was not your destiny and came to the capital instead. I welcome you to my service."

I did not think it possible, but she blushes, then curtsies, even more deeply. "I will draw the water for your bath, My Princess." The girl beats a hasty retreat to the refuge of the bathing pool, which is just as well, since she might have caught fire from the heat of those blushes if she'd stayed in my presence one instant longer.

"And this is Nin," Davith says. "She will superintend your hearth and your bed. And finally, Orla, who will superintend your closet. Of course, it is the privilege of the ladies-in-waiting you choose to select your clothing each day, but ladies are prone to carelessness, if you will pardon my bluntness. Orla will keep your wardrobe organized."

"What am I to do then?" Edda asks, rather frostily. She is not taking to young Davith as keenly as the Squire Wilhelm. "These responsibilities you name are the same I perform for the Princess Thyra, and I am only one person."

"You are, first and foremost, My Princess's treasured companion. And though Helg, Nin, and Orla are quite skilled, they are still young. What just one Edda may accomplish is the work of three maids, I have no doubt."

Davith is also skilled in diplomacy, apparently. I shall have to mention this to Drengr. Mayhap he should send his valet the next time he needs an envoy to forge agreements with another nation.

No, I correct myself forcefully. I will not be mentioning any such thing to Drengr. If I am to make conversation with my betrothed, it should not be because I wish it. But rather, because I wish to manipulate him, to make him spill his secrets.

The three maids speak in the Vagmarian tongue to me, but I must make more of an effort to learn Logalandese. I knew this already, as it would be suspicious if I did not attempt to learn my husband's language. But I find I want to learn it, to communicate with these women. My Language Master gave up all hope in me, but perhaps living here, constantly hearing their words, I will do better.

I am somewhat proficient at reading their language. Many of the scrolls in the Library at Whistletree Priory are in Logalandese. I have always been more gifted with the written word, rather than the spoken.

I believe it is because I like books better than people.

21

THYRA

In the last week, I have endured enough feasts to last a lifetime.

But I have never looked so well in my life, even Edda admits it. She still fashioned my hair, creating an elaborate crown of braids, then allowing the rest of my hair to fall, as befits a maiden. My hair is not curly, nor is it straight. It is somewhere in between and generally gravitates toward messiness. It resembles a bird's nest more often than not, but Edda remembered my curling tongs. She has pulled and poked at my scalp until all my flyaway tresses are tamed, my hair cascading in loose, but artful, waves down my back.

Orla, as it turns out, is a fair sorceress with face paint. It is not the custom of Vagmarian women to wear much make-up, but I have learned it is common in Logaland. Edda was worried I would look like a succuba, Hel-dwellers who can only derive their sustenance from men when they venture into our realm. Because their survival depends on their ability to be charming, Edda reckons it only makes sense they bedeck themselves with face paints.

Orla reassured us both I would look nothing like a

succuba. Though would this be so terrible? I hear they are quite fair of feature. Even Edda approves of the results of Orla's ministrations. She has brushed my lashes with a paste of soot mixed with honey, making them appear both darker and fuller. Using a pomade of crushed and boiled rosehips, beeswax, and juice of lingonberry, Orla dabs at my cheeks with a light touch of her fingertips. I confess, when she is finished, I stare at my reflection in my hand mirror, quite overpleased with myself.

I am reminded of the healing unguents and poultices I prepare in my stillhouse. Mixing ingredients for face paints is not so dissimilar a process. In Rhok, I used the stillroom in the Priory. The monks' and matrons' ingredients were at my disposal. How will I concoct my ointments and potions now? Will I even be able to find the necessary ingredients?

"Hug! Hug!" my craven croaks from his perch in the corner. He has remained quiet, observing me with curiosity whilst I dressed.

"I am sorry, my sweet, I cannot take you down with me."

I wish I could. His presence on my shoulder would be reassuring. I do not think he would be the most well-mannered dinner companion, however, particularly if any rabbit is on the menu. I have discovered it is one of his favorite dishes, second only to the dried mealworms I try to remember to always have in my pocket.

Huggin eyes me disdainfully and flies to the window. I nod to Edda, and she opens it for him so he may fly out. Despite his anger, he will return when he has finished stewing.

I rise from the dressing table, an ornate piece of furniture made from Logalander pine, painted white and topped with a slab of ignatum. To think, at home in Vagmar, the lengths I had to go to just to have a work desk in my chamber.

"Well, then, do I look presentable?" I ask Edda and the other maids, twirling in a circle for their benefit.

Orla chose a beautiful velvet gown for me, an emerald green color that is, though I say it myself, the very match for my eyes. The kirtle she and Helg paired with it is a golden yellow, fashioned of the finest silk. The sleeves are so tight, Helg had to sew them onto the bodice of my gown. But at the wrists, they open into puddles, draping at my sides like wings. It is the fashion, but it is a foolish one.

"You are exquisite."

Edda is the first to speak. She is stingy with praise, so I am pleased. My other maids, sweet as they seem, would likely tell me I look beautiful, no matter what, as they know me little as of yet.

There is a stern knock at the door, and one of the guards bellows the arrival of Master Steward Wilhelm. Nin and Helg open the doors, and the guards strike their pikes against the floor, the sound echoing in my stone chamber. Thank goodness Huggin can fly out the window, for these guards would take note of his travels if he had to exit and enter past them.

"Much congratulations on your impressive new title," I say to Wilhelm by way of greeting.

He flushes, and I sympathize, as only a redhead who blushes often, and always against her own will, can.

"I am commanded by My King to take you to him, so you may ascend to the hall together."

But instead of turning back for the doors through which he just came, he goes to the corner of my chamber, beside my bed, where the secret doorway lies hidden in the wall. We do not descend to the garden, more's the pity, but instead, Wilhelm leads me upwards, to Drengr's chamber. Though Davith had informed me it is Drengr's chamber to where the stairs lead, I have not seen his quarters yet. I do not know what to expect. Headboards and chairs carved into the shape of dragon heads?

As it turns out, Drengr is not in his chamber, so I am able to examine it closely as we stride through it. As Wilhelm leads me to the door on the far side of the room, I notice the similarities in our chambers–same stone floors, windows along the exterior wall–such an extravagance, that, but I do love it. His bed is enormous, covered with furs and an embroidered counterpane in shades of black, red, and gold. Of course, the colors of the House of Logaland. It could fit an entire levy of warriors, if needs be. I feel my cheeks flush.

"Where is the King Drengr?" I ask.

"He will meet you in the solar. It is just this way, through the door."

I am pleased I do not have to meet him in his chamber. There is something so...intimate about it. Where he sleeps, where he dresses. In short, where he is naked quite a bit. Where someday soon, I will have to be naked. Curse my body for the warmth coursing through it, for the tightening of all my muscles, when I think of myself, naked, in Drengr's bed. This is not how it is supposed to be. It is he who must become besotted with me, so eager for lovemaking, he will spill all his secrets without thinking twice.

Drengr's back is to me when I walk through the doorway. I note there are guards on either side of it to prevent anyone from entering his chamber. I feel reassured, for perhaps mine own guards are there to protect me and not just to prevent me from escaping. Since he is bent over a desk, examining what appears to be a map, I can look my fill of him without his notice. His hair is braided as always, but the bottom half of it hangs loosely, past his shoulders. Indeed, our hair is not styled so dissimilarly. I knew Edda would take notes on his braids and try to replicate them. He is dressed all in black, his tunic cut close, so all can see the breadth of his shoulders and the narrowness of his waist. The collar of it is high but austere. Indeed, though the fabric of his tunic and breeches is a fine velvet, he is dressed simply. Nothing like the ornate costumes he wore when in Rhok. Could Davith have been telling the truth, when he said his king cared nought for finery?

I try not to dwell on how he continues to ignore me in favor of an old piece of parchment. Then I realize it is my parchment, the one Brother Matthias gave me the night of the betrothal feast. For one moment, I feel beastly, as I realize I haven't thought of Matthias for an instant since leaving Rhok. I'd given the map to Drengr to examine that night in the tent, then must have forgot to take it back. No surprise there, as I was...distracted.

But I had not said he could keep it.

"I hadn't known thievery was one of your faults."

I must say it. I am compelled to create an argument with him, for he no longer smells like woodsmoke and pine, but I do not rest easy, because now, he smells...even better. Like oil of amber and clove made passionate love and created a scent baby, then named it Drengr. I want to stick my nose in the crook of his neck, behind the high collar that brushes against his nape.

"Do you speak of the map?" he asks in a distracted tone.

This does not bode well, for it seems he is not interested in arguing. I need him to become angry with me. Only when we are fighting am I distracted from how much I want to taste his mouth on mine again.

"I'd planned to return it to you when I was finished with it, though in my defense, you never asked for it back," he says affably.

Logically, too. Damn him. I try again.

"It is not a very secret passage, is it, this staircase that leads from my chamber to yours. Besides you and myself, I count six people who know of it. Davith and Wilhelm, and now Edda and my new maids."

"It is not meant to be secret. Its purpose is to get you to me quickly and discreetly, and vice versa. Also, should the keep ever be attacked, the staircase down to the garden is a quick means of egress."

Finally, he lifts his gaze from the map and looks at me. And finally, he seems to notice me. "I see you are dressed in green," he says, sounding pleased with himself.

"Yes, my maid chose...wait...did you give instructions to my maids to dress me in green?"

"The color suits you. I wanted to see you in it. There is no need to be so angered."

"There is every reason. You cannot think you may command my women, contrary to mine own orders."

"How so? How were my commands contrary to yours? And it was not a command, but more a suggestion, that you wear green. You had not already decided on a gown to wear, had you?"

No, I had not. But Drengr is not to know this. For I've finally roused him to argument. Does he appear even more magnificent when he scowls? Perhaps. Do I forget how well he smells or what his lips can do?

I do not.

But at least I am distracted when we exchange these barbed words, so I do not do something foolish.

Like move closer and smell his neck.

Then he ruins my strategy again by saying, "I had a notion you would look fetching in green, and I was not mistaken."

I have nothing to say in response to such a compliment. Not for the first time, he has rendered me speechless.

"Shall we go down?" He offers me his arm. I try not to stare at it as though it is a wriggling serpent. Touching Drengr is not a wise decision. His arms are strong and welcoming, solid as oak.

They are dangerous.

He sighs. "We must put on a show for our guests. They will expect you to be on my arm, Princess. It is the custom. I am not trying to seduce you, tempting as the prospect is. I haven't the time for it. Our feast awaits."

He is right, of course. Not to mention, I should not be caught being so indecisive around him. I must feign regard for Drengr, no matter how I really feel.

The trouble is, the attraction I feel for him does not need to be feigned or forced. The reason I do not wish to take his proffered arm has nothing to do with distaste and everything to do with fear.

I am afraid of what this man does to me. I can admit it. I must admit it, even if it is only a silent admission. If I cannot be honest with myself, I have no chance of being duplicitous with Drengr.

I take his arm, wrapping mine own around his, feeling the hardness of his muscles, the warmth of his skin, though he must wear at least several layers of clothes. We descend the stairs, and I find I am clutching Drengr's arm in earnest. I have never seen so many people gathered in a hall in all my life. Mine own father's hall could not hold this many people. They are all lavishly dressed. The noblemen's beards and hair are plaited, and the ladies wear cloth of gold and drip with jewels. I notice their sleeves are obscenely long, like mine own. Fashion does not change much from kingdom to kingdom. I hope Edda is able to come to the feast for a while, for she will be in awe of such finery.

Then promptly try to make me copy it.

Drengr's hall glows with the light of hundreds of sconces hung on the walls. The great hearth in its center has a log heaped on it that must have taken ten men, at least, to haul it here. The scent of cedar wafts upwards, and I breathe deeply, trying to settle my nerves. It will be Yule soon, and this cedar log will be replaced with ash.

But I prefer the cedar.

"Princess, do not clutch at me so. You shall break a bone."

I doubt a troll could break his bones, such is his heft, but I take reassurance from his teasing.

"That is the Jarl Merven who waits for us at the bottom of the stairs. I am sure he knocked over at least three other jarls to take the privilege of being the first to greet us. He may have even maimed one, such is his ambition."

This Jarl Merven is small in stature. Once I am standing at the bottom of the staircase, I will still be able to look down upon him. He is also balding and dressed from neck to toe in a violent shade of yellow. He seems lugubrious, like one of the villains in the old tales Edda would tell me when I was a child. I wonder if he is trustworthy and if Drengr should be suspicious of him. Then I realize this is a foolish concern. Drengr is in possession of dragons who do his bidding. Who would dare challenge him?

Then I realize, I would. Or at least, I am commanded to do so.

Would my father have given me such orders, if he could

have laid his own eyes on Drengr's dragons? Would he put me at such risk?

I do not think I want to know the answer.

"Ah, and here comes his loyal lady, who would never miss her own opportunity to be obsequious. Lady Cornela is as ambitious as her husband, though be on your guard if she ever pays you a call. She does not take kindly to women who are prettier than her."

I try to ignore the disgusting warmth that spreads through my belly at his praise. He cannot mean it, though, for whatever faults this Lady Cornela possesses, she is very beautiful, with hair of a lustrous silvery blonde color and a magnificent bosom, which I instantly envy. Her eyes narrow in dislike as she watches me descend. It is a small victory. She would not take such issue with me if she did not think me worthy of her jealousy. My confidence is almost restored.

Which must have been Drengr's goal, I realize. He is trying to make me feel more relaxed by making these fine personages seem less imposing. By telling stories of them. By making jokes. Damn the man. For the thousandth time, damn his considerateness.

As newly minted steward, it is Wilhelm's responsibility to lead Drengr and me to the high table. He pushes past the Jarl Merven and his wife to fulfill his obligations, though it must be said, with a politeness only Wilhelm could muster.

The dais is fashioned of raised flagstones and the table of pine. It must, of course, be Logalander pine. These people and their trees. You'd think they were the ones who grew The Great Ash, the one which holds the Nine Realms in its embrace.

We are joined by the Prince Rufus, whom I am not yet sure I like, though I do know I find him amusing. I am not surprised to see the Jarl Merven and Lady Cornela traipse over to our table as well. I smother a smile, remembering Drengr's words. Who did they have to maim to gain a seat at table with their king?

I sit to Drengr's left, and Rufus is at mine. I do not know the woman at Drengr's right hand, so I am surprised when she asks me boldly, "Tell me, how many times have you wanted to spit in my brother's ale?"

Of course this is his sister. She is a mirror image of him, albeit a more feminine one.

"Princess Thyra, allow me to introduce the Princess Mist of Logaland. I am sure you will find much in common, or at least, if you do not, you will unite in your disappointment in me."

I knew Drengr has a sibling, as I know the ancestry of all the royal houses of Plane. But I suppose I was having enough trouble processing my impending marriage to Drengr to even think of his other family. If I remember correctly, he also has an uncle, the brother of his late father, who is married to a princess of Echen. And I am sure I do remember correctly.

The lineage of the kings of Logaland is in a very fine scroll in the Whistletree Priory. Most all the kingdoms of Plane have a scroll penned in their honor, so we in Vagmar may track their progeny.

To my knowledge, there are still no livestock responsible for furthering the line of the House of Hausen, though I'm sure Harald will try to remedy this, when he is king.

Mist is garbed in a gown of palest violet. It is cinched just below her breasts, and I notice her proportions are generous. In this, she is like her brother. As with him, it suits her. Her hair is only chin length, which is a rarity, even amongst menfolk. This style also complements her, though, as it frames her striking face.

I did not think I would have any appetite, but the food smells delicious. The first course is a frumenty, a strange choice, I think at first, as it is oft times a simple porridge I have to break my fast, but this frumenty is spiced with saffron, an exquisite, but expensive, herb, mixed with bulgur, a grain from the Southlands that is expensive to import.

"The frumenty aids digestion of the feast to come," Drengr says, as if reading my thoughts.

He seems to do this often.

Though it pains me to admit it, my dining partners are tolerable company. Prince Rufus of Echen is far too in love with himself, but he is amusing. Both Mist and Rufus enjoy making Drengr a target of their amusement, which makes it difficult to dislike them. It surprises me that he bears such teasing.

And once again, for what seems like the thousandth time, I find him to be altogether confusing. I hadn't thought any man enjoyed bearing the brunt of others' jokes, but particularly not kings.

Rufus has just finished cautioning Drengr not to overindulge in the dessert course, as his ancestors have tended to fatness in their elder years, whilst smirking and stuffing his own gullet with an alarming amount of the second course, roasted otalarks in a truffle and hazelnut sauce. I suspect Rufus's warning is meant to point out his own ability to remain slim with ease. Then the Prince of Echen's attention is caught by something–or someone–at the trestle tables below us in the hall.

He grimaces. Then he scowls. I cannot help but ask, "Does something trouble you, Prince Rufus?"

He turns to me quickly. Too quickly. His smile is all forced brightness. "Nothing at all, My Princess."

"I think you are lying."

I am not normally so bold when first becoming acquainted with someone, particularly not the heir to a royal house, but some niggling sense of intuition tells me I must press him for the truth.

His smile is genuine this time. "I am going to have so much fun at Drengr's expense, watching him try to cope with your wit."

Emboldened, I command, "Spill it."

Though to be fair, I have not known him long, I have never seen the Prince Rufus nervous. He swallows hard, his throat bobbing, then leans closer to me and says in a low voice–one only I can hear–

"Drengr told her not to come this evening. Indeed, he cautioned her their relations were at an end..." His voice trails away, but I follow the direction of his gaze and see a stunning woman with fury blazing in her blue eyes, eyes so bright I can tell their color even from this distance. A cold fist clenches at my heart.

"What do you mean?" I ask in an icy voice. But it is a rhetorical question. I already know the answer.

"That lady who stares at us so is Drengr's mistress."

22

DRENGR

Thyra stands abruptly, nearly tipping over her chair. Without a word, she leaves the dais, her head bent to conceal her expression.

I thought we'd been getting along so pleasantly. Or at least as well as we ever have done. I turn to Rufus, expecting his support, but his glare is accusing. If even Rufus thinks I have somehow been hurtful to Thyra, gods help me.

"What did I do?" I ask.

"How could you allow Esmina to come to the feast tonight?"

But I didn't. I strictly forbade her from attending. Indeed, I cut off all relations with her. It felt like a great sacrifice at the time, but once I met the Princess Thyra, I confess I've thought little of Esmina.

Actually, I haven't thought of her at all.

Hel. Now I shall have to chase after the princess and plead for her forgiveness. Even more problematically, our guests are starting to notice she fled the high table so abruptly.

As I rise, I say to Rufus, "I must go to Thyra. If anyone

questions our absence, tell them she is not so used to such exceptional wine, and I've gone to check on her welfare."

"Do not be worried," Rufus says. "I shall come up with a far better excuse than your piece of idiocy."

"Thank you." And I do mean this sincerely. Deception has never been a talent of mine.

I stride after Thyra, though I cannot be certain where she went. She fled the great hall through the antechamber near the dais, and I inquire of the carls stationed there where she went. Is it my imagination, or do they hesitate to answer me? One is looking at me as if I have frumenty smeared over my chin. It is as if they wish to protect the Princess Thyra from...

From me.

Hel.

"Out with it," I bark. I am normally not so rude with those who serve me, but these boys try my patience. If all my guards become besotted with her, it will prove awkward if she is still spying for her father and decides to use their loyalty to her against me.

Not waiting for them to answer, I move past them, intent on pursuing Thyra to her chamber, but one of the carls surprises me by saying, "My king, the Princess Thyra ascended the stairs to your solar."

I smile. Perhaps it is not the reaction you expected, but I know why she returned to my solar, rather than her own chamber. She wants the map, the little vixen. I wouldn't be surprised if she contrived her discomposure at spying my mistress–former mistress–just so she could get her hot little hands on my map. Her map. Whatever. I took it, and I need it, and that is all that matters.

Or so I tell myself.

I inquire of the next set of carls, those who guard the

entrance to my apartments, why they allowed the Princess Thyra to enter.

"You did not tell us she was prohibited from doing so."

It is a fair point, but not one I am willing to concede at the present moment.

Deciding to reprimand them later, I push the gigantic doors of my solar open, finding my princess exactly where I expected. At my desk, perusing my map.

Her map.

Hel...our map?

"You have a fair talent for acting, Princess. Here, I thought you wounded at the sight of Lady Esmina, but you only used her appearance as a clever ruse so you could snag my map."

"It is my map."

"You have your opinion, and I have mine own. When we are wed, I shall be merciful and not command you to always think as I do. I may even allow you to disagree with me sometimes, though only on occasion."

"You are a troll."

"If you must be insulting, I prefer you call me an ogre. Much like trolls in appearance, but more intelligent. I have even heard tales they can be taught to use a privy, instead of just dropping their breeches wherever they please and clogging up the streets of Innangard with their steaming piles of turd."

"I do wish it was not unlawful to ban them from the cities. They foul the streets, not to mention they are always instigating brawls in the taverns."

In spite of my exasperation with Thyra, I find myself agreeing with her. But no one, not even kings, can disobey the edicts of the Great Sorceress, Queen Maeve, who created the Ninth Realm of Plane. Our realm was created as a haven for all the persecuted creatures of Midgard, trolls included. To defy any of Maeve's edicts would invite her wrath upon us.

Still, I do so wish it were legal to ban trolls from public taverns.

"What's more, you are a mistaken troll. I am furious you allowed your mistress at this feast. It is an insult to me."

"You are jealous." I am not angry at her antics, however. Indeed, I am rather absurdly pleased.

"Oh please, I do not care that you have a mistress–"

"Had." I am compelled to interrupt and correct her.

Her face mottled with rage, which she must never know I find adorable, she says, "What bothers me so is that you ceased relations with this Esmina before you ever traveled to Vagmar. The Prince Rufus told me so himself. Once again, I am reminded you and my father planned this betrothal without clueing me in. That you assumed my compliance before you ever met me."

"You make a fair point, Princess, but if you do a little soul searching, I am sure you will find jealousy is the genuine cause of your distress. The assumptions I made before making my intentions known to you are mere matchsticks to fuel the fire already burning in your gullet."

Thyra's face is flaming as brightly as her hair. She opens her mouth, and I just know she is going to utter the most delicious of retorts, one that is going to make me want to kiss her senseless, when I hear–

"Hug. Hug."

What in Hel is Thyra's pet bird doing here? How did he get in?

The answer to this puzzle, I notice belatedly, is sitting in one of the cavernous chairs at my hearth. Hug sits on her shoulder, as though they are old friends...which they may very well be. But I have discovered my princess has a rather jealous nature, even if she says otherwise. I do not think she will be pleased at Huggin's interest in our intruder.

She is uninvited, but it does not mean she is unwelcome. She only visits when she has something of vital importance to share with me.

"I was wondering when one of you fools would notice me. It is always the way with princesses and princelings. Noses so high in the air, they cannot see what is two feet in front of them."

The crone's voice is raspy, but strong. She must be older than the volcanoes of Logaland, and yet she is still vital.

Next to me, Thyra stiffens. My bride recognizes that voice, and I know it must come as a shock to her. She turns toward the hearth, and when she speaks, she sounds like a bewildered child.

"Elfgiva?"

23

THYRA

Fury replaces my shock in an instant. How could she? This woman I loved and respected–and yes, often feared–left Vagmar for Logaland. It is a betrayal of my mother's memory.

I open my mouth to shout at Elfgiva, to take out all my frustrations on her, since I cannot do so with my betrothed. But thank all the gods I realize I would be betraying myself with such behavior. Drengr would be suspicious of my intentions if I accused Elfgiva of treason.

Elfgiva was never one for hiding her light under a bushel. Many völvas dress in somber hues, preferring for their magicks to be for what they are remembered. Not so, Elfgiva. My earliest memories of her include silken tunics in exotic shades and chains of gold and silver at her necks and wrists and ankles. She still does not disappoint, wearing a woolen cloak of scarlet, trimmed with squirrel-belly fur.

She is a tall woman, one of the tallest I have ever seen, and I hail from a kingdom where such height is unremarkable. She has allowed her hair to whiten, though I remember when she still lived in Rhok, her receipt for hair dye was more coveted than her magicks by most women and just as zealously guarded a secret by Elfgiva.

Ignoring me, which I realize hurts as much as her betrayal, she directs her attention to Drengr. "I have seen portents in the skies, Your Grace. Ill omens."

"Come now, Elfgiva. You know I put no faith in your auguries. I keep you as my Court Völva because you amuse me. With mine own mother gone, it soothes me to have a matronly, slightly deranged maternal figure at hand," Drengr says.

"Ignore my warning at your peril. In your absence, I witnessed these portents with mine own eyes. Flashes of green lightning in the night sky, shaped like dragon heads."

"It was probably actual dragons you saw, Elfgiva. Bathuba is green, and she does so enjoy a midnight ramble. Besides, in this kingdom, the appearance of dragons in the sky has never been an ill omen."

"Not yet," the völva replies with admirable equanimity. "And though I did not witness it with mine own eyes, the Abbott of Alcun wrote to me to tell of a rain shower of blood that fell on the priory there."

"Yes, well, he was probably drunk off cider. They have a productive apple harvest there, and 'tis the season for it. They brew some rather strong stuff. And being pledged to chastity, no wonder the man drinks. You two must have a great deal to discuss. I will return to the feast and make your excuses, Princess."

He nods and leaves us. He shows a sensitivity which would be surprising in any man, but particularly a king.

We are alone. I may speak to Elfgiva without reserve.

Though she is a powerful völva–one of the few whom, I believe, actually possesses a talent for sorcery–she should fear my wrath. Not because I can harm her. I know I cannot.

But because she loved my mother, or so she always claimed, and she has proven herself to be a liar. In more ways than one. She must have told her sister to relay to us she'd died, rather than say she'd left for greener pastures.

"How could you betray my mother's memory? She loved you. I thought–mistakenly, it would seem–you loved her in turn."

"You are not prepared, yet, to hear why I left Vagmar. You will not believe me when I tell you I never betrayed your mother, and that I honor her memory to this day. That I fulfilled my oath to you, and to her, to always watch over you. So I will not waste my words trying to convince you otherwise. When you are finally ready, you will return to me for the answers you seek."

"Cryptic, as always, Elfgiva."

She smiles. "It is not the business of a völva to be transparent about her doings. We must cast an air of mystery, else no one will trust us to cast the runes and read the future." She becomes pensive. "I know what you are, did you know? Your mother confessed all to me many years ago. I was there when she was bitten. I have kept her confidence...and yours... all these years. Would a traitor protect your secrets so tenderly?"

It still puzzles me, how a Valkyrie came to attack my mother. She was not on a battlefield, nor was she engaged in combat. To my knowledge, the Valkyrie could not have been summoned by the tang of blood or the sounds of violence, for there was none on offer that day. And I've never heard of a Valkyrie attacking a woman. Somehow, we are not drawn to their blood.

We do not enjoy the taste of it.

I suspect Drengr's blood would taste delicious, but I hope never to find out. I am commanded to kill him, if necessary, but I'd rather avoid it. I doubt I would be able to escape this fortress without encountering at least several angry, retaliatory dragons.

But speaking of escaping, it is what I need to do, right this very moment.

Elfgiva, who has already proven false, knows my secret. She could reveal it to Drengr.

She could destroy me.

THERE ARE guards posted outside my chamber, but none at the garden gate. Once I am ensconced in my chamber, the guards will think I remain there. The garden wall is only six feet high, taller than me, shorter than Drengr. It is easily scaled. Once I change into something less…conspicuous…I will be able to exit through one of the city gates, like any other citizen. No one will think I am a princess. The Princess, I suppose. The only one they would be charged with apprehending.

I do not know whether Drengr intends to return soon, though I suspect he will not be able to resist the allure of fine wine and his even finer mistress. Ignoring the churning in my gut when I think on the beautiful Esmina, I tell myself what matters is, he thinks I am still with Elfgiva. Even if someone informs him, one of my maids or the guards perhaps, I retreated to my chamber after my conversation with Elfgiva, he would understand. The reason he gave us privacy in the first place was he knew it would be a difficult conversation.

Which was thoughtful of him. I do not like to think of him as being considerate. He keeps proving my most treasured assumptions about him to be mistaken. But will he be so thoughtful he will want to check in with me, to make sure I am fine after my encounter with Elfgiva?

I try to suppress my snort of laughter, as it is at my own expense. Also, my guards are just steps from me, stationed at the entrance to my antechamber. I give them a nod, striving for as royal a gesture as possible. There are two more at the entrance to my bedroom, and I mustn't let them suspect I have any intention other than retiring to mine own quarters for a break from the festivities.

It is no simple task to undress myself, but after several futile attempts, I manage to reach the ties at my back and loosen them. Pulling the pins out of my painfully tight sleeves, where they attach to my bodice, helps in the matter. Being a well-dressed princess means never being able to lift one's arms over one's head. After I finish removing my gown, which I admit, I take pains not to tear, as I do have every intention of wearing it again, no matter it was chosen for me by Drengr, it is the work of moments to exchange my finery for something more serviceable. I throw on a loose, russet woolen dress, no different from what many women in the city wear. I decide against my fur cloak, though I know I will be cold, for it is a costly thing. Only the very wealthy can afford to own one, and I do not wish to be thought wealthy. Affluent people draw attention to themselves. I do, however, remember to drape a leather hood over my head, one such as any woman in the city would wear, to protect herself against the elements. My red hair is, to put it mildly, a giveaway as to my identity.

As gardens go, mine is quite large, but it is still easy enough to find my way across it in the dark. I have already memorized where the algae-covered pond is and where the hot springs bubble in its corner. The stone wall is in disrepair, like the rest of the garden, and it is easy enough to find several footholds to help me gain purchase over it.

I drop to the other side, exultant. I've managed to sneak away from Edda and my maids, Drengr and his court, even my guards. It is eerily quiet in this small lane, and I am not surprised, for being caught skulking around the royal apartments is unwise for any person. But as I walk toward the courtyard, I hear the voices of many people, some laughing, others bellowing. All sound as though they've had more than one pint of ale. I'd worried the guards would recognize me when I tried to exit the palace gate, but there are so many people gathered in the courtyard, no one pays me any mind. I see fires have been lit, and the citizens of Innangard huddle around them to ward off the chill.

"Another toast, to our King and his Intended. May they be ever merry with each other and bear our kingdom more dragons," slurs a man as I walk by one of the fires. His companions all cheer. These people seem to like their king. It is not a thing I am used to. Indeed, I'd thought it common practice for most subjects to dislike their monarch, especially when taxes are due, or the royal retinue travels through their village and they must labor for days to beautify their homes and their lanes, only for my father and his warriors to trample through, not bothering to notice any of the efforts to which his subjects have gone.

Then again, my father would never allow the citizens of Rhok anywhere near his hall. I realize Drengr must have arranged for the people of the city to come here, knowing they would want to celebrate his betrothal as much as the nobles gathered in his hall. It seems the only person who does not wish to celebrate Drengr's betrothal to me is...me.

After passing through the gate, I turn from the main avenue and make for the Forest Gate. Everyone in this city is either abed or in Drengr's courtyard, so I meet no one in the streets. Though Innangard makes mine own capital of Rhok seem like a hovel fit only for livestock, it still takes little time to reach the gate. No city in our realm is large, except for perhaps the ones in the Southlands, where trade and banking are more important than agriculture. In the Northlands, land is more of a commodity, as our growing season is so short. Most people live in the countryside. To be able to afford to live in the city, people must be well off indeed, for they must buy their food, rather than grow it or butcher it.

The Old Stories tell of the brutally cold lands in Midgard, from where the peoples and creatures of Plane trace their ancestry. I do not see why Maeve had to make the Realm of Plane quite so much like the Old World.

Is it the wisest course of action to run off into the forest in the middle of the night? No. And I knew the answer to this question before I ever set out on this mad dash into the moonlight. I would say I did it to teach Drengr a lesson. But that would be a ridiculous notion. He likely could care less I've hared off to the forest, and not be troubled at all by my anger.

I just needed to get out of the keep. Needed to feel the night wind on my face, see the shining moon, and pretend it is Vagmar's air I breathe. Though I must admit, Vagmar's air is never this sharp or clean or cold, and its forests are certainly not this old and deep.

My reverie of being home is ruined by the dragon flying through the night sky, blotting out the moon. Damned stupid beasts. But they are not stupid. And despite my hatred of them, I am fascinated. Enthralled.

And curious.

How do they know where the boundaries of Logaland lie, and why do they take such care to stay within them?

They are dragons. It seems to me they can go where they bloody well please. But yet, they do not.

Which brings me to the penultimate question. How does Drengr control them? What hold does he have over the dragons? They almost seem to love him, and he returns the affection. Then again, I notice he has a way with animals. Holfnir minds him, and he is an ornery beast. He and Drengr seem to have some strange understanding.

I am caught up in my musings, but not so lost in thought I forget to keep the fire lanterns of Innangard's walls in sight.

Apparently too distracted, however, to notice the Valkyrie who has alighted without a sound to block my path.

24

THYRA

"Why are you alone again? I thought you always traveled with your sisters. There is safety in numbers, I suppose, when you hunt in packs," I say by way of greeting. It is the very same Valkyrie who attempted to prey upon me in the Three Sisters Forest. We are alone, and so I do not fear her. She cannot harm me. Not with teeth or claws, leastways. Only by revealing I am of her own kind to Drengr can she destroy me.

First Elfgiva, now this smirking creature. My enemies–specifically, the ones who can spill my secrets–now outnumber me.

"They are your sisters, too. Are they not?"

Her voice is taunting, but seductive. Raspy, yet sultry. Seductive, even as it is terrifying. It is a voice meant to tempt warriors to damnation, even as they expire.

"They–and you–are more like demented cousins to whom I wish to lay no familial claim."

She laughs briefly, as though she grudges finding humor in my wit. Valkyrien all look very much the same–snow-pale skin, dark eyes, raven-colored wings–except for their hair. Mine own red tresses are not out of place when we swarm around a battlefield, as Valkyrien can be readheads. Blonde or brunette. Curly-haired or straight-tressed. Much as any human woman. This one possesses long, poker-straight hair of a black that matches her wings.

It must be said, we do all have a fine head of hair. I suppose it is nature's way of making up for the blood which seeps from our eyes when we feast.

Valkyrien are also naked when going about their business. I do not know if they choose to wear any garments when not cruising battlefields for new victims, as I must do. But then, they are not princesses required to adorn their fathers' halls, as I am. Also, were I to go naked, I would freeze. I am only impervious to temperature when the bloodlust is upon me. Otherwise, I highly object to the season of winter. If Maeve was so all-powerful, she should have deleted the colder months from the calendar entirely.

It is another reason their victims have no chance of defending themselves. Sexy voices. Naked, heaving bosoms. Shapely thighs, and of course, what lies between them. Most warriors hardly register the eagle-sharp talons or wolf-like fangs tearing their flesh from their bones.

"Has it ever occurred to you, we speed the agonizing process of dying for these warriors? Their passing is inevitable, and we make it less horrific."

"Yes, that is just what I think when I am sinking my fangs into their necks. I say to myself, 'Thyra, aren't you such a do-gooder, helping this nice young man die an excruciating death?'"

She only smirks again in response.

"Why do you keep pestering me? How did you even discover my identity? Have we met before on some battlefield? Did I somehow wrong you? Have you come to take your revenge?"

"I do not know which question you wish me to answer first, but instead I shall tell you the truth, even if it is not what you seek. I am the Valkyrie who bit your mother."

I'd thought I'd felt impenetrable fury before. When I learned I would be Handfasted. Worse, when I discovered it would be to my most bitter enemy. Just moments ago, I learned Elfgiva betrayed my mother. But this. This sensation is an entirely different kind of rage. I want to tear this creature's eyes out and rip her wings from her slim shoulders. I want to wind her hair around my fist and bite down upon her neck until I sever all the purple veins lying beneath it.

For the first time in my life, I want to transform. I want to feel my talons claw their way from my fingers. My teeth poke into my bottom lip until they draw blood. To feel the bottomless hunger I experience when in the midst of a battlefield of dying warriors.

But unlike the creature who stands before me, blocking my path back to the keep, I can only be a monster when I scent the blood of the wounded and dying.

"Why?" It is the only word I can utter. If there were a stray warrior wandering these woods, I would be tempted to slit his throat so the scent of his destruction would fill my nostrils, and I could transform and match this bitch talon for talon, fang for fang.

"Because she asked me to."

"You lie."

The words are unbidden. I say them without thinking. For of course it must be so. My mother would never have done such a thing.

"Thyra!" I hear Drengr's bellow, both furious and yet tinged with anxiety. He has come in search of his bride. He wishes no harm to come to me in these woods, for he must protect his Vagmarian investment.

Only moments ago, my greatest worry was having Elfgiva reveal what I am to Drengr. But now, such fury consumes me, I can barely register concern at the prospect of him discovering this Valkyrie and me in the same wood having a heated argument.

I turn in the direction of Drengr's voice, only to ascertain whether there is time enough to interrogate this creature further before we are discovered, but when I face the Valkyrie again, she is gone.

25

THYRA

"Did you see it?" It is a stupid question, but the only words I can manage.

I debated whether I should keep silent about the Valkyrie's appearance, but if he did see her, he would immediately suspect me of treachery if I do not mention her.

"See what, Princess? Your foolish flight into the forest? No, I'm afraid I missed it. Else I would have prevented it."

Damn. He did not see her.

Foolish. I do not appreciate being labeled so. But at least I forget my rage and my fear for a moment. My fury is for the Valkyrie, but my fear, though for an instant I pretended otherwise, was for being discovered having a conversation with one by Drengr. Explaining to him why we were having a disagreement would be difficult.

"It was a Valkyrie," I explain. "Here, just steps from your keep. And she was alone. You told me they do not stray from their covens."

"You little fool, a stray Valkyrie is the least of your worries in this forest. One false step, and you would be a sacrifice to the bog goddess. And did I mention there are wolves in these woods? Not all of them are of the four-legged variety."

Again, with the insults. Foolish. Fool. Surely he can come up with an insult possessing more creativity. But I must ask...

"Bog goddess?"

"The goddess Mose. She is mistress of much of the more stagnant bodies of water. Swamps and such. Surely you have heard of her. But then, Vagmar is blessed with the seas, not swamps. But what of this Valkyrie?" Now he cares. "They do not travel alone, but rely on their covens for protection."

I decide–wisely, I think–not to explain to Drengr that a Valkyrie has no need for protection. That the notion is laughable. But I must concur on one point. I, also, have always wondered why Valkyrien tend not to stray from their covens. I am an outsider, and I can admit to myself this is by choice. Had I embraced my identity, I would be much like my midnight, monstrous visitor and be flying back to the other women who share my curse.

Except I would not be able to fly, because I would not be transformed. I forcibly remind myself this is why I have never sought out other Valkyrien. We are alike, and yet so different. Together when we wreak destruction on a battlefield, but oh-so-separate when peace looms, and I don the guise of a pampered princess once again.

Not to mention the little detail that they are bloodthirsty killers, and I do not wish to associate with them, except for when I am forced by my bloodlust.

Had I befriended others of my kind, would I now be so lonely?

For I can admit this is what I am. My only friend is my giantess nurse. My only father figure, a thane I shall likely never see again. Same goes for Lyda, to whom I can only now write letters. Love will never be mine either. I shall be lonelier married to Drengr than I was as a maiden princess in Vagmar.

"I do not know how the Valkyrie came to be in the forest," I answer honestly. For I know not from whence she came, nor where she goes now. I only know for certain she sought an audience with me. I am not lying to Drengr. I am just...omitting information. Then I have a stroke of brilliance, even if I say it myself. "The Valkyrien seem to be targeting your warriors, My King. Were I you, I would ensure they know of her visit. They must be on their guard."

"I left my personal carls stationed at the wall outside your courtyard, Princess. You know, the one you scaled to escape the feast. And myself, I might add. And Elfgiva, too. Rest assured, I will make them aware of the Valkyrie's presence upon our return."

"You brought your house guard for protection? I thought you were the mightiest king in all of Plane. Why do you need such stiff security? Are you afraid your dragons will turn on you?"

"It is rarely a keep's defenses that fail, but its people. Treachery will breach our gates faster than any siege."

This man is too clever. And terrifying. Is that a knowing tone in his voice? Has he wondered whether I would try to betray him?

Or does he already know I intend to?

Thyra

26

THYRA

The next morning, when I wake...who am I kidding? I did not sleep. But when I rise, Helg greets me. "May I draw you a bath, My Princess?" she asks.

I appreciate my new maid, even if she is a Logalander. She seems to anticipate just what I need, without being asked. Though I just had a bath yesterday evening, before the feast, my shoulders sag in relief. The breath I did not even know I held releases.

"A bath would be wonderful," I say gratefully.

Just moments later, my hair is pinned, and I am ensconced in a cocoon of liquid warmth, scented with rose-hips from Thisal, lavender, and petals of peony. I do not feel so guilty about asking the servants here in the keep to draw me a bath, as I did at my home in Vagmar, for there are taps with running water piped into my bathing pool. It is a marvel to me. I will miss these baths when I have returned to Vagmar.

If I return.

It is not lost on me that I may die in trying to fulfill my

father's orders. Drengr is not what I expected, which irks me greatly. He is no ogre. Something tells me, though, he would not forgive my deceit. That my life would be forfeit. I shudder to think how I would meet my end. Were it my father's kingdom, the punishment for treason is to be tied at the wrists and ankles to plough horses, who would pull until my limbs are severed. Mayhap Drengr would commute my sentence to a hanging. Even a burning would be preferable to being stretched.

"Will you leave us, please, Helg? I wish to speak privately with my betrothed."

My shoulders stiffen as I hear Drengr's low rumble of a voice. It comes from behind me, which means he used our adjoining staircase to sneak up on me.

Helg leaves the towel she'd been holding on the step and dips into a low curtsy to Drengr. She bustles toward the door, though she has the grace to dart me a sympathetic glance. I try not to feel betrayed, for she cannot defy her king to insist on staying by my side. For that matter, once we are wed, I can refuse him nothing, no more than a servant can.

I hate that he knows Helg's name. That he says please to her. The man is infuriating. It is so difficult to hold on to the hatred I have of him.

Then again, he has interrupted my bath and is making no attempt whatsoever to avert his eyes. Indeed, he stares hungrily at me, or at least the spot in the small pool where he must know my body lies, for the herbs and petals strewn in the water cover me.

Mostly.

"To what do I owe this pleasure?" I ask sarcastically. And perhaps a touch defensively, too. In defiance, I gather up the herbs that lie near my feet and move them higher up my body, in a vain attempt to cover my mons and my breasts.

Drengr only smirks.

"I came to check on you, after yesterday evening's excitement."

"As you can see, I am having a bath. Your visit is ill timed."

"On the contrary, I think it fortuitous I chose this particular instant to come down the stairs. A few moments earlier, and you might still have been clothed. Something tells me you would have changed your mind about the bath, preferring not to disrobe in front of me."

"Whatever gave you such a notion?" I retort.

But I must be careful. I cannot appear too pleased to see him, as his suspicion would be aroused. Drengr of Logaland is no fool. But I mustn't alienate him, either. On our wedding night, he must believe I desire him.

And I must, for the Vales' sake, convince myself I do not.

"It takes more than a stray Valkyrie to rattle me."

"I have no doubt," he says, his voice soft. "I speak of your encounter with Elfgiva. I know it was not easy to see her again."

What remains unspoken is that seeing Elfgiva again is what prompted my mad dash into the forest.

"She betrayed my mother. Elfgiva was her friend, her dearest one, but she came here, to those responsible for my mother's death."

In my fury, I pound the water with my fists, forgetting to care whether the herbs and petals still conceal me. But Drengr does not forget. His eyes grow even hungrier, and his own fists clench at his sides. He takes a step closer to the bathing pool, which is a step too far. I hold up a hand to halt his movement, though I know full well how futile such a gesture is. If he wants, he will just continue inching closer to me. He does, apparently, for in one fluid movement, he walks to the side of the pool and plucks the towel from where Helg abandoned it on the step. With a predatory grin, he unfolds it and holds it out for me, in silent invitation to step out of the bathing pool, to be wrapped in its soft linen. No, it is not an invitation. Such a description is not accurate.

It is a dare.

"Or perhaps, Princess, you are mistaken about Elfgiva's loyalties, and you will realize the error of your ways in due time. You will come to find she is no betrayer, but a loyal friend, as you once thought her to be. Hopefully, this realization will happen sooner, rather than later, for I find your spirit...exciting...but this defiance at every turn grows tiresome."

He shakes the towel mockingly, as if to emphasize his point.

"You will learn there is no denying me. You may think you do not want me, but it is only a matter of time before I will have you, wet and whimpering and on your knees."

I say nothing in response, mostly because I cannot. I am incapable. I am already wet, and I do not mean from the bath. His words alone do this to me.

Feign attraction to him. Get close to him. It is how you will learn his weaknesses.

Except this desire I feel is no pretense. I wish it was. My instructions aside, it's damned inconvenient to lust after my most hated enemy.

"We are only handfasted, not even wed. My body is not yours to claim yet."

"It could be, if I so chose."

I realize there is only one means of proving him wrong. It is to stand up and climb out of the pool, so casually

Drengr will be convinced a king towel dries me after every bath I take. And as an added benefit, I will prove to myself I can resist his touches. I will not fall prey to this desire, but instead use his own as a weapon against him.

I rise from the water. Slowly. Deliberately. My shoulders are straight, the curve of my back arched. I feel droplets of water run down my neck, over my nipples, and on down to my belly. I expected such a display to wipe the smile from Drengr's face, and it does, but I do not think in the manner I intended. I hear a rumble low in his throat. It takes a moment to realize it is a growl, the feral noise a beast would make. Such as his dragons. I realize, too late, I have made a mistake. I made a calculation, and it was in error. I should not be surprised. I never had a talent for ciphers. But before I can retreat to the relative safety of the pool, he wraps the linen around me and scoops me out of the water as though I weigh no more than a wren's feather. He turns me from him, so I face the pool still, with my back to him. I can still smell him. The scents of amber and clove I found so intoxicating last evening still cling to his tunic, but they are mixed with the pine of the forest, from when he came dashing after me.

Then he begins drying me. Slow scrapes of the linen at first. Against my shoulders. My arms. My back. Then he moves the towel lower, to my buttocks. His strokes become less gentle. Every piece of skin the towel touches is alight with fire. I burn hotter than any dragon flame. My nipples peak, and he must know, for he moves the cloth to my breasts, becoming more erratic, rougher with movements. My breasts bounce under his ministrations, and to my utter and everlasting shame, I moan.

I feel him at my back then, pressed against me. Feel his cock through his breeches, hard at the small of my back. As hard as it was the night he pinned me beneath him in his tent, on the road to Innangard after the Valkyrien attack. Harder, even. He bends his lips to my ear, murmurs, "I told you, Princess, you would whimper." Then he catches my earlobe between his teeth and sucks gently. He drops the towel, which I vaguely hear fall to the floor, and cups a palm around my neck.

I am lost.

He was right. I am wrong. I do not care. I just want this endless throbbing to cease, and I know he can ease it for me.

His other palm cups my breast, and his lips move to the left earlobe, where his teeth begin anew their torturous ministrations. "Say it," he murmurs in a soft voice, but even so, it is a command.

"Say what?" I gasp as his mouth moves to the side of my neck, where he nips at me much less gently this time. I likely deserve this, for any fool would know what he wants to hear.

And I am no fool.

I want to defy him. To stalk away from him and fetch Helg to help me dress. I almost summon the will to do it, but then he slips a palm from my breast to cup my mons, and though I could swear it is some other helpless creature keening like a madwoman, I find myself saying, "I want you. You can have me. Now. Please. Now."

And then I am lifted in the air again, like so much gossamer, and placed on my bed. Drengr covers me, as though still unsure of whether I will try to escape. Trailing kisses down the column of my throat, he lifts the pins from my hair. When he is finished, he props himself on his elbows, though his hips still pin mine against the pillows.

"It is brighter than dragon fire."

He sounds awed. Enraptured. Distracted. It is my moment to flee, to tell him I've changed my mind. But then he recovers himself and presses his erection against me. Somehow, the rough woolen of his breeches only drives me more wild. I am slick with need, and as I rise to meet him, my wetness coats the front of him.

Suddenly, I am a frenzied animal, bucking my hips against the hardness of his cock, the roughness of his breeches. All I know is, this is the closest I have come since meeting him to finding some antidote to the need that always burns within me.

He pushes at my shoulders and throws me against the pillows again, moving like lighting to cover me, to pin me. He does not take his hands from my shoulders until he has traced a line with his lips down the center of me, past my breasts, over my ribs, and to my belly, stopping just before his mouth can touch my mons.

Then his palm is spread flat on my belly, clamping down on my skin with the lightest of pressure. Somehow, the touch inflames me even more. He nuzzles my mons, his nose trailing through the slick curls. Then his tongue darts out, licking against me, against a part of me I'd not even known could produce such pleasure.

This is the ache that must be eased.

I am a wild thing, straining ever closer to his tongue. The soft, fleshy part of my thighs rubs against his cheeks, and I feel the stubble there, scraping against my sensitive skin. The roughness of his beard is even better than the feel of his breeches, and I moan with pleasure, a guttural sound I'd not known I could make. Though my vision seems hazy, I look down and see his chin is coated with my slickness. His eyes are open, but heavy, his thick black lashes hiding the darkness of his irises. His jaw is taut, the tendons there flexing as he moves his mouth against me. Finally. Finally. This is how I will find the release I seek. This is the solution to easing the ache between my legs that has not ceased. I feel even more pressure building within me, but it is pleasurable this time, not a burden. I anticipate...what, I do not know. But I am about to discover it, of that I am certain.

Then in one fluid movement, he is kissing me, and I taste myself on his lips, and my own wetness coats my chin, as it does his. His cock is at the entrance of my passage, pushing ever so gently against me. All I feel is fire and slickness, and all I can think is that I must thrust to meet him, for he hesitates, which is not acceptable. This will not do. I must feel him inside of me. He must fill me. Complete me. Quench this fire that has threatened to consume me since the moment he walked into my hall.

Then suddenly, I feel cold air against my slick heat. I open my eyes, which I'd not even realized were closed in concentration. He is gone. More specifically, his cock is nowhere to be found.

"This has been useful instruction for you, and a pleasant enough means of passing the afternoon for my part."

He stands and pulls up his breeches, not deigning to even look at me as he ties his braies, shrugs his tunic down.

"What in Hel are you doing?"

"I didn't think I could be clearer, but I shall explain if I must. You insisted I could not have you, whenever I wanted, and I tried to explain to you, Princess, but you would not listen. Stubborn, as ever. And so, I had to show you. Demonstrate, if you will, how mistaken you were. Now, lie there and suffer."

And with this pronouncement, he departs, walking back to the far corner of my room and opening the hidden door without even a backwards glance.

Sometime later, Helg returns. I am still atop my bed, the pillows stuffed under me, my hair in wild disarray. I am still wet with need, my skin still slick, but growing uncomfortably cool as dusk advances, bringing a chill to my chamber.

"Oh, I am sorry, My Princess. I did knock, and thought you'd either departed or were asleep. I will return later."

She moves to leave, but I find myself saying, "No, stay Helg." Misery loves company.

It is time to dress for dinner. I will not make excuses. I will attend. I will not allow Drengr to think he has bested me. But before I ask for Helg's help in dressing, I decide penning a letter is in order. And for this missive, I do not need Hug to sneak it out of the keep for me. I want very much for it to be intercepted by Drengr's carls and taken to him directly for his perusal.

Dearest Lyda,

Drengr's cock is disappointing. His tongue even moreso. You told me he looked like a man who knew what to do with them both, but you were mistaken.

Also, I hope you are well.

Much love,

Thyra

I've decided it would be wisest to keep my message to the point, as I do not wish to waste time on words which will likely never be read by Lyda in the first place. Besides, the intended recipient is my betrothed, not my friend.

27

THYRA

I am in the midst of choosing which jewels to wear–the Crown's valuables have already been made available to me, so I may impress Drengr's courtiers with my finery, and I confess, I deeply enjoy the process of choosing baubles–when I hear a knock at the door. I tense, but only for a moment. For Drengr would not knock so politely. I cannot guess who it is. Someone not well known to me, but clearly someone considered no threat, as my carls have allowed the visitor to enter the hall which leads to my rooms.

Helg's voice is icy with disapproval as she returns to my side. "Lady Esmina of Heimfeld, My Princess."

Lady Esmina. Drengr's mistress. I was mistaken to relax my nerves. Her expression is serene, her hands clasped in front of her, almost as though she wishes to show me she does not come bearing arms. That she poses no threat.

But as women, we both know she is dangerous, even without being armed.

I mentioned her blazing blue eyes, which stared at me with such fury at yesterday's feast, but I had not yet described her other features. Lady Esmina is–and this will come as no surprise– stunning. Her hair is flaxen yellow, her cheeks and lips flushed pink without benefit of cosmetics. I am tall and spare, and so I feel particularly self-conscious about her petite, curvaceous figure. Tiny women, who are a rarity in the Northlands, always make me feel like a bumbling ogre.

"Which do you think I should choose, Helg? The gold or the silver collar?"

I wear violet satin this evening, mostly because Drengr has told me he would like to see me wearing green. I speak to Helg as though Lady Esmina does not stand before me, waiting patiently for an audience. I would normally not be so rude, though princesses are perfectly entitled to be, but for once, I think no one can fault me for being less than civil.

But Lady Esmina opens the conversation, which really, is quite cheeky of her.

"My Princess, I came to apologize to you. If my appearance at yesterday's feast wounded you, I am deeply sorry."

Her blue eyes are soft and glistening, her expression warm and genuine. Either she is a highly skilled actress, or she means what she says.

I decide silver pairs best with violet, though the gold would pair lovely with my green gowns. I hate that Drengr is right. I would look quite fetching in green and gold. But I cannot ignore Lady Esmina forever. I turn to her.

"Then why did you come?"

"There are several reasons. First, Drengr commanded me not to come to the feast, and this was poorly done on his part. He treated me badly, and he did not give you enough credit. I am not a thing to be hidden away, as though he were a child caught with too many sweets before dinner.

Nor would you be so irrational, to hate another woman simply because she had a relationship with your betrothed before you were even acquainted."

The Lady Esmina may, perhaps, give me too much credit.

"And the second reason?" My curiosity gets the better of me.

"I must find a new protector, mustn't I? Where better than your betrothal feast, where my presence announces I am newly single and there are many jarls and princes present."

"Why must you find a new protector?"

She is a lady, highly born. Surely there are other opportunities for her. Then I remember I am not just a lady, but a princess, and my only option–my determined fate–was always to be married.

"My child, I cannot marry again, and so a protector is, indeed, my only choice. Drengr has stayed with me only because I cannot have children. I am barren, you see. He holds no great love for me, nor I for him."

I find myself soothed when she calls me my child, instead of My Princess. She does not mean to insult me, but to provide comfort. And yet...

"You are not so much older than me, My Lady, surely."

"I am two and thirty, which may not be far from one and twenty by years, but it certainly is by experience."

Now I do feel vaguely insulted.

But instead of allowing my annoyance to hold sway, I say, "What I mean is, you have many years yet in which you could bear a child. How do you know you cannot conceive? Perhaps the problem lies with your partner, not with yourself."

Belatedly, I realize Drengr is her partner, and though I

never wanted this marriage, its only purpose is to produce heirs. If he is sterile, this will pose a conundrum.

"I was married to a man who sired many children with other women, but never with me. When he died, Drengr asked me to be his sole mistress, not because of my personal charms, but because he did not wish to beget a bastard. It is an arrangement which suited us both for many years, but now it does no longer."

Lady Esmina's voice holds no accusation in it, only acceptance.

I wanted to hate this woman, but I find myself liking her. Were she not my natural enemy, I would enjoy being her friend. Indeed, I pity her more than I resent her.

She holds up a hand. "Do not feel sorry for me, My Princess." It is as though she has read my thoughts.

"I want to believe you, Lady Esmina, but something puzzles me. Why did you stare at me so coldly at the feast, if you bear me no ill will?"

"My child, I did not stare daggers at you, but at Drengr. He has not dealt charitably with you, though I am sure he thinks he has."

We share a smile. I know exactly what she means. I do know he had no malicious intent when he made his plans to marry me. When he corresponded with my father.

It would be easier if he was the villain of this story, but the wretched man proves himself to be more a hero with each passing day.

28

DRENGR

My betrothed and my mistress–pardon, former mistress–have just entered the hall together. They are arm in arm, smiling wickedly, as though they share an amusing secret. Which gods did I offend?

I watch as they exchange a fond parting farewell. Esmina returns to the seat she took at yesterday's betrothal feast, but Thyra stalks toward the high table, sporting a gloating grin.

"How is it you are the one with all the woman trouble?" Rufus pokes me with his eating knife, reaching over Mist to do so. "You have one mistress and one betrothed. It is a small number of women to manage."

Had a mistress, I wish to correct Rufus. But then I would be putting too fine a point on the matter.

"Mayhap it is because my brother takes his relations with women more seriously than you, Prince Rufus. He does not just chase anything that moves in a skirt," Mist says. I am touched. It is not like my sister to defend me. "Besides, he's too busy playing with his dragons."

Ah. There it is. I knew there could not be praise without censure, as well.

Rufus and Mist continue to enjoy their bickering, but I confess, I do not pay attention. I have eyes only for Thyra. My rational mind tells me she smirks at my expense, but I do not care. Her smile illuminates her eyes and pins my gaze to her lips. I want to kiss the smile off her face. Or perhaps I want to kiss her so she continues smiling? Just without the smirking. I know not what I want, besides to finish what I started this afternoon in her bed. In a life full of challenges, the hardest thing I have ever done was leave her side without plunging into her first, to feel her heat.

"You have dealt quite poorly with Lady Esmina," she says by way of greeting, flopping into her seat in a decidedly un-princess-like manner, and still wearing that mocking grin.

I feared seeing the Princess Thyra at the feast. I wondered if she would attend. I wouldn't blame her if she chose to stay abed. I am not too proud to admit I had no wish to see her so soon after our encounter this afternoon. It was a delicious experience, do not mistake me, but I may... may...have not behaved very well.

Fine. I was horrible. I can admit it, though certainly never to her.

Had I known she would arrive at the feast with Esmina, arm in arm, and had I thought for one moment she would spend all of dinner chastising me for my behavior toward that lady, perhaps I would have stayed abed.

"How so? Esmina will want for nothing. I have reassured her on this score. She has a house in the city, a carriage, and a pension."

"You make it sound as though she were a loyal servant who is now being rewarded."

"Tell me, Princess, how would you suggest I treat with the Lady Esmina then?"

"For a start, you could convince her that she has more worth than simply being a wealthy man's mistress."

"And what pray tell, is this worth? What else shall she do to support herself? She is a woman of a certain age, albeit a lovely one, who has proven she cannot bear heirs. She was born to a noble family, and so if she cannot remarry, if she cannot rely on her own family for charity, what should she do? Become a merchant? We do have all manner of trades in Innangard, but none in which a gently reared lady would excel."

I cannot believe I am having this conversation with my betrothed. We are speaking freely of my mistress. Former mistress. And the princess is taking her side. Again, I wonder which gods I offended.

"I disagree. You do not give the Lady Esmina enough credit. I am sure she has many talents, beyond those which you have enjoyed."

I do not appreciate the princess's snide tone. I am a generous lover, as she discovered earlier today. Actually, perhaps she didn't. She found I can be a rather cruel one, in point of fact, leaving her desperate. Leaving her wanting.

I cannot regret it, though. The look of shock and disappointment on her face when I left her chamber was deliciously rewarding. Though perhaps our current conversation is my comeuppance. I wronged her, and so she made friends with Esmina. I am an even more generous master and employer. Not that the Lady Esmina quite falls into the categories of either servant or employee.

"Perhaps it is you, Princess, who do not give her enough credit. Lady Esmina was never taught a skill more valuable than embroidery, like many noble ladies, unfortunately.

When her husband abandoned her, she did not falter. She used her wits and her cunning to make her way in the world. Her looks helped, but if all it took to gain financial security was a pretty face, there would be many more wealthy women in the Realm of Plane. Though highly born, she was left destitute. She has secured her own future, despite her husband's perniciousness."

"I just think she should have been able to determine her own fate, without having to put it in the hands of a man. First her husband, then you. I'll grant you, you are a better option than her husband, I have no doubt."

"You are such a flatterer. After seven years of marriage, in which Esmina proved barren, the bastard quite literally dumped her in the streets. Her parents would not take her back, such was their shame. I shudder to think what fate could have befallen her. Had we thralls in Logaland, she may have been forced into some kind of slavery."

29

THYRA

"Did I just hear you correctly? You say there is no slavery in Logaland?"

"We do not have thralls here," Drengr confirms.

"But how are you able to accomplish so much then, within your kingdom? The great fortresses and priories require many laborers for their construction. Your horses need constant tending, if they breed as prolifically as you claim."

"They do, and thank you."

"Whatever for?"

"I believe you are paying me...and my kingdom...a compliment."

"I did not mean to. Do not worry. It won't happen again."

"Believe it or not, employers pay their laborers wages. Fair and honest ones, if you can credit it. It is the law, as laid down by my great-great-grandsire, Dagmar V."

I laugh derisively. "No jarl or merchant or yeoman can afford to pay all his workers, not if he wants to be prosperous."

"But they can. If you pay laborers, they will spend their wages with said merchants and on the produce of those yeomen. A jarl can charge higher rents from paid workers, thus enriching his own coffers."

I muse a bit on what Drengr has told me and conclude I should not have been so quick to be dismissive. I have never liked thralldom and feel pleased it does not exist in the Kingdom of Logaland. Not for the first time, I am forcefully reminded of the contrast in how Drengr governs his kingdom, when compared with mine own father. King Skerr is not the monarch who appears more decent and just in this comparison, I must admit.

I am intrigued by how the economy in Logaland operates. Perhaps there is hope for Esmina. Should she wish it, she could find employment other than being someone's mistress. Though it might not pay so well. I do not judge her if she seeks another protector. There is no shame in her choices. But if this is not what she wishes, she should be able to seek another fate.

What else would she enjoy doing? Her taste is impeccable. Surely she could do something with those skills.

Like become my first lady-in-waiting! Davith and Edda have been bullying me to choose my attendants. I had no desire to do so, but perhaps Esmina will agree to serve me. She would be no replacement for Lyda, but that's fine. She would be an entirely new friend. I make a mental note to speak with her after the feast. Then I wonder–

"If you were not a king, what would you choose to do? Let me guess–dragon tamer."

He barks with laughter, though I am not sure it is genuine. "Being a dragon tamer is part of my kingly duties, so no, I would not choose such a profession."

My words, casual and flippant, have spurred him to

come as close as he's ever come to confessing he does, in fact, control these dragons. That their loyalty to him is not simply innate, because they are from the volcanoes of Logaland.

I may not yet know how he does it, but it is confirmed he does somehow control the dragons.

It is a revelation, and I congratulate myself on this victory.

I should excuse myself and write to my father, sending Huggin on his first mission. This is news of great import. For if Drengr is killed, perhaps someone else can take control of these dragons? But I find myself most reluctant to tell my father. Besides, I wish to know the answer to my question.

"If not dragon tamer, then what?"

Whatever it is, he has no wish to tell me. That much is clear. His eyes are downcast in embarrassment. His lips form an almost boyish pout. Damned if I do not find his reluctance adorable.

"You promise you will not laugh?"

I hold out my hand so he may clasp my forearm, the symbolic gesture for sealing an oath. He looks askance at my proffered arm, but only for a moment before he wraps his own forearm around mine. "I promise," I say, once our arms are clasped. My voice is, admittedly, somewhat breathy, for we are clasping each other tightly and looking one another in the eyes. And so of course, I am forcefully reminded of this afternoon. Drengr must be as well, for his eyes darken and move to my lips.

I remove my hand from his arm, before I do something foolish, like drown in those dark eyes and kiss him in front of the entire court.

"Well, what is it?" I prod him, trying to hide my discomposure.

"A minstrel," he says in a rather strangled voice. Then– "Did you just...snort?"

Even as I pinch my nose to stifle another, I manage to say with a quavering voice, "Of course not."

At that moment, the air rushing through my nostrils dislodges my fingers, and I prove myself a liar. I snort worse than a pig enroute to the slaughterhouse.

I am supposed to make Drengr desire me. I have the strictest of instructions from my father and the Council. This will be difficult to accomplish, now that he has heard me pig-snort with abandon.

"I promised you I would not laugh, and I kept my oath. But I cannot control what my nose does," I say.

"I have a rare singing voice, and a talent for the harp," Drengr says hotly. "Why should I not use my skills as the gods intended, if I had to earn mine own bread?"

Why indeed?

I try not to think about the obvious. I find the man I am supposed to destroy to be funny and charming and attractive. He makes me snort-laugh, which very few people can do. Lyda, for one. Ulf, though his cares have been great in recent months, and I have not heard a single piece of mirth escape his lips in all that time.

"And now I must know, as it is only fair, what would you choose as a profession, Princess?"

There is no harm in telling him.

"Librarian," I say promptly. I do not even have to ponder the question. I know the answer in an instant. "I have no wish to be a matron, but to be a librarian, one must be a matron first. Were it possible to be one without having to be the other, it would be my chosen profession."

Matrons take vows of chastity, but this never bothered

me. It might now, I admit, as I admire the breadth of Drengr's shoulders out of the corner of my eye.

I just simply have never met a matron I like or even admire.

"And of course, if you were not a princess. Princesses can be neither matron nor librarian."

He says this with no rancor. Indeed, his voice is sympathetic.

I find myself confessing all to him. "I am no warrior. Not a shield-maiden of old, as the stories recount. I am a scholar. That is my gift. Or at least, it is where I have talent. There was not much opportunity to hone and refine my gods-given talent in Vagmar. The Priory was more my home than my father's hall, but even their resources were limited."

"You're saying you have no skill with a blade? I find it difficult to believe. Shield maidens are thick as lice on the ground in Vagmar."

"I am better with an axe, but that is irrelevant. What I am saying, if you would only pay attention, is that my true talents do not lie on the battlefield. I repeat, I am a scholar. Or I would be, if given the proper opportunity. My skills in warcraft are merely incidental, a byproduct of being raised a princess of Vagmar. I am no better trained for battle than any other Vagmarian. Indeed, I am perhaps worse prepared, as I paid little attention during my training."

I am, admittedly, being slightly disingenuous, as a Valkyrie has no need for blade or axe when on a battlefield. But the words I speak are truth.

"How do you daydream when there are blades flying at you?"

"I have always been skilled at multi-tasking."

He laughs, and I find I want to make him laugh again.

"Who knows? Perhaps one day you will view my library

as ample enough compensation for being forced into this marriage. And you haven't even seen our priories."

"You have more than one?"

He laughs again, and for the thousandth time, I curse my traitorous blood for warming my veins when I hear his laughter.

"Would you like to visit one? Just outside the city walls is the Priory of Ten Sleep. It is one of the largest in the kingdom, and only a morning's visit, it is so close. Unless, of course, you wish to stay the entire day to peruse their catalogues."

I had to hide my visits to the Whistletree Priory's library from my father, but Drengr is not only offering me the opportunity to visit a library, but tempting me with unfettered access to all its riches.

It is only too fortunate I know the truth of Drengr's history. Of his father's. Of this entire cursed kingdom's. They are to blame for my mother's destruction.

For if I did not know better, I would say Drengr, who will soon be my husband, is not a bad sort of man.

Not bad at all.

And rather easy on the eyes.

But thank gods I know the truth.

Still, a trip to the library with him can't hurt.

I must look pensive, for Drengr says, "'Tis just a trip to a priory, Princess. I am not asking for your blood oath. There is no reason for the decision to take such deliberation. If you scowl for too long, you'll get wrinkles. And it would be a shame, for you are a pretty lass, in your own way."

"Do you ever take anything seriously?"

"Not if I can help it. I spend enough time carrying the weight of a kingdom on my shoulders. Smaller matters, such as your adorable frown, do not upset me. I find your mercurial moods an opportunity for sport."

I try to focus on my anger and not that he calls my frowns adorable. I try, but I fail. I have detested Drengr of Logaland, his kingdom, and everything they represent, for my entire life. And I have known him less than a fortnight, but it is already so difficult to hold on to my hatred.

30

THYRA

When I wake in the morning, Helg is patiently waiting for me to arise. She tells me the King Drengr requests my presence in the courtyard after I have broken my fast.

"Did he explain why?" I ask.

Helg shakes her head, and fear clutches at me. Does he await my arrival only to accuse me of treachery publicly, before all his court? Or perhaps he has decided against our marriage and the alliance of our two kingdoms and wishes for me to witness his departure as he rides for war against Vagmar.

If Helg were not smiling, I would worry.

"The King Drengr said it was meant to be a surprise, and we were not tell you."

Nin serves my breakfast as Orla fetches some garments from the closet for my selection. They are all green, some the pale color of an unfurling fern, others as dark as the pines in the Three Sisters Forest. I have still not asked Esmina if she will serve me, partly because it is my expectation I will not live in Logaland long enough to require her assistance, but mostly because I am afraid she will say no. I do enjoy the company of these three women and Edda, but for once, I wish to surround myself with other ladies as well.

I nibble delicately at a buttered barley cake covered in a generous helping of lingonberry jam–I have never had much stomach for breakfast–and decide it would be wrong of me to take my anger out on Orla. It is not her fault all my day dresses are green.

It is my betrothed's.

Edda arrives to style my hair, which she insists she will always do, no matter how many people I now have at my beck and call.

I hate that I feel excitement at what Drengr has planned. It must be something pleasant, else Helg would not have smiled and Orla and Edda would not be so assiduous in their ministrations. Edda loves me too well to put me in harm's way, and I'd thought Orla and I were getting along famously, so long as I never complain about which gowns she pulls out of the closet. I hate even more how well I look in a walking gown of gossamer-like sage green. It is belted at the waist with a golden-colored sash, and the sleeves are not obscenely long, allowing me to have the use of my hands without having to constantly push up the fabric.

To make up for this effrontery, I shall be sure to wear purple this evening.

Then I become even angrier, for I realize I am already adapting to the courtly routine of this keep and looking forward to the dinner hour. Sighing, I walk out to the courtyard. Without being told, the carls stationed at my door follow me silently. Ever watchful. Ever guarding. But also, ever faithful to Drengr and not myself.

There is a carriage waiting for me in the courtyard, and a smiling king. For a moment, I allow myself to think of nothing but this smile. He is dressed casually, just a tunic and breeches, with soft boots tied below his knees. He looks like any village yeoman, albeit an uncommonly handsome and hulking one. Though his braids betray his status, for they are as intricate as ever, held with golden clasps.

I smother a smile of mine own, because I know enough now to know Davith must not have dressed him, as the valet would insist on arraying him in finery. He dressed himself and came in a hurry so he could be here waiting for me in the courtyard. I am touched. Dangerously charmed. And well on my way to self-delusion.

The carriage is strangely devoid of the trappings of Logalander royalty. No sigil. No crest. The drivers are not liveried. As if anticipating my question, Drengr says, "I travel incognito, rather than have a train of carls take time out of their more important duties to guard us. No one will even know you and I are inside."

His voice holds the barest hint of a suggestion. Drengr and I. Alone. Where no one else can find us. I shiver, and it is not from the Logalander cold.

I take his hand as I ascend the steps into the carriage. The inside of it is such a surprise, it is enough to distract me from the feel of his fingers on mine own. Though simply constructed on the outside, in here it is a plush paradise. The seats are brocaded and covered in furs. Beneath the far window a small tabletop has been constructed against the carriage wall. A decanter and two glasses rest atop it. I notice on the floor is a trunk, its lid open. It overflows with foodstuffs.

"I did not know if you'd breakfasted yet," Drengr says as my eyes fall on the pots of lingonberry jam and clotted cream with appreciation.

"There is enough here to feed me for all the breakfasts, for the rest of my days."

I say this with real regret. I do not know if it is because of my Valkyrie blood, but I have never had much appetite for food. I wish the same was true when I transform. That my hunger for blood would be so easily assuaged. But sadly, it is not the case. When I scent the agonies of a wounded warrior, my appetite rages.

It truly is unfortunate, especially on an occasion such as this, for I do so enjoy clotted cream. Who doesn't?

"I'll eat what you don't," he says affably as he vaults himself into the carriage once I am seated.

I have no doubt of it.

Drengr taps the roof of the carriage to signal we are ready to depart. I am lulled by the sounds of horses' hooves on packed earth and the tinkling of their harnesses. Innangard is a far larger city than any in Vagmar, but we are still soon at the city gates.

We sit across from each other. Drengr has taken the rear-facing bench, which was most considerate of him. It is common to experience nausea when seated behind the drivers. Is he trying to woo me? Or is this all effortless? For regardless of whether he is conscious of what he is doing, he is impressing me.

I am jealous of his appetite. He unwraps a loaf of manchet bread and holds it out to me for my perusal, like a boy proudly showing off his collection of tin warriors. He asks if I wish for some, and it would be rude to say no. He spreads the cream and jam on it for me, places it on a napkin, and hands it to me with an adorable kind of reverence. I take a taste and tell him honestly it is the finest clotted cream I've ever tasted.

He is absurdly pleased at the compliment, as though he'd made it himself.

Outside the city walls, the Three Sisters Forest quickly envelops us. The woods here are different from Vagmar's. Ours is a nation surrounded by seas, and the winds buffet our lands too forcefully for any great trees to grow there. There is no pine or oak or ash, just scrubby beeches and whistletrees and rowans, warped and twisted by time and gales.

It is so different here from my home and so cold. But it is beautiful.

"How close are we to the priory?" I am excited to see it but also content to stare out the window.

"Any moment now, you will see its spire rise above the tree line. The Ten Sleep Priory, so named because when it was first constructed, only ten monks lived here, each in his own cell, holds not just scrolls, but maps and illuminated tomes and compositions of music."

He speaks with a reverence I share. I feel my thighs clench. Who knew speaking of libraries could be so seductive? But his words remind me–

"Speaking of, why do you care so about my map?"

"I'm not sure," he says. It is a strange answer, but I think I understand him. He is so earnest, he does not even bother to correct me, to insist it is his own map. "I stare and I stare at it. I know there is something...missing...from it, though I cannot figure out just what yet. Or perhaps not missing, but...wrong. And I have a feeling once I figure out what the error is, I will have solved an important mystery."

He speaks truth. He is confiding in me.

Again, this would be a reason to write to my father, to send Huggin on a journey. I feel a momentary pang of guilt, as he was left behind once again this morning. But ravens do not do well in a confined space. It is worth informing my father that Drengr puzzles over a map from our own Whistletree Priory. That if my father determines what is wrong with the map before Drengr does, he will somehow have the advantage.

But I find myself unwilling to do so. Indeed, I know I will not write such a letter today. Or ever, for that matter.

The spire of the Ten Sleep Priory rises in the distance, an ornate affair with gleaming tiles and ornately carved reliefs. I am not surprised, as I was when I first arrived in the capital. Logalanders seem to take a pride in their crafts which borders on hubris. Still, it is beautiful, as a place of worship and knowledge should be.

We enter through the gates, which are unguarded, and I am surprised to see it is a hive of activity. Monks and matrons scurry across the courtyard and down the corridors which fringe the perimeter of the building, clutching scrolls or pails of water or, in one monk's case, a loudly honking goose.

The Prime Monk emerges from the priory to greet us. To be received by him, Drengr must have sent word ahead of us. Another thoughtful touch. The Prime Monk is tall and spare, with wild white hair and a ready smile. I find myself warming to him, which vexes me, as I do not have much use for monks and even less for matrons. Then I remember Matthias was a monk, sworn to the gods, and I feel guilty. He, of course, was the exception.

I swear.

The Prime Monk bows to me, and Drengr introduces us. He asks–

"Do you wish for me to accompany you on this visit, My King, or would you rather tour the Priory at your leisure?"

"Leave us to it, I think. Given how much my betrothed

loves libraries, I think we will be here a while, and you are a busy man."

"Never too busy for you," the Prime Monk says, but nonetheless he bows once more, gives us a merry wave and retreats into the priory. He seems to mean what he says. How can it be that all Drengr's subjects actually like him?

I have never heard of such a thing.

But we are entering the library through a smaller entrance to the left of the courtyard, and I am too distracted by the wonders which greet me to think more on Drengr's likeability. I try not to gasp in delight. I think I fail. "This library must rival the ones in Echen with its size. I have always dreamed of traveling to that kingdom, to visit the Great Library of Holl, in their capital. It is said to hold the largest collection of grimoires–magical texts–in all of Plane." The Whistletree Priory's library did not contain a single grimoire, much to my dismay. It is no surprise, however. As I've mentioned, we are not known for our scholarship in Vagmar. Besides, the Vagmarian völvas I know would scorn the use of such written guides. They believe the oral traditions passed down through generations, those tested and honed in practical settings, are the most effective. I smile when I think of Elfgiva using a grimoire. Then I remember I should be furious with her, but I can't seem to summon the effort. Elfgiva was quite...creative...with her incantations.

"Yes, thank you, Princess, I know what a grimoire is. It is lucky I won the tournament, and not Rufus of Echen. It might be his libraries you would be exploring."

"I'd prefer to explore no king's libraries, but rather, stay in mine own, expanding it."

Drengr nods. "Playing around in one's own library is enjoyable, but it is never as amusing as sharing the experience of visiting together."

"Are we still speaking of libraries?"

"No, Princess, we are decidedly not."

"You use your tongue rather cleverly, for such a brutish warrior." Then I realize what I've said, and my face flushes furiously. I have firsthand knowledge of just how clever he is with his tongue. "I meant to say, you are skilled in wordplay."

Surprisingly, he ignores my unintended innuendo and says, "To believe the mind is any less valuable than the sword-arm is short-sighted. There are different kinds of might, and the power you find in a library is far greater than that found in a warrior and his weapons. For knowledge lasts much longer than a man's strength. And while we cannot all be warriors, we can all open a book."

Damn him. Damn him to Hel. I want to rip his clothes off right then and there. I could take him on the stone floor, and it would feel like a mattress stuffed with eiderdown. I shan't feel the cold, for my skin is blazing with heat. With need for this man.

I was so wrong when I thought there was no harm in telling him I wished to be a librarian, if I was not a princess.

For he has so generously planned this entire day for me, and tells me this entire priory is at my disposal. If I had doubts whether I should comply with my father's commands before, I now have almost no ability to commit treachery against this man.

"I am sure you could spend the entire day in this room, Princess–more like the next month–but there is also a magnificent stillroom here. I remember you saying you have a talent for healing. Indeed, you demonstrated it when you stitched me up."

"There is a stillroom here?" I hate how my voice quavers with anticipation.

"Yes, of course. Logaland's finest healers are monks and matrons."

Though I cannot believe it myself, I leave the library behind with nary a backward glance and follow Drengr down a narrow passage which must connect the library to the rest of the priory. We pass the door to the main building and continue to the end of the corridor, where the pale and dismal light of a Logalander morning greets us. But despite its poor showing, the weak sunlight is most welcome, for we are in a room with glass panes for a ceiling, something I thought never to see in all my days. I've heard of priories where there is such wealth they can afford the amount of glass necessary to construct such a roof, but I wasn't even sure the stories of their existence were true. I am happy to be proven wrong. The sunlight which streams through the glass, meager as it is in winter, is enough to force herbs and other medicinal plants to grow out of season, as long as there is sufficient heat. There is a small fire burning in a hearth in the corner, making the room, while not necessarily a comfortable temperature, given all the glass, at least warm enough for cultivation.

Drengr was right. I may not come home for a month, at least. Then I realize I would miss him, and that realization ruins my good mood.

Even as Drengr and I approach, a tiny, wizened old man emerges from the stillroom. He is white-haired and stooped, wearing the serviceable, grey woolen robes of his order. In his hands, he carries a hellebore, blooming early. He must have forced the flowers, which do not usually sprout until after Yule, in the stillroom. Hellebore has many medicinal uses. I often crush its dried petals to bring down fever, if I have not had the time to distill willow bark.

"Would you like your own stillroom?"

It takes me a moment to register what Drengr is saying. I am basking in the light streaming through the glass ceiling, even though it bestows no warmth to speak of. The scents of drying lavender and hyssop and sage fill my head. But when I do comprehend him–

"What? Do you mean of mine own? In the keep?"

"We can construct it in the Three Sisters Forest, if you prefer, seeing as how you have a penchant for fleeing there when things don't go your way. But I think you'll find having your own stillroom within the keep would be more convenient. Perhaps in the garden outside your rooms?"

This day started out so well. But now my mood only sours more. Which begs the question–

How am I ever supposed to betray this man?

Which also begs another question–

How am I ever going to stop myself from falling in love with the King Drengr?

But aloud, I say, "Could this stillroom perchance also have panes of glass to filter the sunlight?"

"If you wish," he says agreeably.

Oh, dear. Does he know he is making it impossible for me to ever leave Innangard?

Worse, to leave him?

31

THYRA

Later that day, I beg directions from Davith for finding Elfgiva's lair. Yes, lair sounds ominous–a hidden dwelling full of dark corners and dried bat wings–but I doubt Elfgiva has changed so much since leaving Vagmar that she would instead prefer a newly built townhouse on the capital's main avenue, complete with modern conveniences.

And I was not wrong. Her abode is just a stone's throw from the dragon pit, a place I learned of shortly after my arrival in Innangard but have had no wish to visit. The pit lies just outside the city's fifth gate. It is the gate farthest from Innangard's main entrance, and therefore quieter. More dilapidated. As with each entrance into the city, there is a guard tower above it. Elfgiva has fashioned (or more accurately, had someone else fashion) a wobbly hut constructed of timber, which rests (more like tips) precariously atop the crenellations.

Against my will, I smile fondly at her antics.

My fist hovers at the door, ready to knock, but before I have the chance, Elfgiva bellows, "Come in Thyra, but you'll have to wait a moment for your answers. I'm in the middle of something, and I cannot stop now."

I enter, despite her warning. Her home is, as I expected, snug and charming, if one overlooks the dead newts floating in distillation bottles and the bat wings pinned to the rafters, drying like herbs. And yet, nothing like herbs. There is not a speck of dust in sight, which one would normally expect with a batty old völva like Elfgiva. And yet, she has always been fastidious. Her back is to me, and she stands over a steaming cauldron. From the small folding table which stands next to it, she takes a few sprigs of what looks to be rosemary and dumps it in the pot.

Elfgiva removes her staff from the sleeves of her capacious robe–a lovely turquoise color with sleeves and hem and collar trimmed with the feathers of a peacock–sourced at great expense, no doubt–as peacocks are only to be found in the warmer climes of the Southlands.

Her staff is fashioned of dwarf-forged iron. At its tip is a triskele, which is quite remarkable for its craftsmanship, given the metalworker who forged it must have had to split the iron into three strands at the tip, without cracking the rest of it. The triskele is the symbol of female power. Maiden. Mother. Crone. The stages of a woman's life, and how each one is no less important than the other, however different those stages may be.

Elfgiva used to tease me, that I was the maiden and she the crone. Of course, the mother was absent. Mine own. She was dead.

A völva's staff is the lifeblood of her magic. As Elfgiva used to say, It does not matter how much magic a body holds, if there is no means of conducting it.

This was when she still called herself a friend to my

mother, and I loved her as I love Edda and Ulf. She was like a mother to me.

And then she left me.

I concede it is, perhaps, my anger, my hurt, which makes me want to shut my ears to her.

Now I am willing to listen, and I think the reason has less to do with Elfgiva, and more to do with Drengr. He told me I was mistaken about the manner of my mother's death. They both warned I should not trust my father. Initially, Drengr's claims only helped to make me resent him more. But though I can barely countenance it, I have grown to trust him.

Edda always says it is easy enough to judge the character of a person. That people overcomplicate the matter. If a person shows themselves to be kind, then they are likely kind. If, on the other hand, they are unforgiving and supercilious to others, it is a waste of time to think they might be hiding a better nature.

Which begs the question–why, all these years, have I put all my faith in my father, who has mostly ignored me and rarely had a kind word for me? Whose people obey him out of fear and not love?

Why should I not trust Elfgiva, who only ever showered me with affection and taught me right from wrong, when she echoes what Drengr has said about my mother's death? I suppose it is because I am still like a little girl, vying for my father's affection and approval, though I know it to be a thankless task.

"I am ready to listen, if you are ready to talk," I say to Elfgiva.

"Yes, yes. I knew you would come. But give us a moment. This concoction always frustrates me. I never remember in which order to add the ingredients, and I always forget at least one of them."

"Goodness, it sounds like a fearsomely complicated spell."

Elfgiva finally looks at me, her usually gleaming hair in disarray, her cheeks rosy from the cauldron's steam. "What? No, child. I make stewed lamb. Not a spell. Please. A spell is no trouble at all. Old Nasmell's receipt for this casserole reads longer than a grimoire. But it is worth it, if one gets it right."

She takes her staff and moves it above the cauldron. The stew moves in a circle, though there is no ladle dipped in it. Then she does dip in a spoon and holds it out for me to taste. I oblige, and try–unsuccessfully–to suppress a grimace.

Elfgiva sighs. "I can foretell the future, cast the runes to change one's fate, and summon the gods. But I cannot make a damned stew." She wipes her hands on a towel, even though they are not dirty, and turns to face me. "Well, do you want to hear what happened to your mother or not? I have a lamb casserole to finish and a war to prepare for. I haven't much time for reminiscing."

She gestures for me to sit by the fire, where two stools lie. I lick my lips, which are dry, and tug at my braid, which suddenly feels heavy at my shoulder. I am nervous. Partly because I have not seen Elfgiva for so long. Does she remember me as fondly as I remember her? Did she miss me? And mostly because I am not certain I wish to hear what she has to say.

There are so many questions I should ask.

But the one question which burns in my mind is the only one she perhaps can't answer.

I am the Valkyrie who bit your mother.

Why?

Because she asked me to.

"Who is she?" I ask. It is an incoherent question, of course. And yet, Elfgiva seems to know exactly of whom I speak.

"Before you want to take your vengeance on Brunna, you should know I sent her to find you. I thought it was past time the two of you...connect."

So Brunna is her name.

"Why would you send her after me? I swear she wanted to kill me."

"Her means of locating you was...regrettable. There were needless deaths...on both sides, mind. There were just as many Valkyrien killed as Logalander warriors."

"Am I supposed to feel sorry for them?" And yet, curse it all, I do.

Ignoring my question, Elfgiva begins her tale. "Your mother was in her confinement, just weeks away from labor. She was much weakened by pregnancy and feared you would arrive early. Even in the womb, you were an ornery child. Merlina felt your quickening at less than four months."

"You call it ornery. I choose to call it precocity."

"Do not interrupt. As I was saying, her labor was still some weeks away, or at least, it should have been. But she sensed an urgency to enact the plan she'd concocted whilst idling away the hours of her confinement. She asked me to locate the nearest coven of Valkyrien and to bring to her one willing to provide a service for her.

"Of course I knew where the nearest coven was to be located already. I always make sure to know such things. And yet, her commission would still not be an easy one to achieve. I knew it would be difficult to find any Valkyrien willing to visit a human queen in her palace, unprotected by her coven, let alone provide her a service."

"Let me guess, for some nefarious reason of her own, Brunna was willing."

"Stifle your racket, or I shall box your ears," Elfgiva says mildly. "All Valkyrien are vicious and powerful, but only some are cruel. Brunna...she is different from the others. They tend to have a hive mentality, never wishing to be parted from each other, always operating in a cohesive manner when infiltrating a battlefield. Almost as if they share each other's thoughts. You would know better than myself of what I speak."

Yes. Try as I may to escape their clutches, when I hunt a battlefield, the camaraderie of the other Valkyrien tugs at me. Pulls at me like a magnet. When alone, I can resist transforming, even if I am in the presence of the wounded.

But in the company of other Valkyrien, I am a thing possessed. I feel no guilt. I sense no shame. I revel in each bite I take. Every chunk of warrior flesh.

For the first time. I feel something like pity for Brunna. My words to her stab at my conscience. I am no better than any other Valkyrie when I take such pleasure in my battlefield destruction. Who am I to feel so superior to Brunna and the others?

Elfgiva continues her tale. "Brunna is able to understand what many Valkyrien cannot comprehend. The human politics of Plane affect their covens, just as their actions can sway the outcome of battle in return. It is a mistake for the Valkyrien to be so secretive. To never mix with the outside world. Such aloofness breeds resentment. Brunna recognizes this.

"There is no means of explaining to you the next bit of this story without wounding you. It grieves me to cause you pain, but I think you are as ready as you will ever be to hear the truth. Your mother wanted you to be able to stand up to your father. She knew one day you would need to." Elfgiva pauses in her telling and eyes me speculatively. "Do you know why Valkyrien only feast on the blood of male warriors?"

"I assumed it was because they have little use for men." It is one of the few aspects of being a Valkyrie I can support wholeheartedly. Though I admit, I find the King Drengr to be rather useful. His tongue, in particular. How when he speaks, he can make me laugh. Or when he licks me, he can make me moan.

Elfgiva laughs. "That is perhaps part of the reason. But no. It is because long ago, the Valkyrien discovered they make more of themselves when they bite woman warriors, whereas men simply die and go to the gods. Believe it or not, they do possess consciences and had no wish to create more of themselves, to create more cursed and damned beings to roam the earth, never able to satiate their cravings."

Understanding, sudden and terrible, dawns.

"You tell me my father has lied to me. I am not so naive as to insist on his innocence. He has ever been a distant father, quick to judge, quicker to express his disappointment. I have known for some time I would never be able to meet his expectations. Known longer that he is a king who is feared by his subjects, yet never revered. But tell me, what did he do to earn my mother's undying hatred?"

"I suppose you wish for a simple answer. One cold, clear, obvious reason she detested him. But the truth is, his transgressions were small, yet many. There was no distinct reason, no particular incident, which earned her resentment and distrust. The King Skerr hides his basest instincts, and yet, he can never manage to fully conceal his petty cruelties.

Hour by hour, day by day, Merlina came to realize her husband was...unnatural. I am sorry, my child. You have always been distant from him, but I know you loved him and ever held hope your relationship would somehow be mended. I must tell you, there is no hope."

Elfgiva only confirms what I already knew, deep in my gut.

Still, she has not told me why. Or how.

"King Skerr is a distant father, and though he is feared, not loved, by the people of Vagmar, he is not the cruelest monarch in Plane. Arno of Dervnonia, though he is a wretched little turd, could probably give my father lessons in depravity. So how is it my mother came to discover his true nature? Why did she have a Valkyrie turn me?"

I cannot comprehend it. Not yet. My mother believed my greatest chance of survival was to make me a monster. The only solace I have is she felt she was doing what was right. That she was giving me what she believed was my only means of defense against my father.

"Merlina feared your father would treat with you as he had with her. I cannot say for certain the reason he never harmed you was because he feared your retaliation, but I suspect it is exactly why. Your father is a warrior king. At some point, you would be on the battlefield together, allowing you to transform. Allowing you to rip him to shreds. I believe this is the only reason he never harmed you. And even when not transformed, you possess an unnatural strength, do you not?"

I shrug. Perhaps. It is a robustness that is nothing when compared with Edda's, but yes, I suppose I am stronger than most women. As I have little talent or inclination for warcraft (it would not do to transform into a Valkyrie and start biting the other warriors in the training yard should they incur a wound), it has never mattered to me. My unnatural vitality was just another abnormality I wished to conceal. To forget.

But now, I see it in a whole new light. Almost as if it is a gift.

"Do you mean to say my father harmed my mother? That he would beat her?" My heart pounds with anger.

"It is exactly what I am saying, my child. Even then, she suspected she would not always be there for you. That either by his hands or through illness, to which she was prone, she would die before you grew to adulthood. Her lungs were never strong. She readied you for this life in the only way she knew how."

I share this weakness of the lungs. And yet, I have never been wholly troubled by it. Only occasionally, when the seasons change or I have caught a cold. Obviously, when I am fanged and clawed, my lungs work just fine. It seems my mother wanted to spare me this fate as well.

"Why did she never tell anyone? Elfgiva, if you knew, why did you never tell Ulf or some other worthy member of my father's council? They would have intervened."

"When the Great Sorceress Maeve fashioned our realm, she did not demand there be edicts barring men from abusing their wives. This was not deliberate, but an oversight. She did not realize such a law was necessary. As time has progressed, many local governments have, of course, made such laws. But who makes the laws for an entire kingdom?"

"A king," I say morosely.

"Exactly. In many ways, there is no one with less rights than a queen. A thing you know all too well. I think, perhaps, the King Drengr is a bit more worthy of your consideration, given all you have learned. He would never harm a hair on your head. And it is a lovely head of hair."

I smile at her compliment. No. Drengr would never intentionally harm me.

But still, he could break my heart.

"But my father was not responsible for my mother's death. She died in Logaland. How can you explain this? Perhaps it is true, what Drengr says, that his father did not murder my mother. But still, her death cannot be laid at Skerr's feet. So how did she die?"

She smiles sadly. "This is not my part of the story to tell. You must ask the King Drengr. Perhaps you are now finally ready to hear what he has to say as well."

She is right. I stand, ready to depart in search of Drengr. I am about to say my farewells to Elfgiva, and thank her as well, but then I realize I have one more question.

"You could have gone anywhere. Served any king or queen you wish. Served none, if that was your preference. Why Logaland? Why the King Drengr?"

"I would have thought the answer obvious. Because I knew you would come here one day, and I would not be parted from you."

A great, heaving sob wracks my chest and erupts from my throat in a strangled cry. Elfgiva opens her arms, and I rush into them.

I am home at last.

32

DRENGR

Sometimes, I play with my dragons. Yes, my sister was absolutely on the mark when she made fun of me at dinner the other night. But the reason I do so is simple. The bond we have is not because of my dragon magic alone. Nor in my blood.

It is based on something far more powerful than blood or magic.

Friendship.

Harig, Bathuba, and the others live in Mount Muspel. It is the source of their power. Their very existence. A dragon can only be born in the fires of its volcano. But there is also a pit constructed below the keep where they may come and go as needed. Harig, in particular. I summoned him so I could discuss the current predicament I face with Thyra. And when I say discuss, I mean I talk, and he listens. Not well, however. He is more interested in our game.

Sitting on the steps which lead down into the pit, I take a gold coin and toss it in the air, whistling casually, pretending Harig does not sit below me in the dragon pit. I ignore him. He eyes me beadily. Intently. Though to be more accurate, he eyes the coin as it travels into the air, then back down to my palm. Dragons are ever avaricious, even mine own. Though Harig heeds me, I suspect I could not stop him if he wanted to sit under Mount Muspel for a few hundred centuries, guarding a horde of treasure.

Gold, in particular, is his favorite. Silver is beneath his dignity. He is also partial to gems, but gold is what attracts him the most. I suspect this is because he is a male dragon, and men have simple tastes. Bathuba would likely have a keener sense of appreciation for rubies and emeralds and amethysts.

We both know how this game will end. I will toss the coin. Then toss it again, casually catching it a few hundred times before I finally throw it to him. He could take it from me any time he wanted, but he knows I would be displeased, and I would not bring him more treasure.

Harig snorts, but he is not angry. Dragons have no concept of time. They are intelligent creatures and can understand the passage of hours well enough. They just do not care. Dragon time is what my father called it.

It is easy enough not to care about time when you are immortal.

Finally, I decide it is time to end his torment and throw him the coin. With a rumble of exultation, he catches it nimbly in his mouth and swallows. I do not think the means by which he carries and...deposits...his treasure in the caverns of Mount Muspel requires further explanation.

I descend down the stairs, further into the pit.

"I did not take Thyra to the Ten Sleep Priory with ulterior motives in mind. I swear," I say to Harig. To the air, really, but I like to pretend he is an attentive audience. "But her shifting loyalty to me, and away from Vagmar, is an added bonus. She may not yet even realize her allegiance is to me, and not her father, but I see it in her eyes when she looks at me."

I taste it in her kiss, which is pure innocence and unadulterated passion, all at once. But Harig does not need to know this. I could allow him into my mind easily enough, but I do not wish to. It was not the visit to Ten Sleep's library or stillroom which helped to sway her. Nor, even, was it my tongue and its skill at bringing her pleasure.

She is an intelligent lass. She knows she has been lied to. All her life, in point of fact. She just needs to come to terms with it, which is not an easy thing to do. I will give her the time and space necessary.

Or at least I will try.

Harig snorts again, this time in amusement. Perhaps he is listening. Or mayhap he can simply sense I feel frustrated and is enjoying my discomfort. This latter explanation is more likely.

I did not take Thyra to the Ten Sleep Priory with ulterior motives in mind. But her shifting loyalty to me, and away from Vagmar, is an added bonus. She may not yet even realize she believes her father less and less every day and begins to view my keep as her home. My people as her people. My sister and friends as her sister and friends.

If books are all it takes to woo her, perhaps I can get something far more exciting than loyalty from her. That slick heat. Her, willing and wanting.

But in all seriousness, I must know where her loyalties lie before I indulge myself in her heat. I am rather besotted with the Princess Thyra, and I know myself well enough to know I may grow to love her once I have been inside of her. That I will never be able to be objective where she is concerned ever again. I could doubt her loyalty and yet still love her. It is a dangerous prospect, indeed.

33

THYRA

Drengr is singing to his dragons. And to be absolutely transparent, he did not exaggerate his talents. His voice is a low baritone, dripping with honey and spices and smoke. It is a voice to captivate. To mesmerize and hypnotize.

And I find myself falling. Falling into a chasm from which there is no escape. The chasm is Drengr, and I am his willing sacrifice.

Harig snorts his approval of Drengr's tale, much as a faithful hound would do.

Deep in the caverns of the mounds o'er hills,

a maiden, she waits for her dragon e'er still...

I was taught dragons eat maidens, and so I cannot imagine a girl waiting for one's visit with any kind of anticipation, but nonetheless, I continue to listen intently. He sings in his native tongue, but I know just enough of Logalandese to understand most of his words.

Shy as a blossom, still scared of the frost,

will she keep her vigil anon?

I resist descending the steps which lead down into the

pit any further, lest I am discovered, but I find myself wanting to know if this princess will keep her vigil. Instead, Drengr ceases singing and says–

"Fancy meeting you here, Princess. I did not think you would ever brave the pit."

"How could you know I was here? I was silent as the grave." Also, I was intent on eavesdropping, but this is neither here nor there.

"Harig told me."

"He did not make a sound. He didn't even look at you." Actually, I think he has fallen asleep. His eyes are closed, his breath rises and falls in a rhythmic, somnolent tattoo.

That's a gentle way of saying he is snoring.

"He doesn't need to." Drengr rises and ascends the stairs until he is just a step below me. He sits, motioning for me to join him. I do so without argument, because I wish to know how Harig communicates with him, without making a sound, nor even a single movement.

And I do not want to know so I can write to my father.

I desire to know this part of Drengr, for it is the last piece of the puzzle. The mystery I must solve before I can understand him.

"I still do not understand why they all listen to you." I speak truth, but I also wish to focus Drengr's attention on his dragons, not on my father. Nor on my treachery.

"It is only Harig who heeds me. But he is the leader of this conquer. If I give him a command which involves the others, he passes it to them."

Now I am angry. "I see. So you tell Harig to lay waste to the people of Vagmar, and he does it?" This is helpful. Though I know in my heart I will never be able to hurt Drengr, he recalls for me how he is responsible for so many needless deaths.

"Believe it or not, I do not enjoy unleashing dragons on my enemies. They tend to kill the innocent, as well as the guilty. Those caught in the crosshairs, if you will. Women. Children. Cattle. And horses."

"Should it concern me that you mention the slaughter of livestock in tandem with innocent people? As though they are equally disagreeable. Most people, even those of the kingly variety, would regret the loss of human life even more."

"Yes, of course, though I do hate to see good horseflesh go to waste. And if you think most kings are concerned with the fate of the innocent, you are much mistaken, Princess. Just ask your precious father."

It is not the first time he has broached this topic, implying my father and the Kingdom of Vagmar are not so much victims of Logaland's violence, but instigators of it.

But this is the first time I believe him.

And yet, as I have done on each preceding occasion, I ignore him. I refuse to rise to his bait. If I express any doubts about my father, Drengr will see it as an opportunity. An opportunity to continue speaking ill of Skerr, instead of explaining how he has this connection with Harig.

Also, it is a dangerous subject to discuss, my wavering allegiance. He knows I did not wish for this marriage. But he hasn't the faintest notion I was sent here as a spy. If I fulfill the promises I made to my father, to Vagmar–which, of course, I have no intention of doing–I face the wrath of Drengr of Logaland. This did not seem so terrible a fate.

Until I met the man. He is more intimidating than his dragons, and what is irritating is that he does not utter a word or even lift a hand in anger. Ever.

I have seen him lose control on several occasions

though. Or perhaps it is more accurate to say I have felt him let go of the iron control he wears like armor.

It was with me.

Though perhaps this is not strictly accurate. For even when he plucked me from my bath and rendered me a flaming puddle in my bed, he possessed self-control. He knew exactly what he was doing. It was I who was a frenzied animal.

"I knew the moment my father died, though I was many hundreds of miles away." Drengr speaks softly. Sadly. He is telling me a tale he'd rather not recall.

"But how could you? No messenger could reach you so quickly, not even a raven."

"Because it is the very moment I became the dragon."

I try not to roll my eyes, though not too hard. "You really are quite full of yourself. You have dominion over dragons, I know. I do not know how you do it, but I am no fool. They listen to you. But to call yourself 'the dragon' is a touch presumptuous, is it not?"

Drengr sighs. "There is only one way to show you. To make you understand. Though I do not enjoy the process. It is usually a transformation I undertake only when absolutely necessary."

Harig's eyes open, the reptilian, amber slits malevolent with annoyance. This time, when the dragon snorts, he sounds insulted.

"Do not be like that, Harig. You like it no more than I," Drengr says to the dragon.

Drengr commands me to be silent, then closes his eyes. He is still, preternaturally so, his hands clenched into fists. I am so absorbed by him, it takes me a moment to realize Harig is also still as a statue, his eyes also closed.

But the dragon is not asleep, and neither is Drengr. I

hear his breath, soft, but deep and steady, and realize Harig is breathing in and out at the same rate. Breath for breath, they match each other, until it sounds as if it is the same being inhaling and exhaling. As though dragon and man are one.

Then Drengr opens his eyes. I suppress a scream, not of terror, but of disbelief.

His eyes are the same color as Harig's. Gone are his soft black eyes, which hold such a merry glint when I amuse him (usually at mine own expense). In their place is the glowing, lazy gaze of a predator.

Of a dragon.

He stares straight ahead, his body still tensed and utterly still. For a moment, I think he is staring at me, but really, he is looking through me. Then I am frightened, for it is as though Drengr no longer sees me. Does he even know I am here? For he is not himself. It is as though his body is still here, but his mind is elsewhere.

Below us, the dragon stirs. Breaking my gaze from Drengr, I look down to Harig.

His eyes are milky-white, strangely rounded orbs. No iris. No pupil. It is as though he is blind.

How could I not see it? This entire time, the means by which Drengr holds dominion over dragons was self-evident. When I finally realize what he has done, I curse myself for being an idiot. The reason he is able to control the dragons is so very obvious. And yet, I did not think his kind actually existed. I believed them to be tales from the Old World, the Realm of Hjartagard, where I suspect, even there, his kind were just a myth.

"You are a Shadow Master. A warg." Though, really, I speak only to myself. I do not think Drengr can hear me.

. . .

Shadow Masters are able to invade the minds of beasts. Or to be more accurate, just one. They are the 'shadow' of this beast, as Drengr is to Harig. Whenever he wishes, a Shadow Master can inhabit the body and mind of this creature. It is a great gift, a fearsome power, and also a terrible curse.

And I am furious.

Never able to curb my temper, I am nearly shouting my words as I speak. "I have never understood why the dragons of Logaland are so loyal to the rulers of your country. No one has ever comprehended it, not in thousands of years. But now I know it is only by your command they lay waste to the peoples of Plane. You and your ancestors are murderers, all of you. I'd always believed your father to be one, but only of my mother. Now I know his transgressions–and yours–are even worse than I believed!"

I truly have no notion of whether Drengr or Harig are aware of my presence. Will he–or they–sense a threat in my words, in my very presence–and harm me?

But then Drengr's eyes open, and they are that soft black color again I know and am coming to love. I look to Harig, and his own eyes are insolent amber slits, before he closes them and promptly returns to snoring.

At some point in the last several days, I forgot to hate Drengr. I do not know when I decided I could never betray him and play spy for my father, but it was a resolution I made. And I will not change my mind. I cannot. For no matter how much I hate him in this moment, I think I am growing to love him. Can a person fall in love with another after so short an acquaintance? Maybe not. But what I feel for the King Drengr...call it obsession, call it infatuation, or choose to think of it as a fledgling sort of love...is not going away, even if he is a cruel conqueror.

And now I think my heart is breaking.

Or at the very least, cracking.

"If you would only think a moment, Princess, no dragon has attacked the levies of Vagmar since I became king. Since I became Harig's shadow."

"Then where were you at the Battle of Dale's End? I have heard all about this battle from Ulf, and he tells me the Vagmarians won–a rare enough occurrence–because your dragons decided it was time for their dinner break."

Ulf has made me cry with laughter many a time when he recounts the story of the Battle of Dale's End. It was a tiny hamlet in one of the southwestern provinces of Vagmar, full of farmers.

And where there are farmers, there are cattle.

And goats.

And pigs.

And sometimes, even sheep...a dragon's preferred dish.

Our Vagmarians fought valiantly in that southern valley, but they were, of course, no match for the dragons of Logaland.

Until those same dragons caught the scent of a certain shepherd's sheep. They were Eider-Dales, bred primarily for their meat. As it is warmer in the southern provinces, their wool was nothing to speak of and easy enough for the dragons of Logaland to gnash through on their way to the sheep's' juicier bits.

Battle, quite literally, ceased while the dragons of Logaland held a feast, ignoring the frustrated oaths of the Logalander commanders.

The Vagmarians retook the field with little further bloodshed, as Logaland conceded. They had only a fraction of the warriors that Vagmar possessed.

The shepherd, a Master Robisson, was knighted and granted fifty hectares from the crown.

"Are you telling me you were one of the brainless horde of creatures who feasted on Farmer Robisson's herd while Vagmar took the field? I would have thought you have some semblance of control when in your dragon form."

"If I recall correctly, I was seven at the time, and nowhere near the battlefield."

"Oh."

"But my father, through Harig, of course, may have been a member of that brainless horde, as you so eloquently put it. He was ever so fond of a mutton chop, was my da."

I find myself jealous when Drengr calls his father 'Da' in the course of his reminiscences. As though true affection existed between them, and it was not just duty that bound them to each other. If I dared to call my father 'Da,' he might have me committed me to the convalescent ward of the Priory, rather than marry me to Logaland.

Just days ago, I would have chosen the company of the patients in the Priory over marriage to Drengr, and some of the wards' inhabitants believe a giant serpent will one day swallow the earth whole. One, to be more accurate. But I cannot help but smile when I think of Old Nasmell. I miss him, as I miss many of those who make the Priory their home. I would say I miss the library, but since I now have what I believe may be the most magnificent library in all of Plane at my disposal, the Echen priories be damned, I cannot mourn the loss of the Priory's tomes and scrolls overmuch.

Then again, I have recently discovered some men can transform into dragons.

I suppose anything is possible.

"So is it true, then, that you lose all human ability to

reason when you are in the mind of a dragon?" This is what I fear most.

He frowns. "Why would you think so?"

"You just told me your father enjoyed a mutton dinner after a long morning of laying waste to the people of Vagmar."

"I jested. Well, perhaps not. I would not put it past my da to indulge himself, though I doubt he would do so in the midst of battle. But why is this so important to you? I would think you would rejoice at Vagmar's victory that day. Many lives were spared."

"If you were transformed, would you recognize me? Or would you have me burned? Or Hel, have Harig eat me as though I were a piece of mutton?" I think on his gaze, unseeing and feral, and shudder.

"Do you think that is what happened to your mother? That when she came here on a diplomatic mission, my father ate her? For I do not know all the particulars, but I can categorically tell you this is not how she met her end. And I will also tell you this, the sins of the father should not be revisited upon the child. My father did not murder your mother, this I know, and even if you choose not to believe it, it is wrong for you to presume I would act in such a manner, that somehow murderous intent is passed on from father to child. Are you anything like your father?"

Dear gods, I hope not. Even before my conversation with Elfgiva, I fervently prayed to never be like him.

"Now, if you are done with accusing me of being a murderer, Harig would like to get back to his family. There is a young swain–only five hundred years old or so–who is currently courting his daughter, Drusila, and he does not wish to leave them unattended for overlong. Mind you, I cannot blame the lad. Drusila is a pretty minx."

"Wait, I had thought you doted on Drusila as a father would. You are not...romantically involved, are you?"

"Don't be disgusting. Of course I'm not. She is like a daughter to me. Besides, she is my sister's favorite dragon. Such a relationship would be positively incestuous. Now, her mother is a different matter. Many a time have I been tempted."

It takes a moment to realize he jests. At least, I think he does.

"Dragons mate for life, which means virtual eternity for their kind, and Bathuba is already spoken for. Besides, I am a king first, a man second, and a shadow dragon only third. It is my duty to produce an heir to the throne."

A king first? I do not like this admission. If he is a king first, and a man only second, he will never forgive me for my deceit. He will choose the well-being of his kingdom over any lingering affection he holds for me.

"Are you saying you would no longer be a warg if you had a choice? How can you stop? Is there even a way?"

"There is." He nods solemnly. "For me to no longer be a shadow, my dragon must needs die."

"But you would never wish for this." Not to mention, it is nigh impossible to kill a dragon.

"No, of course not. Harig has served the House of Logaland faithfully since my forefathers planted the first timbers of their hall in the valley below Mount Muspel. He is older than the blood elves of Vale, and likely as old as many of the gods."

"There is a most practical reason you do not wish for Harig to ever perish as well." Distaste crosses his features. He does not appreciate the accusation. "Without your shadow magick, Logaland would no longer be the most powerful kingdom of Plane."

He nods. "And if you think I should not take our power into account, you are a fool."

"I am no fool."

"I love Harig, more than any other creature living, except perhaps my sister and...and...well. I would never see him harmed. But also, if Harig dies, I die. And though sometimes even I dislike myself, I do not wish to leave this mortal realm until I've achieved a ripe old age."

Fear clutches at me, but then I remember–

"You cannot kill a dragon. They are immortal. Their hides are impenetrable. No blade can pierce them."

"There is one substance in all the Nine Realms that is poison to them. It is not even found in Plane, but Hel. The water of the River Nifl, where the dead travel when the gods have judged them not worthy of The Vales. If a dragon drinks from it, they die."

"But dragons are intelligent creatures. Surely they sense it is fatal to them."

"They do. But if their shadow master commands them to drink it, they will. They are powerless to oppose us."

"Whyever would a shadow master do such a thing? You said it yourself, if their dragon dies, they die."

"Is it so hard to believe some shadow masters would wish to break this curse? To try to save the next generation from its fate? Make no mistake, if we have a son one day, he will belong to Harig, and Harig will belong to him."

I hold out a hand, as if to ward off the images his words inspire. "Enough. I get the picture. But would you really give it up? It is the gift of your forefathers. Their legacy."

"It is also a curse."

"I do not believe you. Without the might of dragons behind you, Logaland would be just any other kingdom, with nothing to distinguish it throughout the Realm except a self-important conceit for its prize horseflesh."

"Pay attention. I did not say I wish we did not have dragons. They're dead useful, and I'm quite fond of them. It is being the Dragon I mind. The transformation I am forced to endure is indescribable."

"Try," I say through gritted teeth.

"What, describe what it feels like to inhabit the mind and body of a dragon? Bloody awful, as one would expect. When Harig breathes fire, I feel it. It is like molten lava being forced down my throat, seeping into my guts. He does not mind it, as he is impervious to temperature, but as I still have my wits about me...my human wits...I feel the lick of each flame. It is like I am drowning in a river of melted ignatum."

"So you are still fully aware of all that happens around you. It seemed as though you do not. I will not lie, your stillness, your eyes...I was frightened."

"I am aware, but all my attention must go to Harig when I am his shadow. My Princess, you did not risk the perils of the dragon pit merely to hear me sing. Why have you sought me out?"

I try to ignore how warm I feel when he calls me My Princess and explain. "I was not expecting to find you with Harig when I sought you out. Nor was I expecting to discover your secrets, or to have you learn some of mine own in turn." I say some, because I still have more to tell, unfortunately. "I came to tell you I went to see Elfgiva. She told me much, helped me to understand even more, but said the final part of the story is not hers to tell. That it is yours."

He looks so hesitant. I have seen him angry and happy, but not nervous. I'd not thought it was an emotion he experienced.

"I do not wish to cause you pain."

"This is exactly what Elfgiva said as well, when she began her tale." He still does not know I am a Valkyrie. So much of Elfgiva's tale had to do with my mother's choice to make me one. If I expect truth from Drengr, I shall have to give it in return. I take a shaky breath. "There is much I must also tell you, My King, and I fear you will also not enjoy the experience. I suppose we may as well both spill our secrets."

"Do you speak of your unwillingness to comply with your father's orders? Which, undoubtedly, involve my assassination and committing treason against your new kingdom. Though I suppose, since we are not yet wed, it is not strictly treason. We are only betrothed, and though it is very poor manners, we could break a betrothal...you do not wish to break our betrothal, do you?"

He seems nervous again. I do not know whether to reassure him or flee in terror. "How...?" It is all I can manage to speak aloud. If he knew treason and murder were my father's commands, why has he allowed me to get so close to him? Why the lovemaking? Why the trip to the Priory? Why even bother trying to make me laugh?

"I knew you would do none of what he wanted. I knew it from the very moment I met you."

My confessions flow from my lips in a tangle, but once I begin, I cannot stop.

"My father...he never had any intention of honoring this alliance."

"Well of course, he didn't."

"No, you don't understand. His instructions were quite clear. He wanted me to gather intelligence for him, so he could learn how to destroy you. He insisted no detail was too small to be included in my reports."

Now that I am revealing all to him, I can't seem to stop

my fool mouth from running away with its words. "I was supposed to feign a regard for you, so your guard would be relaxed and you would share information with me. I was to always act overjoyed when you came to my chamber."

"My Princess, there is no feigning your pleasure at my touch. All the demons of Hel could be trying to force their way through the ceiling, and we wouldn't hear them over your moans of pleasure."

"You knew those were my orders? How long have you known?"

It is difficult to follow the thread of his words, for he just called me My Princess again. A thing he has never said to me before, with the exception of our first formal introduction. It is better than any endearment. It is how princesses are addressed throughout the Nine Realms. Instead, he has always said Princess in that insolent way of his, part insult, part appreciation in his tone.

Is it because I have shown he can trust me?

He moves to hold me, which I know will soon lead to a kiss, but I cannot embrace him. Not yet. I must tell him I am a Valkyrie. All must be openness and truth between us, if we are to face my father together.

I hold up a hand to ward off his advance. "No, not yet. I must tell you–"

Suddenly, Harig's amber eyes open. He is alert, aware of a danger I can only guess at, even with my heightened Valkyrien senses. With a roar he spreads his wings and vaults himself into the air, toward the opening of the pit. I hear his massive talons scrape the floor as he alights, the rasp of his wings as they beat the air furiously.

Then trumpets blare in the distance. One long blast, followed by a shorter, almost staccato one. It is a foe, calling Logaland to battle.

I suspect I know who the encroaching enemy is. Vagmar. Led by Ulf, I have no doubt. My father does not command his own levies, not when Ulf is so much more capable.

And dispensable...at least in his view.

"Drengr, what will Harig do? He will not lay waste to the levies, will he?"

"Not unless I command him to do so. But I cannot control his anger. He goes to ensure the safety of Bathuba and the others."

Drengr and I take the stairs carved into the stone wall of the pit, following Harig, albeit more slowly. By the time we emerge into the full light of day, Harig is only a flash of tail in the distance.

But he flies toward Mount Muspel, not battle. Drengr was right, it seems. Harig will not attack the oncoming levies unless he is commanded to do so.

By Drengr.

And only Drengr.

And if Harig somehow dies in battle–which seems impossible, and yet there is always a chance–Drengr also dies.

But if Drengr dies at a ripe old age, Harig will begin heeding the commands of...

Drengr's child.

Our child.

Suddenly, I want this child very much.

More specifically, I want Drengr's babe.

We emerge from the dragon pit into the light, but also into chaos.

Children crying. Mothers calling to them, frantic to locate them so they may seek shelter should the invaders make it to the capital. And above the shouts and screams, the steady rhythms of pounding drums and the blare of battle horns. Drengr's levies are as well-trained as any of Vagmar's.

And this is what frightens me.

The horns of war summon the levies of Innangard to battle. Their trumpeting is deafening.

Shield for shield. Warrior to warrior. The levies of Vagmar, trained by Ulf, and those of Logaland, led by Drengr, are equally matched. Equally loyal to their commanders and their kingdoms.

It is the dragons of Muspel who render Logaland undefeatable.

"Drengr...please. Do not call your dragons. These levies only follow the commands of their king. There are those in their ranks whom I hold dear."

Not just Ulf. Many of them have served as my personal guard. Some I trained with when we were children.

"I vow I will not, but only so long as I can keep the Vagmarian levies at bay. If they are able to take the bridge, I will not choose their lives over mine own subjects. They must not destroy Innangard."

I understand, but I hope it will not come to that. Even without his dragons, Drengr is the most fearsome warrior I have ever seen. His carls are the best trained, and what is more, they revere him. They will fight to the death to defend their king and their kingdom.

But then again, though mine own father may not enjoy the same loyalty from his subjects, Vagmarians also love their country. And what's more, Ulf is their commander. He is as worthy of respect and loyalty as Drengr.

"Come," bids Drengr, and I follow him as he strides toward the keep's tower. Huggin squawks overhead, alighting on my shoulder. Either to comfort me or to seek protection. Perhaps both.

We hurry up the steps until we are atop the tower. Drengr nods at the pair of guards who guard this tower, who seem awed to have their king in their midst, in this, the most dilapidated of the twelve towers of Innangard. Beyond the dragon pennants swaying in the breeze, we look out to the Three Sisters Forest, then past it to the River Ignis. From this distance, it is a gleaming sliver of ribbon cutting through green fields.

But on the other side of it, looking like ants from this distance, are the warriors of Vagmar, marching toward Devil's Bridge.

If they cross the bridge before Drengr and his levies can ride out and meet them, Innangard will be overrun.

"There is a rotating guard always posted near the bridge, at the entrance to the forest," says Drengr. "Pray to the gods they can hold the Vagmarians back until we arrive."

"I am coming with you," I say without thinking. It is a dangerous decision, as I do not know how I will avoid transforming once blades clash and blood spills.

"Of course you are." And though there is a tense stillness in his stance, he still flashes me a grin. "Though you, yourself, have admitted you are not much use in battle, I want you there with me. Not, however, in the shield wall."

Elfgiva emerges from her hut and joins us, staring out at the levies of Vagmar. Her wild hair blows in the wind. Her face looks as if it is frozen in granite. She turns to Drengr. "I did tell you to heed my warning," she says imperiously.

"Now is not the time for I-told-you-so's," he says.

"You'd best hope they did not bring their siege engines," Elfgiva retorts. "They are the finest in all of Plane, designed to launch invasions from sea. They can launch missiles from many hundreds of yards away."

"You exaggerate, I think, though I take your point."

Turning to me, Drengr holds out his hand. "Come," he commands. "We have no time to waste."

I grasp his hand, realizing just how right it feels to take it.

A bedraggled-looking woman climbs the steps and emerges atop the rampart, three small children hanging on her apron. Two girls and a boy. Elfgiva seems to recognize them. The woman, gesturing to one of the guards, says, "We was just bringing supper to my man when the horns blasted. May we stay here with you 'til it is safe again?"

The carl who must be her husband hurries over to usher his family further from the edge of the rampart, away from danger.

But it is too late.

A fiery ball of stone, covered in pitch so it stays aflame, crashes into the tower above us, showering rubble into our midst. This keep is well-constructed, and most of the tower withstands the onslaught, but Drengr wraps his arms around me and ushers me away from the destruction, retreating to Elfgiva's hut. The others follow.

All except the young woman, who screams in agony. I think she must be hurt, but no. It is far worse. Her son has toppled over the crenellation. He grips it, his legs thrashing against the stone for purchase, his cries of panic echoing against the tower. We watch, helpless, too far from the edge of the rampart to catch his hands and pull him to safety. Drengr moves toward him, but even he cannot get to the boy in time. I know this. Then I smell it. Blood. I sense it. A warrior suffering. The scent of a warrior's pain is like no other's. Sweat and fear and courage meld, creating a perfume a Valkyrie finds intoxicating. I turn to the pair of carls who guard this gate tower. One is wounded from the siege engine's detritus. Judging from his agonized bellows, he is the boy's father, as his injury is minor. His helmet is askew, and his temple oozes. He is dazed but still standing.

It is enough. My fangs push against my gums, my ankles and shoulder blades itch with the anticipation of sprouting wings. One of the boy's hands drop from the crenellation. His mother wails; his sisters clutch at her skirts.

I know what I must do.

And I can only pray to the gods Drengr and I have reached enough of an accord, he forgives me.

I rip the bodice of my gunna so my wings may sprout unimpeded, forcing Huggin to alight from my shoulder with a squawk. Kick off my shoes so the feathers at my ankles, so like Huggin's, may bud. They are of the utmost importance, as these tiny wings at my feet add speed to my flight. Elfgiva, knowing just what I intend, only says, "Hurry, Thyra. He holds to the rampart with just two fingers."

Drengr gazes at me in shock. I am bared to the waist, my breasts visible to all who stand in the destroyed tower. But I see the moment understanding, sudden and terrible, dawns in his mind. His eyes narrow in anger, then...wonder.

My fangs fill my mouth, so I find speech difficult. Instead, I scream. It is the cry of a Valkyrie. Triumphant. Terrifying. Plaintive and cursed. My gunna still clinging to my lower half, I alight from the tower just as the boy loses his battle with the crenellation and plunges to the rocks below. My wings beat furiously, the sound echoing in the air around us and blowing detritus from the blast into my companions' faces. With another scream, I race after the boy, head directed toward the cobblestone pavement many hundreds of feet below. We are not ten feet from the street when I finally gain purchase over his ankle. Deftly, I grasp it and pull him to me. With barely a foot to spare, I turn and glide over the cobblestone, only landing on my feet once the motion of my wings slows.

I want to ask the boy if he is harmed. If he knows how to find his mother and sisters again. But he only looks aghast at me and screams. He flees toward the tower stairs, presumably to reunite with his family.

I try not to feel offended. His reaction to seeing a Valkyrie is to be expected. I must look hideous, and let us be honest, the ruined gunna falling from my torso and trailing down my legs does not help to make me look any less terrifying.

Once this battle is over, Edda is going to have something to say about this garment. It is irreparable.

With a sigh, I watch the boy go. At least he is safe, no matter what consequences I may endure. I could not have stood idly and watched him plummet to his death, knowing I could save him. My conscience would not allow it.

I wonder if Brunna and the other Valkyrien ever feel such qualms. If they do not, I almost envy them.

Drengr descends the stairs and emerges into the street just as the boy disappears up it. They must have passed each other. His expression is, as expected, grim. I suppose the invitation he extended to accompany him to Devil's Bridge, to support him during the battle, will now be rescinded.

I just hope he does not choose to also rescind the invitation to marry him.

I breathe a sigh of relief as my fangs and wings retract. Once the bloodlust has left me, my wings feel heavy, my fangs burdensome. I pull my gunna up over my shoulders, doing my best to cover my breasts. At least I am in human form by the time Drengr joins me.

As expected, he is fuming.

"Drengr, please, battle calls, but later, if you will only let me explain–"

"You could have been killed," he says in a tight voice, one which barely contains his fury.

"Pardon?" It is all I can think to say. If I am not mistaken, he is less angry about the fact that I am a Valkyrie and more outraged I risked mine own life to save the boy's. His concern is laughable, but also reassuring. Perhaps there is a chance he will not detest me after all.

"There was an inch of air left between you and the cobblestones when you finally switched direction. How could you know you could get to the boy in time?" I open my mouth to answer his question, but apparently it is rhetorical, for he says, "You couldn't know, that's how."

It is at this juncture, I do laugh. No man who intends to throw his betrothed in the nearest dungeon shows such tender regard.

I throw my arms around him and give him a loud, smacking kiss on the lips. My bodice falls again, and my bare breasts crush against his tunic.

"King Drengr, I think I love you."

The shocked look on his face is worth the price of my admission.

34

DRENGR

My betrothed is a Valkyrie. Even more shocking, she claims she loves me. More to the point, the woman I am coming to care for–to love as well, I think–is a Valkyrie.

But I haven't the time to contemplate the enormity of this revelation, for the levies of Vagmar are almost at our very gates. I speak hyperbole, perhaps. But they are on the other side of the River Ignis, and the entire Realm of Plane knows Ulf's history with bridges.

That is to say, he is like an unscalable wall, and I do not just mean metaphorically.

I hear in the distance the screeches and roars of Harig and Bathuba and their kindred. They know I need defending. That all of Innangard needs protection. But they will not descend upon the Vagmarian levies unless I command them to do so. They are frustrated, and I understand.

This battle would already be over if I summoned Harig. But I swore to Thyra I would not unleash my dragons on Vagmar's levies. Her father may have betrayed her, but she still holds Ulf dear. And the levies consist of warriors who have pledged their fealty to Thyra since her birth.

One of my guards has already thought to saddle Prunella for me. Holfnir would be useless in such a battle. My mare's only (albeit crucial) responsibility is to take me to the bridge as quickly as possible. From there, only a shield wall can defend against Vagmar's onslaught.

Thyra rides beside me, and damned if I do not find her presence a comfort. Nay, a necessity, almost. Like breathing or taking food and drink.

"You never had the chance to tell me about my mother," she says mulishly.

"You never told me you were a Valkyrie."

"No, nor that I was sent as a spy. I suppose we're even."

"Not even close, My Princess. You owe me, and rest assured, I shall collect on your debt at a later date. After we have won this battle."

"But first, you will tell me what you know of my mother."

"It is a bargain. Furthermore, you will stay out of the shield wall. You will give me your oath on this matter."

"Fine," she says sulkily. "But I am not so terrible a warrior you must prohibit me from picking up an axe. You do not give me enough credit."

"You mistake my reason, My Princess. I cannot worry about your safety and also lead the levies into battle effectively."

She smiles, seeming somewhat pacified, but then says, "You do realize Valkyrien have little to fear in a shield wall, do you not, My King?"

"But you will avoid transforming, will you not? Which is another question you must answer for me, My Princess, when this battle is over. I have never heard of a Valkyrie who can transform between woman and creature at will, nor one who is not member of a coven."

"I can only transform when I scent the blood of wounded warriors. It is the sole reason I could transform to save the boy. His father, your carl, was wounded. As to the rest, I am not like most Valkyrien. I shall explain another time."

"Hmm. If you did change into a Valkyrie during battle, it could be dead useful."

Her only response is a baleful glance, but no matter, for we are here. We emerge from the Three Sister's Forest, blocked from viewing the Vagmarian horde by our own River Guard. They have formed a shield wall in front of Devil's Bridge. Mist is here already, barking orders and yelling both insults and praise to the levies, which can oft be equally effective in the midst of battle. I give command to my adjutants to have my best warriors join the front line of it. I also make certain there is a reserve waiting in the rear, supporting both the left and right flanks, should they fail and need backup.

This would normally be when I summon Harig and the others, but I have vowed I will do what I can to avoid doing so.

The warriors part for me as I walk through their ranks, promptly clanging their shields together again once I have passed their rows. I take my place in the front line, squarely in the middle of Devil's Bridge.

Surprise, surprise. The Thane Ulf Olafsson is directly opposite me. He wears a helm, but still, I know it is him. He wears the very same armor he wore during the Handfasting Joust, though it is muddied from the no-doubt hurried journey here, toward Logaland, toward battle.

Besides, he swaggers in a manner no one his advanced age should ever attempt. 'Tis unseemly.

Mist pushes through the wall as well, joining me. You might wonder at how I am able to lead the shield wall without worrying for my sister, as I do for Thyra, but Mist is terrifyingly vicious in the wall. Though she is as tall as most men, she is more nimble. She is very good at cutting warriors at the ankles. She is a handy shield partner. There is no one I'd rather have at my side. Except perhaps Rufus.

As if reading my thoughts, she says, "Rufus wanted to join us, but you understand, he cannot."

No. Echen is not a traditional foe of Vagmar, nor do I wish it to become one. If Ulf were to see Rufus standing by me in the wall, it could mean the Vagmarians attack the people of Echen next. It would not do to spread even more bloodshed throughout the Realm. By showing his support for me, Rufus could do more harm than good.

Warrior for warrior, the levies of Vagmar and Logaland are equally matched. Their numbers match our own. And yet still, they have no chance of success. The King Skerr is many things, none of them favorable, but he is no fool. Why would he endanger his levies so? For he must know they have no chance against my dragons. Did he think I would abstain from using them in Logaland's defense, to spare Ulf and the other Vagmarian warriors for Thyra's sake?

Then I realize, damn it to Hel, the bastard was right. I am holding back my dragons for Thyra. He made a calculation, and it was a correct one. Truly, he is a fearsome opponent. I find myself smiling, for a less formidable enemy would be boring.

Speaking of formidable enemies, Olafsson clangs his axe against his shield, signaling he is prepared for battle. I answer with a clang of Dragonspear on mine own shield, painted with the sigil of the Kings of Logaland.

Then I hear screeching in the skies and know immediately who it is. The Valkyrien have arrived to feast on the wounded and the dying. They drift around the battlefield, appearing like wraiths in the Logaland mists. Will Thyra join them? I wonder if, when she transforms, she has any control over who she attacks? For as I said, targeting the Vagmarians would be dead useful. Perhaps she could sway the other Valkyrien to remain on the Vagmarian side of the river?

A thought occurs to me, and though I say it myself, it is a very good one.

"It seems as though it is you and I, old man, who shall decide the outcome of this battle. For I shall not allow you to cross this bridge into my kingdom. Not while there is still breath in my body."

By gods, it feels good to call him old man again without worrying about offending Thyra. It is small compensation for engaging in battle, but rewarding nonetheless. Then I recall the Valkyrien have exceptional hearing. She is not eavesdropping, is she?

"Then I shall make certain you have no breath left. Enjoy your last few inhales of the Logaland air, King Drengr, for today I send you to Hel."

Thank the gods Thyra is still atop her palfrey, protected by the rearguard, for if she heard our exchange, I believe she would be angry with both of us. Worse, disappointed. But it was not I who began this fight. Then again, it was not Olafsson either. It was his master, King Skerr.

I am no coward. If I can prevent the slaughter of warriors who are only doing their duty and fulfilling their oaths, not just the Logalanders, but also the Vagmarians, I will. If one death–my death–saves hundreds of other lives, it is worth my sacrifice.

And the Thane Ulf Olafsson is one of the few warriors in existence who can send me to the gods. He strides toward me, axe aloft. I quickly unsheathe Dragonspear, just barely meeting his first parry. His axe is every inch as long as my sword, and what is more, he is just as capable with his weapon of choice as I am with mine own.

The Valkyrien keen in the skies around us, angry they are being denied their feast, for no warriors but myself and Olafsson engage in combat. There is no blood spilled yet in which they can revel.

I dodge his axe, but it glances against my gauntlet. It stings enough so mine own armor makes a divet in my skin. It causes only a momentary pang, but I know the impact of the metal must have drawn blood.

The Valkyrien know it, too. With a triumphant howl, one of them dives for me. I wonder if I am hallucinating, for all I can think is, My, she has lovely blonde tresses, but I recollect myself in time to deflect another of Olafsson's blows and also prepare for the Valkyrie's coming onslaught.

But it never arrives. For suddenly, there is another Valkyrie in the air above me, darting like lightning toward my blonde attacker. With a flash of flaming red tresses and a cry of unmistakable fury, she slams into the other creature, knocking her from the sky to the bridge below.

Between Olafsson and myself.

My betrothed has arrived.

Both of us retreat to the safety of our sides of the river, realizing our combat is nothing when compared with the savagery of two Valkyrien bent on killing each other.

Ulf and I watch, both awed and horrified, as the two women claw at each other, talons scraping against each other, fangs gnashing at exposed flesh, but not quite managing to gain purchase.

My betrothed has saved me.

I look briefly at the Thane Olafsson, who looks stunned, yet somehow curious. He examines Thyra as she battles the other Valkyrie with a perplexed air. Is it possible he did not know of her secret?

Then he looks to me again, and his face hardens. He is determined on victory, and given he is the only one who has yet drawn blood, he just may achieve it.

I promised Thyra I would not summon Harig and the others, if I could avoid it, but I will not risk the invasion of Logaland, as well as the almost-certain destruction of our capital. I must summon the dragons.

But then the battle horns of Vagmar trumpet three blasts, which means they are prepared to pause fighting and try to negotiate.

We have fought to a standstill. From across the bridge, I see Ulf Olafsson scowling, heaving with exertion even as he clutches his axe, ready to plunge back into battle if the horn blows again.

Thyra will never be able to reconcile with her father. There is no doubt. But if Olafsson and I can treat with each other, she may be able to salvage her bonds with him. I know she does not wish to be separated from the country of her birth forever, particularly since one day she will be its queen.

"Are you ready to admit defeat, old man?"

Thyra, fangs protruding and skin a ghastly translucent color, glares at me.

"Are you?" Ulf bellows from across the bridge.

I am about to shout Never without pausing to think, as it is the expected response of the kings of Logaland, who of course, do not concede. But perhaps, just perhaps, I should try what I have never done before and attempt to negotiate a peace. Ulf and I know each other better now, since my sojourn in Vagmar. I even made him laugh once, and not at mine own expense, but because he found my wit amusing.

Peace is possible, and the old man seems to sense it as well, for he takes one tiny, hesitant step onto the bridge and nods his head at me, urging me to do likewise. Just us two, meeting in the middle of Devil's Bridge, talking out how best to precede.

To my surprise, I find I am not opposed to the idea, particularly since Thyra is suddenly right next to me. I do not know how she arrived at my side, as she agreed to stay away from the shield wall, and she is no oath breaker. She is smiling tentatively at Ulf, who cannot restrain himself from grinning at her widely when he spots her. I lift a boot, prepared to take that small, but significant step toward Olafsson.

But then a dragon roars above the clouds overhead. No one can see the beast, but there is no mistaking its presence. We all hear its great wings beating through the sky, louder than any ship's sail in a storm-tossed sea. The terror on every Vagmarian's face is evident. And for once, I share it.

For it is not one of my dragons.

Not only do I know this because I have not summoned Harig or the others, but also because I know the sounds they emit as well as I know mine own.

Which can only mean one thing, for a Shadow Master must hail from the House of Logaland.

I have a brother.

A Note from Faith

As I'm sure you've guessed, this series is loosely based on Viking culture. Vikings are having a moment, and I am here for it, as I am actually half Swedish with a very Swedish father who taught me to eat all kinds of tinned fish and enjoy it before I was too old to know better (but it is also the best skincare tip I have). Before making my foray into Romantasy, I wrote Viking Historical Romance (see Eliza Carter, another of my pen names). I am obsessed with Viking history, and when I first began typing up this manuscript, I couldn't get away from it. It sounds both nerdy and pretentious, but I feel a deep connection to it. But I also enjoy being able to diverge from actual historical fact, as only a fantasy world will allow one to do. Thyra and Edda take tea together, which would be a total idiosyncrasy if this were the real Viking world, but since gorgeous men and women who inhabit the minds of dragons are part of my fantasy world, why can't caffeinated beverages also be, I ask you? Maybe they were already importing tea leaves from the Eastlands, whereas Europeans didn't think to do this with Asia until the seventeenth century.

My fictional characters are just more precocious.

Also, I don't want you going away thinking jousts and massive stone fortresses were part of the Viking world either. I mean, sometimes they sacked stone fortresses, but mostly, they were too mobile a culture to take the time to construct such edifices. And jousts were very much a later medieval invention, but I couldn't help including them in this book. Again, it's the beauty of an alternate realm. I do what I like!

However, I try to keep actual battle tactics (you know, minus the dragons and Valkyrien) accurate. Shield walls were a messy, bloody business. Knights on horseback were not a thing in the Viking era.

Another thing I fudge a bit (OK, a lot) is the mythology of the Valkyries (I use the German plural for the book, –en). They were not pseudo-vampires with a taste for solely male flesh. I just...am feeling perimenopausal, I guess?

My poor husband!

Faith xo

Another Note from Faith

THANK you so much for reading Crown of Fangs. It is my first foray into Romantasy, and I have enjoyed writing it so much. This book ends on a cliffhanger (sorry! Or not?), and there are two more books coming out to accompany it. For this new adventure, I've created a new pen name to help readers differentiate my Romantasy books from my other work. Faith is, in fact, my "real" first name, but James belonged to my Nana.

Edith James was her maiden name. She was my favorite person in the world. She went by Betty (her middle name was Elizabeth, as is my own–mine own?). If a person dared to call her Edith, she would insist her name was Betty until they complied. She could not understand why she was not allowed to use the name Betty on all life's pertinent documents, but she had her revenge by always signing her name Betty E. Torkomian.

It is to her I owe my love of hearing and sharing stories. I was often sick as a child, and she would tend me and tell me the amusing anecdotes of her childhood, and how her family and my grandfather's came to be in America. We would also play Go Fish, which is probably why today I enjoy the card tables at casinos far too much.

She was convinced there was nothing I wasn't capable of

achieving in this world (she never paid attention to my math grades), and I firmly believe everyone deserves to have at least one such a person in their lives.

If you enjoyed Crown of Fangs, I would so appreciate a review. Even just telling other people how much you liked it is so helpful for us writers!

Also, if you enjoyed it, I would love to hear from you! Insta (@elizacarterwrites or @faithjameswrites) and my Facebook group (Hot Nerds Reading) are the best places to find me. There are many more books to come in the Chronicles of Plane, so I hope you'll stick with me for the adventure. Thanks again!

FAITH XO

EXCERPT FROM COURT OF FIRE

Lust. Hate. Love. These are the emotions I feel for Drengr of Logaland. Both chronologically—before I knew his identity, I lusted after his muscles and his dark eyes. Then, when I discovered he was the son of the man responsible for my mother's murder, I hated him. And finally, I grew to love him, for how could I not? But also, I feel these emotions in tandem. For even when I want to pound his handsome face into a volcano wall, I still burn for him. And though I love him, I hate having divided loyalties.

However, there is nothing complicated about the hatred I feel at this very moment. It is for the Valkyrie swooping toward my betrothed, a malevolent, hungry expression haunting her features. I say haunting, because I understand she only follows compulsion. It is one I share, for I am a Valkyrie also.

More accurately, I am a human, able to transform into one when I smell the blood of a wounded warrior. Which, I remind myself, I currently do. Drengr's. The Thane Ulf Olafsson has wounded him whilst in the midst of single combat on Devil's Bridge. It is a sensible means of deciding the outcome of battle, one of which I would normally heartily approve. But usually, the combatants are not two of the people I love most in the world. Drengr has stationed me in the rearguard, out of harm's way, as I am rather useless in the shield wall. But the stray waft of his blood I inhale is enough.

I run around the warriors grouped in the shield wall. They are in hogshead formation, dense in the frontlines, more narrow toward the rear, where I am. As I run, my wings cut through my shoulderblades, and I rip the bodice of my gunna apart to accommodate them. It seems I am rendering myself topless in public more frequently than is my wont, since I became betrothed. My fangs erupt out of my gums like vicious little blades. It is a painful transformation, but a necessary one. I feel the wings at my ankles sprout, and I am off, alighting into the air with a screech of glee, one I cannot contain, for though I hate being a Valkyrie, it is an emotion I only feel when in human form. But still, on this occasion, I would be joyful no matter what, because I am able to save my beloved from a horrible fate.

I fly at the Valkyrie who dives toward Drengr. With a sickening thud, I batter her with the force of a gale. We both crash in a tangled heap in the middle of the bridge.

In between Drengr and Ulf, who stare at us in wonder.

Drengr has seen me transform. He knows I am a Valkyrie, and yet, he still seems to want to marry me. Even if I were not one of the gods' cursed bloodeaters, I would still be surprised by his tenacity. A Valkyrie is a rather hideous creature. Seeping, bloody eyes. Winged feet. Talons in place of fingers and toes. Translucent, bluish skin. Bare breasts.

Well, perhaps Drengr doesn't mind that bit.

But Ulf, though he is like a father to me...no...this is not an accurate description of the Thane Ulf Olafsson. He has been better than a father, for mine own has ever been distant toward me, not to mention treacherous. He is the father I wish I'd had. One whom every child deserves. Though he is the father I never had, he did not know I am a Valkyrie.

Until now.

My father, King Skerr, and my nursemaid, Edda, concealed my abilities from all. They have been the only two privy to my secrets for twenty-one years.

Though I recently learned Elfgiva, my kingdom's former court völva, as well as the leader of the local coven of Valkyrien, also knew.

I wonder if Brunna, that raven-haired chaos-maker, is somewhere on this battlefield, soaring above us, searching for prey. However, I cannot wonder overlong, for I must deal with the more proximate, pertinent Valkyrien threat in our midst.

"Sister," she rasps. "Why would you prevent me from feeding?" The other Valkyrie is furious, as expected, but also confused.

I grit my fangs, ignoring the blood I draw from mine own lips. I hate it when these creatures call me 'sister'. Though I suppose it is an accurate moniker, for we are no different from each other when cruising a battlefield for victims. I am no better than them, ever hunting for the wounded and the suffering, hurrying their deaths so they may meet their makers, whether it be in The Vales, where we all hope to rest when this life is over, or in Hel, where of course, no one wishes to tread.

I stand, fluffing my wings and placing myself between this other Valkyrie–I shall call her the blonde, as she has a fine head of glowing tresses (it is our one mark of beauty, we all have excellent hair, though I say it myself)--and Drengr.

I bare my fangs at her and hiss, "Not today. This one is not for eating." My voice is garbled, as it always is when I am transformed. These fangs feel like so many marbles rolling together in my mouth.

"Stand aside, sister, for I shall not hesitate to destroy you to get to him. I claim this one for mine own. I found him first."

I have no doubt the blonde means what she says. Though she stands in the middle of two armies, she is fearsomely capable of killing both Drengr and Ulf, crushing them like they are so much gossamer, before flying off to escape the retaliation of the other warriors.

But I vow, she will have to get through me first, and this will not happen.

"Actually, Thyra found me before you. I know you may believe this is just semantics, but I think it important you know she and I have been acquainted for several weeks now, and so her claim is older than yours."

It is Drengr who speaks. Trust him to make light of the situation. To use humor like an army uses a siege engine to hurl missiles. He is not trying to deflate the tense dangerousness of this situation. He is throwing a firebomb into it, hoping it will spark.

The blonde only cackles. It is a rather nefarious sound. I do not think she laughs with genuine mirth. Only malevolence. "Thyra of Vagmar. I should have known it was you. The red hair. The disdain you do nothing to conceal when I call you 'sister'."

It must be said, she speaks more clearly than I ever could when transformed. I suppose this is because she must live all her hours and days with these hateful fangs stuck

in her skull. Not just on occasion, when a bloody battlefield calls for me.

I ignore her insults, saying only, "Will you heed my warning, or must I destroy you?"

She smiles in that ghastly way only a Valkyrie can manage, licks her lips, and simply stares. But not at me.

At Drengr.

I sigh, preparing to fight. To the death, if needs be. Because I love Drengr. Because I love Ulf. Because of my loyalty to the Vagmarian warriors, and my growing allegiance to the ones of Drengr's kingdom as well.

But mostly, because no one gets the better of me. It is unacceptable.

Then Brunna appears, her black hair glowing like a raven's. Like mine own pet raven's Huggin, who stayed behind at the keep. It was not difficult to convince him to do so, he is a bit of a coward.

She lands softly next to us. Next to me, more accurately. I hate the warm glow of appreciation I feel for this gesture, particularly since Brunna and I have such a complicated history. It is a display of her allegiance toward me, and not the blonde.

"Svava, stifle your racket and find other prey," Brunna says.

Svava only pouts in reply, but she does finally turn from us and fly off into the misty skies.

Brunna turns to me to speak. Ulf stares at me, and though he is doing his best to conceal it, a look of revulsion passes over his face.

But I never hear what Brunna intended to say, nor am I able to speak with Ulf, to apologize for keeping my secret from him, to make him understand I am still the same Thyra he bounced on his knee when I was a child, who has roared with laughter many a time when he has recounted tales of his adventures.

For there is a dragon in the sky. I cannot see it. The mists are low today, the sky full of clouds. But I hear the flap of its giant wings as it beats through the sky, its roar of frustration, as it searches for its battlefield quarry. Suddenly, the Valkyrien disappear from the battlefield, fading into the mists like wraiths.

For even a Valkyrie cannot defeat a dragon.

ACKNOWLEDGMENTS

Thank you to Janet Jones Bann, my editor extraordinaire. Thank you for not only being so wonderful at what you do, but also being so considerate and kind. You may not realize how much I rely on the fact that I know my books go to you when they are done. It helps keep me going!

Thank you to my daughter, Nora, a rabid Romantasy reader, who alpha read this (until she got too busy living her best teenage life) and told me I needed to make Edda 'something.' She suggested a troll, but they're a little unhygienic. Still, a genius idea. Giantesses rock!

Thank you to both my daughters for being so proud of me. I love you. Now that you are older, you are as much best friends as daughters. Our conversations are my favorite part of each day, besides my writing time and my reading time, which I do not appreciate having interrupted. Still, for you, anything...

And thank you to my besties, JC Brown and Lena Lane. I couldn't have befter besties and better writer buds. Our group chat gives me life. Thank you for forcing me out of my shell when we are at signings, and thank you most of all for always being there. I love you.

And finally, for the man Drengr is based on, my husband, John. Romance authors are often asked if they base their MCs on real men. Yes. My husband. He really is that guy. We are disgustingly in love, and he is disgustingly handsome and successful. But so much more importantly, he is funny as hell (Hel?) and has the biggest heart of anyone I know. He is also sometimes an idiot, but nobody's perfect. Romance authors are also often asked if they write their sex scenes based on personal experience. Most authors hotly retort they do not. I, however, will remain mute. Thank you for being so inspirational (and my tongue is only partially in-cheek there) and thank you for being so proud of me, even if you don't tell anyone you work with what I do, lest you have to tell them I write smut for a living. I love you.

ABOUT THE AUTHOR

Faith James, who also writes Historical Romance as Eliza Carter, lives on an island off the coast of Massachusetts, where she tries to meet as few new people as possible. Sadly, her husband is an extrovert, though otherwise a most excellent person, and she is often being forced to socialize. It's like jogging or hot yoga–thinking about doing it is horrific, but once one gets started, it becomes enjoyable. In every other respect, she and her husband are of like mind, which is unfortunate, because neither serves as a check to the other when taking in homeless animals. They have a collection of four-legged freaks and geeks that would rival the one on Dr. Moreau's island. Some of them are very good-looking, however, and all of them are sweet-tempered. And when they are not, whoever their victim is, they deserved it.

They also have children of the two-legged variety, but it does not do to dwell on them here. When singing their praises, the author becomes positively obnoxious.

As she moves firmly into middle age, she has set her sights on becoming a woods hag who grows her own lavender and turmeric. She may even let her hair go grey.

She loves to hear from her readers. Socializing online is much better than doing it in person. Go to www.faithjamesbooks.com to connect on all the things.

www.ingramcontent.com/pod-product-compliance
Lightning Source LLC
La Vergne TN
LVHW100515110826
845146LV00002B/650

9798995194903